For Love,
For Lust,
For Friendship

For Love,
For Lust,
For Friendship

Lady Sharp

authorHOUSE®

AuthorHouse™
1663 Liberty Drive
Bloomington, IN 47403
www.authorhouse.com
Phone: 1-800-839-8640

Published by AuthorHouse   01/08/2013

ISBN: 978-1-4670-2426-6 (sc)

ACKNOWLEDGMENTS

I am so grateful for the support that my family and friends have given me. I could not have completed this book without your belief in my GOD given talent.

Thank you Sonny for giving me the space I needed to achieve my dream.

EPISODE ONE

Barbette

B arbette heard about these two young men who were giving a party tonight at the hottest club in Atlanta, the Two Twenty-Two Club, to showcase their new talent. These young men at the early age of twenty-five were fresh on the scene as producers, widely known and often discussed in Atlanta and Barbette wanted to see if they had the skills that everyone was raving about. She could not decide whether to ask her brother to go with her to protect her from the desperate young unattractive, crazy men or to take a chance on entering the den alone. As she got out of the shower and dried off her body, she thought about the last time she had seen Lee. He had been her boyfriend for two years. However, six months ago, he decided that he did not want to be committed to her and moved to LA to live with a doctor he met on one of his many business trips there. Dr. Rachel Martin was perceived by many to be a very attractive and evidently very alluring woman. Since Lee, Barbette had not dated or had sex with anyone, devoting herself to her work at the law firm and teaching dance at the downtown community center. The Deana Butler's Community Center was opened eight years ago. Her dad and three of his colleagues donated the money to have the center built after the murder of his friend's daughter, Deana Butler, who lived in the downtown area of Atlanta. She was a student at Stone Mountain College. On her way to school one fall morning she was attacked, shot in the head and died instantly; her murderer was never found. It bothered her father for a long while. He had been very close to their family and had watched Deana grow up. Barbette and her brothers donated their time to the center as much as they could; based on the request of her father.

Barbette chose to wear her black wide leg pants and a black see through blouse that accented her full bust, which appeared larger than they actually were because of her slim, but curvaceous body. Deciding on what shoes she could dance in was the problem. She finally chose the black patent leather hi-heels that she purchased on her last business trip to New York. The high heels made her look taller and she always felt a need for height since she was only 5'2". They looked sexy on her feet and felt pretty comfortable. She had just gotten her hair done in a bun style pulled up on top of her head, exposing her beautiful neckline. She chose her diamond hook earring to accentuate her oval shaped face and strong cheekbones. Barbette checked her caramel complexion deciding not to apply any facial makeup but highlighted her lips with the cranberry red lipstick and gloss that she often wore. As she applied the finishing touches, Barbette stared at herself in the mirror for a moment and with a pucker she stated, "Damn, my lips look so good; they make me want to suck on them my damn self—mmmmmwha you go girl." After spraying on some perfume she stood back to admire her body and wondered if she should wear something more revealing when suddenly she heard a knock at the door.

"Come on in. I'm dressed." It was her father Raymond Jackson, Attorney and owner of the L.R.B. Law firm. Raymond had started his career with nothing and had managed to build a million dollar law firm. He had always been a very handsome black man that had attracted young women, causing him to pay out plenty of money to help clean up situations and to protect his name. He opened Barbette's bedroom door and peeked in.

"And where are you going tonight, looking so dolled up?" he asked.

"I am going to the Two Twenty-Two Club. I thought I might check out those new producers everybody has been talking about, and maybe run in to a good looking man to bring home." She replied in a seductive tone.

Raymond laughed. "Good luck baby," he said. "But I'm probably the best looking man on earth and I'm already taken."

She laughed out loud as she headed towards her bedroom door. "Ok Daddy out of the way. I'm on a mission." Barbette said.

Barbette marched passed him and started down the hall towards the stairs.

"Hey baby," her daddy shouted after his daughter.

"Yes." Barbette answered.

"Do me a favor, don't stay out to late. I need your help on some briefs in the morning."

"Okay Daddy."

She carefully started down the stairs, watching to make sure that the sole and the heel of her shoes made full contact with each step. The winding stairs case had become a caution sign to Barbette after falling down and breaking her arm several years ago.

When her family first moved in to this six-bedroom and six-bath mansion, Barbette felt that the house was a bit too much for them, but after living there for so long she had learned to accept and love the house as much as her dad did. Her dad especially liked the down stairs private area, where he had access to his office and a large bedroom and bath. He spent most of his time there, entertaining his very attractive young guests.

Her family consisted of her and her two brothers, Raymond Jr., the eldest, who lived in the suburbs of New York with his wife Sylvia and Lance the youngest of the three, who lived in the house with her and their father, Raymond. Lance was the brother that everyone in the family acknowledged as the twenty-four year old wild child. Lance was known for the wild parties he gave and Barbette believed that he knew every stripper from Atlanta to New York.

Her dad had never remarried after their mother had left him for another man, Mr. James Jenkins, a very wealthy Caucasian male. Mr. Jenkins is a Banker and owns several small businesses. The majority of his wealth came from his family. When her mother left, her dad went through a lot of changes financially and mentally, but was able to pull through it all. He had come close to marriage several times and decided to put his career as a lawyer in front of everything in his life, including his two wonderful sons and daughter. They were raised by many nannies, sent off to private schools most of their lives and all three ended up drawn in to the world of Law, partners in his 500 million dollar law firm, L.R.B. Attorneys at Law with offices located in New York, LA and Atlanta. Their clientele consisted of the rich and famous; actors, actresses, rappers, and singers to name a few. The family law firm handled Entertainment Law in the LA and Atlanta office and Criminal Law in the New York office. In many ways the Law Firm can be very entertaining at times.

As she walked out the front door on her way to her car that was parked in front of the house, she noticed a full moon and checked her watch for the time. It was 11:00p.m. The club was located downtown and it would take about an hour to get there. Right then she decided that she would stay in her dad's downtown condo for the night. To drive all the way home would be risky knowing that she would probably have a few drinks. It was a warm June evening, warm enough to drop the top on her XKR Jag. She loved her car. Her dad and younger brother Lance presented it to her the day she passed her bar exam. Her older brother, Raymond Jr., better known as Ray to family and friends, gave her money to invest. Ray is the family miser. He saves every dime he earns. He won't even purchase a new car. He is still driving his old 1999 BMW that was purchase in 2000. His wife Sylvia, wears the same outfit every time the family meets for dinner. But Barbette loved her brother and his wife and thought of them as wonderful, funny people to be around. They were just not into material things. Barbette's mother had abandoned them when she was eight years old. Since then she had had no one to talk to about boys and the things daughters and mothers talk about. Barbette had been delighted when Ray announced his engagement to Sylvia. Sylvia had been like a big sister to her from the day they met six years ago.

As Barbette pulled up to the Club she saw the sign, Parking Lot Full/ No Valet Parking. That meant she had to find a parking space that would put her in walking distance to the club. She circled the block twice and finally found one in the parking lot across the street from the club. Once the car was parked, she put her money, a small tube of lipstick and her keys in a small black purse. She seldom carried purses so she kept this one in the car just in case she needed one. As she started across the street to the club, she let her mind wonder about the two men that were supposed to be the talk of Atlanta. She wondered what they looked like and even though they were giving the party would they even be there. Her dad had mentioned that the young men were trying to put some talents together to produce but had already established a pretty profitable business. He also

4

mentioned that the father of one of the boys had died and left him enough money to start the business.

There was a line at the door. Barbette started up to the door of the club hoping that her bartender friend, Wayne, would be working tonight and could get her in so that she wouldn't have to wait in line. She had met Wayne about three years ago. He was a bartender at a club she frequented at that time. The crowd started pushing and it became too much for her. She stepped out of the crowd and pulled out her cell phone. She dialed Wayne's cell number and prayed he would answer.

"Hello," Wayne said, over the noise of the crowd.

"Hey, this is Barb, I am at the door. Can you get me into the club?" All of a sudden, she heard nothing and assumed that she had lost connection or Wayne had hung up on her.

A man came to the door of the club and shouted, "Barbette Jackson. Is there a Barbette Jackson out here?" She held her hand up and waved to the man and his hand motioned for her to follow him. He directed her in the club and to the bar where Wayne was working. Wayne had saved her a seat and had already set her up with a drink.

"How's my pretty girl doing tonight?" he asked in a deep voice. Wayne was an attractive twenty-nine year old Italian divorced man. He examined Barbette from head to toe and smiled.

"Just fine now that I'm in the club. Thanks a lot Wayne. I owe you." She replied.

"Oh, that's alright. They need some pretty women in here anyway," Wayne said with a big smile on his face. "What brings you down this way tonight?"

Barbette looked around the club as she answered. "Well, I came to see what those two producers were about since they have been causing such a stir."

"Oh, you mean Dean and Carl?" Wayne asked.

"Oh, I didn't know their names," Barbette said showing her surprise. "Do you know them and are they here tonight?"

"Yes, somewhere around here, I'll introduce them to you when I see them," Wayne replied as he poured vodka for the customer who was seated next to her.

Barbette smiled and said, "That would be great. Thanks, Wayne."

She then looked around the club to see if it had changed since her last visit. Nope! No changes other than the cover charge. The first group was up and sounded great. Barbette was enjoying the music and wanted to dance. A young good looking black man approached her and asked if she would like to dance. "Of course," she said. As he led her to the dance floor she noticed that most of the crowd consisted of young women. She wondered if they had come to see the bands or the new producers. She felt lucky to be asked to dance do to the ratio and thought, she should have brought her brother with her. He would have truly enjoyed himself.

After the dance the young man escorted Barbette back to her bar seat and offered to buy her a drink, which she declined. Then he thanked her for the dance and walked away. Wayne winked at her and said, "So. I see you still got it, girl." Barbette smiled and positioned herself in her seat.

After a few more dances and three shots of Cognac, Barbette decided it was time to go. The bands had been great but now the music was starting to give her a headache and she had promised her Dad that she would be up early to help him with some research.

"Well, Wayne, I think I'll be going now, I have to get up early to help my dad out."

"Hey, it's only 3:00, you might as well stay till closing," Wayne insisted. She thought about getting up early and knew she should go, but she had not seen Wayne in a long time.

"Okay, I'll stay for 10 more minutes, but I got to go pee." She got up to go to the ladies room and bumped into a very nice looking young man. His voice was deep and smooth.

"I think we should dance," he said

He took her by the hand and led her to the dance floor. It was a slow song playing "My Lady."

As they started to dance, he introduced himself.

"My name is Carl, Carl Hunter. What's your name, baby?" he asked

"No, my name is not 'Baby'," she said with a smile on her face, "it's Barbette, but that was a good guess." This man must be one of the producers giving this party, she thought. He was dressed in a nice gray wool blend striped suit, which he had hooked up with a tailored white shirt and a Versace Tie. Everyone knew those ties are priced at $200 or more. Carl was of a light brown complexion with hazel eyes and wore his hair in a very close and neatly trimmed faded haircut. He smelled like he had just jumped out of the shower.

6

Barbette was impressed but not pressed to know him. A dance was all he was going to get from her. She was not about to put herself in a bad situation, since she had just come out of a big mess about 6 months ago.

He whispered, putting his mouth so close to her ear that she could almost feel the tip of his tongue entering and moving making her uneasy.

"Are you with someone?" He asked.

Barbette was hesitant to answer and replied. "Why do you ask?"

He pulled her closer to him.

"A friend of mind is giving an after-party for me and my partner at the Peachtree Hotel. Would you like to come—or would you like to CUM?"

Carl did not smile nor flinch. He was very serious.

Barbette pulled away slightly while feeling so turned on she was having a hard time keeping herself in check. She was losing it and loving it at the same time. She admired his straight forwardness and the power he had over her, but she knew she had to leave before she allowed herself to venture into a place of no return.

"Are you one of the producers giving this showcase party?" She asked.

"Yes I am. Have you enjoyed yourself?"

"Yes I have."

"Well, what about the party?"

"Thank you for inviting me but I was just about to leave. I have to be somewhere later today." Barbette replied as she pulled away.

He pulled her back towards him and said, "Maybe some other time."

Barbette looked into his hazel brown eyes and said in a sexy but demanding tone, "Please, let me go."

Carl let his hands and arms fall down to his side, he stepped back, positioned himself, adjusted his tie while never losing eye contact with her. With a devilish smile on his face he said, "My bad."

As Barbette turned to walk away she looked back and said, "If fate will have it maybe you will see me again, Mr. Hunter."

Carl watched her as she walked away and thought to himself, "She is one FINE ass woman. Oh yeah, fate will have it and I will definitely have it. Yes, I will."

Barbette finally reached the bar from the dance floor.

Wayne approached her from behind the bar. "Hey, I guess you didn't need an introduction?"

"I guess not," Barbette said. "I still have to go to the ladies room. I will be right back, and then I'm leaving."

"Gotcha," Wayne said as he proceeded to wipe down the bar top.

Barbette smiled all the way to the bathroom carrying thoughts of Carl and what had transpired between them feeling pleased that she didn't give him the impression of being an easy prey. Barbette suddenly thought about the days when she was unable to control her lustful desires. She was hoping that she had lost some of her jezebel ways. She was now treading the road less traveled of her promiscuous past. She was becoming a lady with much respect for herself and high morals, instead of what some people considered a whore. The year before she met Tim she had just about done everything a woman could do sexually causing her to lose most of her dignity and self-respect. She would pick up men every day and anywhere, for one night of sexual bliss. She went to the raunchiest bars in Atlanta and hung out with the roughest of the rough necks and thugs. The only thing that she could think about was sex back then. She constantly prayed that she would become a changed woman.

As she was drying off her hands, the bathroom door opened and a red head young lady appeared. She stopped to check herself out in the mirror, interrupting Barbette's thoughts of her past life. The young lady spoke to her and proceeded into a bathroom stall. Barbette exited the bathroom and headed back to the bar.

"Well Wayne, it's been a pleasure. I'll check you later." She said.

"Okay be careful out there." He replied with a wink while waving his hand.

"I will. Bye-bye," she said.

Barbette walked out of the club and then remembered that she had parked across the street. As she started towards the curb Carl came up behind her and asked, "Would you like me to walk you to your car? It could be pretty rough out here and you may need my help."

Barbette spun around and looked at him with a startled look on her face and asked, "Where did you come from?"

"I've been following you," Carl replied with a smirk.

Barbette shook her head as if to say, "This man is crazy." They both remained silent while they crossed the street to the parking lot. As they approached the space where her Jag was parked, Carl's face lit up as he checked out her fly ride. "Wow!" Was written all over his face.

"Nice. Who do you work for?" he asked with excitement in his voice.

Barbette smiled and replied, "What do you mean?"

"You know what I mean. You have to make at least $100,000 a year or more to drive a car like this baby."

Barbette started to laugh. "Oh really?" she said, "Well, it was a gift."

"A gift? Nice gift!" Carl replied.

Barbette checked him out under the lights of the parking lot. She liked what she saw. "I'm a lawyer." She confessed.

"That's nice to know. I might need you one day, for legal assistance as well as for other reasons." He smiled at her as he opened her car door. "May I have your phone number?" he asked.

"Sure, if I can have yours."

"Why would you think you would have to ask?"

"Why? Because you haven't offered to give it to me that's why!" Barbette replied with a wry smile crossing her lips. "Okay, let me ask you this—are you married? Have children? Beaten women?"

Carl stopped Barbette in the middle of her next question and answered 'No' to every one of them.

"So, what's wrong with you?" Barbette asked.

Carl hesitated for a minute and said, "Only one thing."

"And what is that?" she asked, wearing a puzzled look on her face.

Carl looked her in the eyes and said, "I love to love women."

"*Women?*" Barbette said in a sassy tone.

"Yes, I love women!" Carl repeated.

"So, tell me, Carl, how many *women* do you have?"

"Right now? None," Carl replied.

"Sure, Carl, I believe you," she said sarcastically. "But I'll still give you my number because I like your style."

"Thank you, Queen Barbette. I feel honored."

"Here's my card." she said.

They exchanged business cards then Barbette got in her car. Carl leaned over the car door and asked, "Would you mind if I kissed you good night."

Ooh no, not at all, Barbette thought. Suddenly she snapped out of her little fantasy to regain her composure and said to Carl, "Yes, I would mind. But, but . . ."

"Yes? But what?" Carl asked with raised eyebrows, still gazing into her eyes.

Never mind, Barbette thought; *I almost lost control. One kiss and I know he'll end up in my bed. Stop while you're ahead girlfriend,"* she said to herself and smiled.

Barbette started up the engine of her car, a soft purr, and pulled off in the direction of the condo. After she turned the corner and went through two lights, she looked in the rear-view mirror and noticed a white mustang behind her. She turned left down Peachtree towards her dad's place She checked her mirror again and the car was still there, so she decided to find out if the car was following her. She pulled in to a 24-hour gas station a block from the condo and the white car followed. Once in the station the car pulled up beside her. It was Carl.

"Damn man! What the hell do you think you're doing?" Barbette said while shaking her head. She didn't know whether to be scared or flattered by his persistence.

"Just following you to make sure you get home safely." He yelled from his open car window.

Barbette could not believe it.

"Sure Carl," she said. She wondered if this man was crazy or desperate.

He got out of his car and approached her.

"Hey, I got an idea," he said

"Yes?" Barbette was wondering what Carl had in mind.

Carl went on to explain that he thought Barbette should invite him to her place for coffee. He made it clear that this would be an opportunity for them to get to know each other and to find out if she was capable of making a decent pot of coffee.

Barbette also wanted to get to know Carl and felt that sharing a cup of coffee at her place at 4am in the morning would not be too detrimental. Carl was very charming, confident and so convincing.

"Okay," she said, "only coffee and conversation."

"I promise," Carl replied.

Barbette allowed Carl to follow her to the condominium, which was located in the Buckhead area of Atlanta. The two bedrooms, two-bath penthouse was perched at the top floor of a high-rise building. A view of the Atlanta skyline showed through the ceiling to floor windows that covered the entire wall on the south side of the building and the large kitchen filled the best part of the north side area. Her dad had recently purchased the condo as a tax write off and she and Lance had stocked it with clothing, food and other necessities for those nights that they didn't, and couldn't make the drive home.

Carl pulled in behind Barbette as she went through the underground security-parking gate and parked his car in the guest parking space adjacent to hers. As they walked to the elevator, Carl using a joking tone, asked Barbette is this a gift too?" Barbette just looked at him and smiled.

Barbette opened the door to the condo and once inside had second thoughts about this "little interlude." She considered that it might have been a bad idea to invite Carl in for coffee, but continued with her plan anyway. Carl looked around the place and decided that this woman was very wealthy. The condo was decorated with cream furnishings and drapes with hardwood floors that ran all through the house except for the entrance, which was covered in peach and gray marble. Carl wondered who she was and to whom where her people. He knew, and mingled with, most of the wealthy black and white families in Atlanta but he had never met her before this night. He decided not to question her on her family history and would just focus on getting her in the bed, on the floor, or anywhere else he could possibly get her.

Barbette invited Carl into the kitchen and he followed her enjoying the view of Barbette's shapely ass. He took off his suit jacket and rested it on the back of one of the bar stools that match the kitchen island furniture. Barbette immediately noticed Carl's muscle definition and assumed he was a man who worked out often.

She said in an inviting tone, "You may have a seat if you wish."

"No, that's alright, I prefer to stand."

"How do you like your coffee?" she asked

"Black with a little bit of cream and no sugar will be fine." Carl replied.

Barbette poured the water in to the coffee maker and set two coffee cups with matching saucers on the island.

"Where are you from?" she asked, as she went to the silverware drawer to retrieve spoons.

"Texas," he replied.

"What brought you to Atlanta?"

"My brother got into some trouble and I came to help him out, I found that I liked the city and decided to stay."

"Where are you from, Barbette?"

"I was born in LA but we've lived in a lot of places. Most of my teen years were spent in boarding schools and seven years ago, we moved here.

Barbette reached for the coffee pot and poured coffee in both cups while Carl stood at the end of the island in silence. Barbette looked up from pouring coffee and asked in a faint warm tone, "Carl would you like a donut or *something* with your coffee?"

It seemed like it was taking forever for Carl to respond to her question. He walked slowly towards Barbette, came up so close behind her that they seemed to have become one. Barbette did not move an inch. Carl leaned over and feeling his hot breath in her ear, whispered in a sensuous tone.

"I don't care much for a donut but I would definitely like to have the *something*, if I may, please. How about it baby? Right here, right now?"

Barbette started breathing so hard she felt faint. Managing to get control of herself, she said in a strong controlling voice, "Carl, we agreed you were coming up for coffee and conversation only, *remember?*" She slid past Carl, and in doing so, rubbed up against his body causing her excitement to increase to the point of bursting. She walked towards the refrigerator to get the cream and tried to settle her jumbled senses as best she could. Carl leaned against the island and watched her for a while not saying a word.

This girl is so damn sexy and I will have her ass before the night is over. Yes, Yes, Yes, he thought. He finally spoke in a low masculine tone and smiled at her as he said, "Sure, I remember our agreement, but you were the one that offered the *something* with the coffee.

God, this man is as smart as I am. A relationship with him would never work, Barbette thought.

Barbette put the coffee cup in front of Carl and handed him the cream with the hopes that he would not touch her. She was starting to feel afraid of her feelings and wondering if the moistness that he had provoked between her legs was seeping through on her pants. She maintained her cool as she sat on the bar seat next to him and began stirring her coffee.

"Tell me some more about yourself Carl," she asked.

"Well," he said. "I have three brothers and I'm the middle child. We grew up poor. My mother was, and still is, a secretary and my father he was never around much after they separated."

"But, I thought he died and left you money?" Barbette spurted out without thinking.

"Who told you that?" he asked outwardly disturbed by the question.

"My father, He knows all about your business and how you and your partner started it. My father knows a lot of people." She said by way of an explanation.

Carl didn't want to ask who her father was. He wanted to concentrate on the matter at hand. "Yes, my dad did leave me and my brothers some money. He was a plant worker for most of his life. My mother and father separated but never divorced and we pretty much raised ourselves."

"I'm sorry to hear that," Barbette said lowering her eyes and feeling truly sorry for Carl's circumstances.

"Barbette, enough about me; tell me some things about you," he requested.

"What is it that you would like to know?"

Carl shifted his body around in his seat in order to face her. As their eyes met, she could feel her heart beating faster, in anticipation of what he was about to do. His hazel eyes were hypnotic and she became overwhelmed by his presence.

"I want to know your likes and dislikes and what you would like me to do for or perhaps to you baby girl," he said softly.

Barbette realized at that moment if Carl did not leave she would do something that she would probably regret.

"You might want to leave now," she said it so fast; she surprised herself.

"Now?" said Carl bewildered.

"Yes, Now!" Barbette insisted in a demanding tone.

Carl knew he had ruffled her feathers and felt that he had her just where he wanted her. Carl had learned from previous experiences with other women, how to play his hand to get what he wanted.

Barbette got up from her stool and Carl grabbed his jacket and followed her. They walked to the door and Barbette leaned against it. "Well, it was nice meeting you Carl." She was feeling like she was about to explode.

Carl spoke in a low seductive tone, "Thanks for the coffee baby and I have just one request. I've made this request once tonight already".

"I'm afraid to ask what that might be," Barbette replied nervously.

"Please allow me to kiss you good night? Please, just one little kiss, just one" Carl said, as he displayed mass sex appeal while licking his lips.

Barbette knew she wanted to feel Carl's lips on hers if only for a second and although she was afraid, she felt that it would be all right since he was already at the door preparing to leave.

"Okay, just one kiss," she answered.

Barbette leaned against the door; her hand clinching the doorknob. Carl took his tongue and licked her lips in an extremely slow and circular motion going from top to bottom. Barbette wanted to escape the fire of her sensual desires as she felt her body heat up, but her legs would not allow her to move an inch.

Softly he whispered, "Don't move. Oh God, please, don't move, baby." He put his tongue in her mouth sucking and nibbling on her lips like they were candy.

Barbette continued to fight back the feeling, but she knew he was winning. Carl placed one hand around her waist and pulled her close to him, and with his other hand managed to unbutton her blouse. "Relax, just relax," he whispered softly in her ear speaking in a low seductive tone. "I only want to make you feel good, that's all." Carl gently pushed Barbette against the door and while continuing to kiss her, managed to unbutton and unzip her pants.

Barbette could not control the passion within her and knew that if she did not get out of this position she would be in trouble. As Carl slid his hand down her pants and begin rubbing the wetness between her legs, Barbette started to tremble, and Carl realized that he had her at a point of no return. He had won and she could not do a damn thing about it, except relax and bask in the pleasure.

Hearing her moan he realized that this woman had totally surrendered to him and was hot and ready for what was yet to come. Carl stopped kissing her and looked into her eyes.

"Hey baby," he said, "why don't we go to your bedroom and get comfortable."

Barbette was speechless and overwhelmed by his seductive power. Carl took her hand as she led him to the bedroom then sat on her bed, transfixed, as Carl unbuttoned his shirt exposing his perfectly sculpted masculine physique. Her eyes followed his every move. She knew this was wrong but she didn't want to make it right, at least not at the moment.

He continued to undress until he was naked. Barbette lay back on the bed as he undressed her and positioned her legs so that he could climb between them. Suddenly, Carl stopped and backed away making eye contact with her. As he leaned over her, he asked, "Barbette, has it been a long time?"

"Yes," she answered. "How did you know?"

"By the way you where trying to fight it. Relax baby. I promise I won't hurt you. All I want to do is please you. We won't do anything you don't choose to do. I do understand that 'no' means 'no' in many languages: English, Chinese, Spanish, Italian and also sign language, *okay?*" Carl said with a chuckle.

"Okay," Barbette replied with a smile.

He had already pulled out a condom; he put it on and entered her very slowly while gently caressing the walls of her jade gate.

Barbette started to moan and tears rolled out of her eyes.

Carl stopped and asked, "Am I hurting you"?

Barbette answered softly, "Yes. But please don't, don't stop."

Carl proceeded to enter her more intensely and began moving in a more rhythmic motion. He leaned close to her ear and said, "I will not cum until you do. I want to please you first."

Barbette let go of all her fears and totally succumbed to Carl. After a while he realized that she was about to reach the top and breathlessly asked her, "Is it good; huh? Huh? Talk to me baby. What's my name girl? Ooh shit you're so fucken wet; girl you feel so good. Cum for me, baby.

"I'm cumin! I'm cumin! Oh shit; ooh shit . . ." Barbette screamed out, as she grabbed Carl's ass tighter, pushing him deeper into her as her climax got closer. At last she reached her peak. Carl controlled himself until he felt the wetness from her release and then he couldn't hold it any longer. His body began to tremble and he arched his back till he released himself fully allowing his body to scream with pleasure.

As Barbette lay there completely satisfied. She thought, *why did I allow this to happen?*

Carl lay on top of Barbette. He wasn't able to move at all. Barbette whispered in his ear. "Carl?"

He answered the best he could, "What baby?"

"Carl, what's my muthafuckin' name?"

They both laughed softly.

*   *   *

Barbette was awakened by the radio alarm clock on the nightstand beside her bed. The song playing on the radio was one of her favorites, an old classic by Aretha Franklin, Dr. Feel Good. She reached for the knob of the radio and managed to turn the volume down just enough so that she could still hear the words of the song.

Barbette knew that Carl had spent the night, but wasn't sure if he had already left or was still in the condo. She lay in bed looking up at the ceiling thinking about the evening and how hard she tried to stay away from men like Carl. She regretted what had happened but at the same time loved every minute of it.

Barbette knew, from what he had done to her, that Carl was a true ladies-man and had been with many women. She recognized him as a risk-taker and knew that he could not be tied down to one woman; especially not someone like her, who had the same needs and experiences.

Barbette heard the bathroom door open and looked in that direction. Carl stood there, looking at her with a smile on his face. "Did you sleep well?" he asked.

Barbette looked at him and remembered the thrill of reaching her climax and the way he was able to accommodate her needs several times. He stood naked in front of her and she was turned on again. She finally spoke, "Yes, I did"

Carl sat on the bed next to Barbette and caressing her hair, leaned over to gently kiss her lips. He removed his lips from hers and smiled.

"Barbette," he said. "Can I ask you a question?"

"Sure," she replied, wondering why he was smiling.

"Is your hair a weave or your natural hair?" Carl started to laugh and she realized how pretty his teeth were.

Barbette pushed him away and could not help but laugh with him.

Carl said, "I just realized that you have very long hair. You see, last night, your hair was pinned up and now it down. As a matter of fact it's down your back."

"Now tell me the truth because I will find out—is it your hair or not?"

Still laughing she answered, "Yes, Carl this is my hair, I grew it on my own. Tell me, Carl, do you not think that black women are able to grow long hair?"

Carl kept smiling . . . "Don't get me wrong. That's not what I'm saying. I just didn't realize that your hair was so long," he said apologetically.

"Maybe you shouldn't pickup women in bars and sleep with them until you know the length of their hair and other things about them."

"Is there something else I should know about you?"

"Yes," Barbette answered with a silly look on her face.

"And, what's that?" Carl asked with a worried look on his face.

"You didn't notice? I only have one leg!" Barbette answered with a smirk on her face.

They began laughing uncontrollably.

Carl started to get dressed while explaining to Barbette that he had to meet with his partner, Dean. But Barbette was not buying it. She knew who Carl was. She was Carl in female form. She felt that he was lying, but played along with it. She walked him to the door; her body draped in her bathrobe. Carl leaned up against the door and pulled her close to him.

"Hey," he said, in a low voice, "you know this is where we started last night?"

Barbette couldn't help but admire Carl's facial features. He had a perfect nose and mouth. She liked his strong cheekbones and enticing hazel eyes. Carl pulled her to him and began kissing her and Barbette found herself wanting him again. She wanted him to stay but didn't want him to know how she felt. She pulled away. "Bye, Carl."

He opened the door and said, "I'll talk to you later."

Barbette closed and locked the door after him and went back to bed. She lay in bed thinking about what had happened. She tried so hard not to let herself go. She thought about the way Carl made love and knew that, if she could, she would have sex with him every minute of the day. He had opened Pandora's Box, and once it was opened, she felt that it would be hard to close it again. Barbette was afraid that she would go back to her old habits of sleeping around. Picking up strange men and doing things sexually that she could not even speak about was definitely not a path she wanted to walk down again. She said aloud to herself, "I probably need help," and fell asleep once again.

Barbette heard the phone ring and thought she was dreaming and then realized it was her cell phone on the nightstand. She reached over to answer it and found her dad on the line.

"Hello, daughter, I thought you were coming home last night?"

"Oh!" Barbette said startled into quick recall of her promise, "I'm so sorry Daddy. I was supposed to help you today—"

He cut her off in mid sentence. "That's OK. I didn't get up till late anyway. I'll have Clara Mason work on it tomorrow." Clara was daddy's top Paralegal. She had been with the law firm from the beginning.

"So, how was the party," he asked.

"It was fine. I had a good time and even had the pleasure of meeting one of the producers, Carl Hunter."

"Carl?" he asked surprised at this unexpected news. "What did you think of him?"

"He seems to be a very nice guy," she said, while thinking, *he is a bad ass muthafucka.*

"That's good, that's good," her dad replied.

"What time do you think you'll be getting up?"

"What time is it?" she said softly.

"Twelve noon!"

"Oh, I think I'll get up now, get dressed and spend a couple of hours working on the Patterson file."

"Okay then. If you need me call me. Hey, Barbette, are you okay?" he asked.

"Yes daddy, I'm fine," she answered quickly, hoping that her dad would not ask any more questions.

"Okay then. Talk to you later."

"Okay Dad, I love you, bye." Barbette was happy to be ending their conversation, finally.

"You too, baby," he said.

Barbette got out of bed and headed to the bathroom. She began brushing her teeth, looking in the mirror at herself, wondered what she should do to her hair. The phone rang again and she hurried to answer it with toothpaste in her mouth.

"Hello!"

"Hello baby."

She knew right away it was Carl.

"Yes, Carl, what can I do for you?" she asked, feeling excited about him calling.

"Everything you did last night and more," he replied. "But I can hold out till later. Hey, I called to invite you out tonight. My partner and I have to go check out this jazz group on the south side. I'd like you to come with us. He's bringing his lady friend, so, it's a double date kind of thing—How about it Ms. B.?"

Barbette thought for a minute and said, "Okay that might be fun—What time?"

"I'll be by to pick you up at 7:30. Is that Okay with you?" Carl asked.

"Sure," Barbette replied foaming at the mouth with toothpaste.

"See you then baby," Carl said and hung up abruptly.

Barbette replaced the receiver and finished brushing her teeth. She jumped in the shower and let the water pour down on her from the four showerheads. While lathering up, she thought about how Carl had touched her between her legs and how good it felt. She began rubbing her stomach with her hand and couldn't help letting her other hand rub between her legs. She wanted to pretend her hands where Carl's hands. Barbette closed her eyes and tried to imagine Carl touching her but realized that she could never touch herself the way he had touched her. She continued lathering her body and thinking about how Carl had given her such a feeling of ecstasy and she wished that she had never met him. Barbette finished soaping herself down and as she began washing her hair, she smiled as she remembered Carl's inquiring about her hair.

While rinsing her body and hair, Barbette realized that the shower had been what she had needed all along. She felt relaxed and refreshed. Looking in the mirror, she noticed a passion mark on her neck that was put there by Carl and she smiled. She knew she liked him a lot and was trying to be cautious but it was not working for her at all.

*   *   *

Carl stepped out of the shower and began drying off. He decided he would lie down for a few minutes to rest his eyes. He lay on his back; letting the air from the ceiling fan brush against his body. He was thinking about his evening with Barbette. Carl wondered—what type of name was Barbette? And who was she? He loved the sex he had with her, but knew he wasn't ready to make a commitment to any woman in his life. Carl's cell phone rang and broke his daydream. He reached for it lying on the other end of the bed.

"Yes?"

"Hello, Carl." The voice on the other end was his lady friend, Terri. Terri was fine. She was about 5'6 inches tall, shoulder length black hair, long legs and could give head better than any other woman he had ever met. Carl got excited just hearing her voice. He prop his head up on the two pillows behind him and continued listening. Terri was asking him to come by later. She explained that she had been out of town and now she was back. Terri worked for a major airline, as a flight attendant and had been in Chicago. She insisted on seeing him, saying that she had missed him and needed him. Carl knew he had made arrangements to take Barbette out that evening and could not change his plans. As a matter of fact, he did not want to change his plans. Carl was curious about whom Barbette was and wanted to spend more time with her to find out what else she could offer him sexually. He ended the call and laid there with a smile on his face, thinking, "Why am I such a DOG?"

Carl cell phone rang again while he was looking in his closet. He decided on a navy blue pin stripe suit and a white shirt as he walked swiftly out of the closet towards his bed, answering the phone on the third ring.

"Yep!"

"It's me, man." It was his partner, Dean Jenkins.

"Hey, man. What's up?"

"Did you choose a date for tonight yet?" Dean asked.

"You know I have, man. I'm bringing the lady I met last night" Carl replied.

"Who is she?"

"Man, why you all in my business?" Carl said with laughter in his voice.

"Come on, man, you know I don't have fun no more since I hooked up with Dee. Come on now. So tell me man who is she?"

"Ok, Ok," said Carl, "her name is Barbette Jackson and she is a fine ass lawyer"

Dean was quiet for a moment.

"Hello, Hello! What's up with you? You got something to say, man?" Carl asked.

Dean answered, "Hey, man. Is she the Barbette Jackson whose daddy owns one of the largest black entertainment law firms in the world? If so, man her father is worth over 500 million or more . . ."

"*What?*" Carl couldn't believe his ears. "What do you mean, man?"

"Carl, if this is who I think it is; we have hit the jackpot, man." Excitement was in Dean's voice.

"Her father, Raymond Jackson, has all the connections. Everybody knows and respects him. Man, she can help us pull together investors and sponsors for that Tribute to Ray Charles Christmas concert we want to do in December."

Carl held the phone in his hand and tried to remain cool. He was in shock; now he knew who Barbette really was and began to smile.

"Hello," said Dean

"Yeah, man," Carl replied. "I'm here."

"Would you mind if I talked business with her tonight?" Dean asked.

Carl smiled to himself and started to think about how well Dean could put business deals together. "Knock yourself out, man. It's cool, it's cool," Carl finally uttered still in shock at what he had just heard.

"All Right," Dean said, excited about the opportunity of talking business with the daughter of the famous Raymond Jackson. "I'll meet you later."

Carl hung up the phone without saying bye. He started to wonder if Barbette was ever going to tell him who she is. He knew she could help them, but he also knew that he would not be committed to her just because she was in a position to help them.

Carl looked at the clock and realized that he needed to finish getting dressed so that he would not be late picking up the "million dollar woman." He smiled as he thought about how damn fine Barbette was.

Carl arrived at Barbette's condo at 7:45. She had given him the entry code to the security gate which allowed him into the parking deck. Carl parked his car in the same spot he had the night before. Carl pressed the intercom buzzer in the elevator and adjusted his tie while he waited for Barbette to answer.

"Who is it?" Barbette asked.

"It's Carl," he replied

She released the lock that allowed the elevator to bring him up.

Barbette opened the door and waited for Carl to reach her apartment. He walked in wearing the navy pin stripe suit he'd picked out earlier and smelling like he just got out of the shower. Barbette was dressed in a black low cut geometric style Suzy dress.

Carl took Barbette in his arms and said, "You are so beautiful."

"You look pretty damn good yourself," she replied. Carl began kissing Barbette, sticking his tongue down her throat and sucking her lips as he had the night before.

Barbette began to feel excited once again.

Carl pulled away and sat down on the couch. He looked at her body draped in that black dress and began thinking about how bad he wanted to tap that ass again. He asked in a sensuous tone, "Want to stay home and make a movie?"

Barbette smiled, "Later. You made a commitment to meet your partner so, come on let's go before we're late."

EPISODE TWO

The Club

On the way to the club Carl talked about the jazz group that he and Dean were going to be checking out that night. He talked about how he and Dean had met. Carl explained that he had dated Dean's sister, Donna, for a couple of months and after realizing it wasn't going to work between them, the two of them had became good friends. Donna had introduced Carl to her brother Dean, when she discovered Carl was trying to put together a production company. In no time, Dean and Carl realized that they had similar educational backgrounds, degrees in business, and were on the same page when it came to business ideals. Finally they got together and everything clicked.

Dean and Carl had been in business now for three years and there business was worth about two million dollars which did not include the profits from the investments they had made purchasing several pieces of property in the city.

One of the properties they owned was an old house located in the Piedmont area, which they had renovated, and were using as their residence. They also owned a five-story office building located in the Virginia Highland area where their office was located. Dean and Carl were fast becoming well known by Atlanta's elite and a recent Atlanta magazine said that they were giving the best events in Atlanta.

Carl pulled up in front of the club and Barbette was surprised to find herself in front of the JJ Jazz Club. She knew the owner of this club very, very well. Barbette never thought to ask Carl the name of the club before leaving the condo. The club had valet parking; a young man hurried to open her car door.

Barbette stepped out of the car and stood on the curb watching Carl retrieved his parking ticket. Carl walking up to Barbette and taking her hand in his, Carl said, "Come on beautiful."

Barbette walked hand in hand with Carl towards the doors of the club. As they entered, a lady seated on a stool at the bar noticed Barbette and smiled. She quickly got up and coming towards Barbette and Carl said (practically screaming at the top of her voice), "Barbette Jackson, how the hell have you been?"

Smiling broadly, Barbette hugged the lady and replied, "Wild! Wanda girl, how you been doing? Girl you look good."

"So do you," Wanda said.

"Hey, Carl," Wanda said, looking in Carl's direction. Barbette assumed they knew each other, but was not sure how well.

Wanda added, "Let me show you to your seats." She looked towards Carl again, "Dean has been waiting for you about 15 minutes."

The club was packed; every table full. Barbette assumed that the group they came to see was very good and started to feel excited about hearing them. As they walked pass the bar, with Wanda leading the way, Carl dropped Barbette's hand and walked over to talk to a black woman with red hair sitting at the bar. The woman was wearing a purple tank dress and purple shoes to match. Barbette turned to look at Carl and wondered whom this woman was, that she could cause Carl to leave her in order to talk to her.

Carl returned to Barbette and told her to follow Wanda and that he would be right behind her shortly—Picking up on Barbette's attitude. Carl looked at the women at the bar, then back at Barbette and said, "Just business baby, just business." Barbette was so angry she wanted to scream. She managed to retain some composure and continued to follow Wanda to the front table where Dean and his lady, Dee, were sitting. When Barbette reached the table, she introduced herself to Dean and Dean introduced Dee to her.

Barbette took the seat next to Dean and thought to herself that Dean was one dark chocolate, very attractive, sexy brother. Dean talked about his pleasure in meeting her and how impressed he was with the manner in which her dad had managed to build a million-dollar business.

Barbette was distracted and found herself looking back at the bar while listening to Dean. She saw that Carl had his hands on the redheaded woman's leg and just as Barbette was about to turn around to give Dean her full attention, Carl bent over and kissed the woman. Barbette thought, *"You cannot get mad. You knew what you were getting into when you met him. It is you're dumb ass fault for being with him."*

Barbette turned around to face Dean and asked, "Who is that lady Carl is talking to at the bar?" Dean stretched his neck to find Carl at the bar, then, he hesitated for a second and said, "I don't know, why?"

"No reason, just thought I knew her," she lied. Barbette did not want Dean to know that seeing Carl with another woman had upset her.

They ordered drinks and just as the show was about to start, Carl arrived at the table. He pulled his chair close to Barbette and asked, "You all right"?

"Why wouldn't I be?" Barbette responded, even though she was mad as hell.

The band came up on the stage—four fine back men. They began to play a jazz song that sounded familiar to Barbette. She got into the song, feeling every note and liking it.

Barbette directed her eyes towards the trumpet player and realized that she knew him. It was James Cole. James had gotten into trouble dealing drugs and had spent two years in prison. She caught his eye and he smiled at her. After the set, he motioned his head towards the back hallway and Barbette took it as an invitation to talk to him. Barbette excused herself from the table and Carl asked, "Where are you going?"

"To the ladies room, I think." She answered. Carl looked at Barbette wearing a confused look on his face. Barbette walked to the hallway towards the bathrooms and met up with James. He reached out took her hand and pulled her to him. James kissed Barbette softly on her lip and said "Hey, baby." Barbette returned his greeting.

Barbette asked, "When did you get out?"

"About nine months ago," he said. "Hey. Barbette," he added quickly, "I wanted to thank you for all you did for my family while I was gone and putting money in my account while I was in there."

Barbette said, "No problem, I owed you man."

Back in the day, James had supplied Barbette and her friends with free drugs many times. They had even slept together a few times.

"Is that your man you're with?" James asked.

"No. I just met him."

"Well," said James in a sexy tone, "if you need a real man don't hesitate to call me." He took a pen and a matchbook out of his pocket and wrote his number on it and handed it to her.

Barbette replied in a sexy voice, "You know I will."

"Are you staying for the next set?" James asked.

"I think so."

"Okay," said James, and if I don't get a chance to talk to you again before you leave, give me a call sometimes. It's cool, I don't live with a woman anymore, I roommate with my brother."

"I will, good seeing you man," Barbette replied gently—she liked James. She walked to the table wearing a smile. Carl pulled out her chair and assisted her in sitting down.

"I saw you talking to that guy," he said, "what was that about?" Barbette said in an icy voice.

"Just business baby; just business!"

She could tell Carl was hot. He did not like it at all. Barbette felt that this was payback for his stop at the bar to talk to the red-head woman. They were even now. She smiled and crossed her legs.

The show was great but Barbette could not wait to get home and spend some time alone with Carl. As they walked through the crowd towards the exit, Barbette saw a familiar face standing by the bar. It was Jerry Jones, the owner of the club. She was hoping and praying that he would not see her when Carl hollered, "Jer! Jer!, Man, over here!"

Barbette could not move; she should have realized that Carl would know Jerry since they had come to see the jazz group in his club. Jerry motioned Carl and Dean to the bar. When they were able to reach each other, they shook hands followed by a quick embrace, and Jerry said, "Man, I'm sorry I'm late. I wanted to talk to you guys. Did you enjoy the show?"

Barbette kept her face turned away, pretending she was looking for somebody in the crowd. She was hoping they might get to leave before Jerry saw her. Jerry turned towards Dee and said, "What's up Ms. Dee?"

"Nothing man. How have you been doing?" Dee replied.

"Just fine, for an old man."

Barbette knew that Jerry was 18 years older than she was. She had met Jerry through her father when she was eighteen and Jerry and her dad played golf together. In fact, her father was once part owner of his club but her father had allowed him to purchase the interest that he owned in the club, a year earlier.

Jerry had been Barbette's sex-partner and she would never forget how good he was. Being older and more experienced Jerry had taken every opportunity to teach her everything he knew about sex. Also, just being around him had put her in a great position to learn a lot about running a business; he owned three clubs in Atlanta. Barbette remembered how he used to love to have her in his office—on his desk. She always thought that might have been a power thing with him, but had to admit that she loved it herself.

Barbette assumed Jerry knew Dee pretty well from the brief conversation they had. Dee had said more to him than she had to Barbette all night.

Jerry turned towards Carl and asked, "What's your lady's, name Carl"

"Oh yeah," Carl said almost distractedly as he pulled Barbette by the hand forcing her to face Jerry. Jerry looked shocked. He stared at Barbette, wearing a surprised look on his face. Carl noticed the way Jerry was looking at Barbette, but continued with the introduction. "Barbette this is Jerry, Jerry this is Barbette." Jerry put his hand out and Barbette took it in hers.

"It's been a long, long time," Jerry said.

Barbette just smiled. They never took their eyes off each other.

Carl quietly asked, "Do you two know each other?"

Jerry spoke up, "Very well . . . We met a long, long time ago." Jerry still had Barbette's hand in his and their eyes were still on each other.

Carl said, "Hey man—you want to meet tomorrow to talk about the group?" Jerry let go of Barbette's hand and brought his attention to Carl and Dean.

"Oh . . . yes," he said. "Can you come by the club around 1:30 in the afternoon?"

"Sure, we'll see you then," Dean replied in a hurry, noticing that Carl was upset about what just occurred between Jerry and Barbette. Dean could see that Carl really liked Barbette from Carl's actions but Dean also knew Carl and knew that Carl would not allow himself to be committed to Barbette or any woman.

The ride home was not a great one. Carl did not say a word. He turned the volume of the music up really loud, so that Barbette couldn't hear herself think nor have a conversation with him. As he got closer to her condo, Carl turned down the music and said, "Barbette can I ask you a question?"

"Yes, what is it Carl?"

"How well do you know Jerry?"

"I guess I can say, very well."

"Do you know his wife?" he asked.

Barbette looked at Carl face to look at the expression on his face and wondered where he was going with his questioning.

"Yes, I do know her," Barbette answered.

Carl then asked Barbette if the guy in the band and Jerry were old boyfriends of hers.

Barbette thought for a minute and decided that she couldn't call James or Jerry boyfriends; they were just man she fucked a long time ago and so she answered, NO!

Carl was still pretty upset so Barbette asked, "Are you upset or something?"

Carl answered, "Hell no, why would I be upset?"

Barbette said, "That's what I was wondering, but your facial expression tells me that you're not pleased with me knowing these men."

Carl didn't say anything as he pulled into the parking garage. He parked his car and walked with her to the elevators in silence.

Barbette assumed Carl was thinking about what he was going to ask next. He did not say a word as he grabbed her around the waist and kissed her so hard and long that it took her by surprise and threw her off-balance. Carl moved his hand up the side of Barbette's waist till he reached her breasts. Using his thumb, he began rubbing her nipples, going back and forth like a car windshield wiper. Barbette was so hot she couldn't wait to get him upstairs and in her bed. Carl slowly pulled away; allowing Barbette to punch in the code for the elevator then began kissing her again until the elevator arrived.

Suddenly, he stopped kissing her and said, "Barbette, I enjoyed your company tonight." He gave her a concerned look and added "Would you mind if I didn't walk you to your door tonight? I have some business to take care of."

Barbette turned and hurried into the elevator before Carl could see the tears welling up in her eyes. Wanting to get away from him, she pushed the button that automatically closed the doors, wanting them to shut even faster than they did.

Barbette was pissed off and wondered if Carl thought that turning her on and leaving her hanging was punishment.

"I hate him," she said.

Once in the condo, Barbette headed straight to her bedroom and began undressing. As she walked into her closet to hang up her dress, she thought about how she was not proud of her past but knew that she could not change it, even if she tried.

Barbette walked over to her vanity and started combing her hair trying to forget how horny she was, but could not stop thinking about the release she so desperately needed. She decided that she didn't have to do it herself. She knew many men that wanted to fuck her.

Barbette picked up her purse from the dresser and pulled out the matches with the trumpet player, James', phone number on it. Barbette held the phone in her hand and looking at the card, remembered the times she had with James. She remembered; the times they got high together, smoking dope and doing coke, and the orgies he used to have at his huge house in College Park. She wondered if he was still as wild as ever or if prison had set him free from hoes and drugs.

Barbette put down the phone deciding that she did not want to take the chance of getting wrapped up in that kind of life again. It was bad enough she had to deal with "Mr. Carl." She got on her knee and began to pray. *"Heavenly Father, please help me, please help me, Lord."*

Barbette was crying uncontrollably now. She knew that she had to walk away from Carl and that would not be an easy thing to do. She also remembered that she had committed herself to helping Dean by turning him and Carl on to some "Big Ballers" who could invest in the Tribute to Ray Charles concert. There was no way she was going to be able to get Carl out of her life right now.

Dean was not able to rest. He knew Carl was pissed off, and knew the things Carl could do when he was angry. He wondered if Barbette had gotten home safely, so he decided to call Carl on his cell.

"What?" Carl answered in a mean tone.

"Hey, man, this is Dean. Where are you?"

"Man, I'm over Terri's. Carl had decided to finish his night out with Terri. He knew Terri was going to please him and he didn't have to do anything, just lay back and LET IT FLOW.

"What do you want, man?" Carl asked, speaking in a low tone of voice.

Dean started to express his concern for Carl and let him know that he was worried about how pissed off he was when he left the club.

Carl was standing at the foot of Terri's king sized post-bed as Dean spoke to him, while watching Terry as she laid in the middle of her bed, wearing nothing but a garter belt with black stocking and black suede high-heel shoes. She was playing with her nibble rings and moving her body sensuously. Carl could not even hear with Dean was saying.

"What do you want, man," Carl demanded. He was starting to get really pissed off with Dean.

"Man. Are you alright? Carl, Carl . . ."

Terri had moved her hand down between her legs and inserted a finger in her very wet private area. As she brought the finger to her mouth and started sucking it, Carl said, in a shaky voice, "Dean, man, I got to go," and hung up.

Dean was still on the line. "Hello, hello, Carl." Dean realized that Carl had hung up. He knew that Terri and Carl had been kicking it off-and-on for two years and he knew Carl would be there all night—maybe two.

Dean wondered if it would be proper to call Barbette 11:00 at night to make sure she had made it home safely, after all, Carl had been known to drop a bitch on a corner and leave her there. He took the business card out of his pocket and looked at it and started to think about how Barbette looked as she walked up to the table. Dean remembered—the way she talked to him and how turned on he was by her. Dean tried to brush it off and decided that not having sex with Dee for four days, on top of drinking all that liquor, was probably the key factor in feeling aroused. He didn't want to admit that he was attracted to Barbette and was jealous that Carl had her attention.

EPISODE THREE

The Week

Barbette stepped off the elevator that opened to the law office which was located on the twenty-first floor of the building. With her briefcase in one hand and a cup of coffee in the other, she walked right by the administrator's who were busily working at their desks.

"Hi, Daddy," she said as she peeked in his office door. She walked in wondering if he was too busy for her, he didn't even look up from his work.

"Hey, Lady, how was your weekend?"

Barbette put down her briefcase and took a seat in front of his desk. "It was good," she said in a heartless tone.

Her dad had not heard a word she had said to him. He was trying to put together some last minute reports for the Monday morning staff meeting that was about to start. Finally he looked up from his laptop and noticed that his daughter was wearing a very attractive red suit and wore her hair loose hanging down her back.

"What's up, Barbette?" he asked, with a curious look on his face.

"What do you mean Dad?" she asked. She crossed her legs and adjusted her skirt.

"You're wearing a short skirt, high-heels and your hair is down. You never wear short skirts and your hair down to work anymore. What's going on?" he questioned. Barbette just smiled, stood up, grabbed her briefcase and left his office.

"I'll see you in the conference room," she said, as she closed his door. Barbette knew that nobody knew her better than her dad and younger

31

brother and she was debating if she should tell him about her date with Carl.

Barbette walked into the conference room. She believed was the prettiest conference room of all the office locations. The walls were painted in a warm gray and had accompanying gray and peach striped chairs to match the large executive conference tabletop carved and smoothed out of a dark gray marble slab.

"Barbette, sit in the chair to the left of her dad's seat, and leaning back, admiring the beautiful German chandelier he had purchased especially for this room.

"Barbette, where have you been all dam weekend?" Lance walking in the room carrying donuts and a bottle of milk in his hands.

"Hey, Man!" Barbette burst out all smiles. "I was at Dad's condo, relaxing."

"Sure you were," he said, "I heard you met Carl Hunter."

Barbette's smile changed into a surprised expression. She pulled herself straight up in her chair. "How do you know that?"

"You know, I know everything that goes on with you," he replied, with a grin on his face. "I hear he's an awesome lover, so tell me how was he?" he asked with a smart-ass tone.

Barbette, sometimes, hated her brother. He seemed to know everything she did. He was only one year younger than her, twenty-four, but acted like he was fifteen most of the time. Barbette and Lance used to hang out together, doing drugs and going to sex parties. The difference between the two is that Lance never stopped.

Barbette decided not to address his question and instead, began setting up her laptop to look over her reports. The other staff members started to arrive with—Beth Jenkins and Bobby Martin coming in together. Rumor had it that they were sleeping together. (They were both married—but, of course, not to each other.)

"How you folks doing?" Bobby asked. Barbette nodded an acknowledgement and continued looking at the reports. Mack Pain, Jamal Jefferson and Kerry Martin came in and walked over to the table on the left side of the room to help themselves to coffee and donuts before going to their seats. Ms. Star, at least that's what Barbette called her, walked in wearing a white Chanel pant-suit.

"Hello everybody," she said. Barbette called her Ms. Star because she was the best dam attorney in the firm and she looked like an old movie star. Jerome came in with a cup of coffee in one hand and his laptop in the other. He sat next to Barbette, as he always did, she was glad to see him. He was her favorite person. Jerome was a good-looking black gay man, but no one knew but her. They were good at keeping each other's secrets.

"Hi baby girl," he said

"Hello, Jerome," she replied.

"I tried to reach you on your cell phone this weekend. I had two tickets to that Sound the Horns play you wanted to see."

"Oh really?" Barbette said, turning to him in surprise.

"Yep, Marcus was not feeling well," he said in a low tone, "so he suggested that I should ask you."

Marcus was Jerome's live-in partner. He was an attorney at a downtown firm; he handled divorces for very wealthy people. Marcus was the top lawyer in his firm.

Barbette whispered in his ear, "I'm so sorry I missed it. I was busy."

"Doing what?" Jerome enquired curiously.

"Fucking," Barbette whispered.

Jerome pulled back his ear with a shocked look on his face. He looked her in the eyes and said, "You must tell me all about it and I want details."

"Oh I will, I will." She smiled, knowing that she had made his day.

At that moment Barbette's father walked in the conference room carrying his laptop.

"Hello ladies and gentleman," he said with authority, "I have great news, we have picked up four new clients and one of them is Matthew Walker." Matthew Walker was one of the top-ten singers in America.

Everyone showed their excitement by chatting amongst themselves.

Her father had reached his seat and continued delivering the news. "Jerome, you will be handling Matthew Walker."

"Me?" said Jerome, raising an eyebrow.

"Yes you. Do you have a problem with that?" Raymond asked.

"No sir!"

Jerome had a big smile on his face as he looked at Barbette for approval. She was hoping that he would get the account. She and her dad had discussed the account last week and she recommended Jerome because she knew how much he admired Matthew Walker and would do an excellent job handling his legal concerns.

Barbette's dad went on about the new business and she started daydreaming. She was thinking about Carl and if she would see him today or not. Jerome kicked her on her leg under the table to bring her attention back to the meeting, when at the same time, she heard her dad announcing that she would be going to the New York office the following week to assist Mr. Winston with the yearly audit. She was surprised and pissed-off at the same time. She did not want to leave town anytime soon. She had just met Carl and was trying to build a relationship with him.

Who am I kidding, she thought, *I don't have a relationship with that man, nor will I have one later. Staying here in Atlanta will not change anything. Anyway going to New York will give me the opportunity to do some shopping.* She began to pay attention to the rest of what her dad was saying. He was now talking about the accounts they had lost during the year and the reasons for these clients leaving the firm. Nobody was saying anything now.

While walking back to her office, Barbette stopped in the ladies room to check over her appearance and was happy to be alone giving her a minute to think about Carl. She took out her lipstick tube and applied a little on her lips until she felt it was to her satisfaction. Then she decided that she had better use the bathroom before going back to her office and went into one of the stalls. Closing the door, she wondered what Carl was doing this time of day and where he was. Barbette wanted to see him badly and was hoping that he would call her before lunch. She promised herself that she would try to stop thinking about him and concentrate on her work for the rest of the day. She had several contracts that were requiring her full attention.

She walked into her office happy to be sitting down. Her red shoes were starting to hurt her feet. She started her laptop and checked her messaged. None were from Carl. She wondered if he had lost her number, but remembered he knew where she worked and would be able to look-up her number in the yellow pages if he wanted to call.

She looked out of her large office windows that overlooked the highway and wondered, *where are those people going.* She loved her office. It was almost as large as her dad's, with a seating area that she chose to furnish herself. She had chosen a cream leather sofa and two wingback leather chairs to match. She selected a round glass top cocktail table, which sat in the center of the area in front of the sofa, placing a large vase on the table that held a purple and gold flower arrangement, which accented the purple and gold throw pillows she had placed on the leather sofa. There were two floor lamps on both sides of the sofa and a small glass end table that was stationed on the left side of the sofa that she had placed a candy dish filled with chocolate kisses. Her desk was placed on the opposite sided of the room. Her brother had purchased it from Demark Office Furnishings along with several other pieces of furniture for his office. He decided that the desk did not fit his style and offered it to her. Barbette loved the sleekness of the desk, the thin wood and the glass top that accented the wood. Two up-straight, goldish-tanned leather chairs were placed in front of her desk with a small wood table in between, on which her guests could put their drinks.

The ringing of her phone startled her. Her mind had been far away, daydreaming while looking out the window. She answered it on the second ring.

"Barbette Jackson . . ."

"Hey, Barbette, this is Dean Jenkins with CD Productions."

Barbette hesitated for a minute trying to figure out who he was and realized it was Dean, Carl's friend.

"Oh! Hey, Dean; how can I help you today?" she asked.

"First of all," he said "I'm glad you could join us last night and hope you enjoyed yourself."

"I sure did," she replied. "I really enjoyed the jazz."

Dean was relieved to know that she was all right. He remembered how mad Carl had been last night.

"Secondly, I just wanted to confirm our meeting for Saturday. I hope it's still on."

"Of course," Barbette replied.

"Good; so we'll meet at your condo about 1:30?"

"Right" and I plan to make lunch for us," Barbette offered. She wanted to ask were Carl was but didn't want Dean to know he was on her mind and wanted to keep their conversation on the business at hand only.

"You're going to make lunch? That's great!" he said with excitement. "I'll bring the wine."

"Okay then. It's all set."

"Okay, we'll see you then," Dean replied.

After hanging up, Dean thought how sexy Barbette sounded on the phone and how different she was compared to Carl's other lady friends. He couldn't wait till Saturday. As Carl walked in the office he realized Dean was hanging up the phone.

"Hey, man; who were you talking to?" he asked.

"Barbette," Dean answered reluctantly. "Just confirmed our Saturday meeting with her; she is going to make lunch for us."

"Great! Man, that woman is something else. I never met a woman that was good in bed and smart out of bed."

Dean knew that Carl liked her but thought that he might be a little intimidated by her cleverness—and she had not called him today. He was not used to women not calling. His ladies called him all day long.

Barbette sat behind her desk, wondering why the hell Carl didn't call to confirm the meeting. He knew she would want to hear from him instead of Dean, especially since he had fucked her. She felt like she had been used and wanted to go back in time to eliminate the day she met Carl from her life. She started working on a contract when Jerome poked his head into her office.

"Hey, girl, you got time to talk?"

"Come on in and have a seat," she said in a joyless tone. Jerome came in and walked to the opposite side of the room towards the leather sofa. He sat down and asked her to join him over there. Barbette got up and started walking slowly towards the sofa, when suddenly, it hit her. She could not hold it back any longer and began to cry. Jerome rose from the sofa and walked towards her.

He asked in an urgent tone, "What's going on with you?"

Barbette could not stop crying. She sat down on the sofa and started telling Jerome how she felt and what had happened with Carl. Jerome took her in his arms as he sat down again beside her and tried to comfort her.

"Barbette; I never seen you like this before, girl. Hey, he is just a man. Come on now pull yourself together." He kept hugging her and rubbing her back. A few seconds went by and Barbette finally regained control of herself.

"So, you fucked him, you made a mistake. Don't worry about it. Life goes on. Okay?" Barbette nodded to acknowledge his comment.

"Why don't you go home for the rest of the day? Oh, I know . . . why don't you go shopping?" Barbette smiled. She knew that shopping was always Jerome's way of solving problems.

Barbette packed up her laptop and went home. She walked in the house and went straight to the kitchen, pulled two quarts of Ben & Jerry ice cream out of the refrigerator and went up stairs to her bedroom. Looking around, she finally found the remote and clicked on the TV, flicking channels to find something to watch. It was only 12:30. After putting on her nightgown, she got in bed, opened her quart of ice cream and began eating. She thought about her past relationships being like Ben and Jerry. They were here long enough to make her feel good inside and then they were gone. She decided right then that she would only deal with Carl in a business way. Anyone that could make her feel the way he did need not be a part of her personal life.

Tuesday was like any other Tuesday. Barbette worked till 7:30 hoping that the gym would burn down so that she wouldn't have to go. Tuesdays and Thursdays were her workout days and she hated it. She had chosen to join the gym instead of working out at home in hopes of meeting a man. On the way to the gym she stopped to purchase Walker's new release, to listen to it while she did her 30 minutes on the treadmill. The gym was crowded giving her an excuse not to do her full workout program. She did her 30 minutes on the treadmill and left without saying a word to anybody. On her way home she finished listening to the CD and stopped at the Kroger to pick up more Ben & Jerry ice cream. When she arrived home no one was there. She went up to her room and took Ben & Jerry to bed with her.

Wednesday went by fast. Barbette was so busy; she had not had time to think about Ben & Jerry or Carl. But Thursday was different; she was caught up with her work and had an easy day before her, allowing her to think about Carl. She had not heard from him. She was glad, she thought, until the phone in her office rang fiercely.

"Barbette Jackson," she said. It was Carl.

"Hey baby, what's going on?"

Barbette was surprised to hear from him and asked him to hold on. She got up and went to close her office door so that no one would hear her conversation.

"Okay, I'm back," she said.

"How have you been doing baby? You know I missed you."

"If you missed me so much why haven't you called?" Barbette asked, trying not to sound emotional.

"I'm calling you now. I wanted to invite you to have dinner with me on Friday. I'm cooking. I realized we both have been busy, and I really didn't want to disturb you. You're not mad at me, are you?" Carl asked.

"Oh no," said Barbette, "I have been busy." There was a silent, almost ominous, pause between them.

"So, I'll see you Friday?" Carl asked

Barbette said, "Yes," holding back her excitement.

Carl gave her his address and told her to be there at 8:00 o'clock. She agreed and he hung up. He knew he had her where he wanted her.

He lay back in his chair, thinking about the last time he was with her and the way he had made her holler his name out. *"Carl, Carl,"* he said to himself while wearing a pleasing smile.

Barbette was trying not to think about her agreeing to have dinner with Carl when Jerome knocked on her door and peeked in. "Hey; is it alright to come in?"

Barbette smiled and said, "Yes, it is. Come on in."

"I was thinking about going to check out that new restaurant in Colony Square for lunch. Want to go? I'm buying."

Barbette agreed to go. She took a cigarette out of the pack she kept in her drawer to smoke on the way. Jerome saw her as she slipped it into her suit jacket pocket. He asked if she was a smoker again. Barbette used to smoke for a time, at least a pack a day, when she was studying for her bar exam.

"I only smoke once in a while," she answered. "I'm not a smoker."

Jerome started to laugh. "You are a smoker," he countered, chuckling.

The restaurant was excellent. Jerome could not get over how good the food was and how decent the prices were. As they left the restaurant and walked to the car Barbette ask Jerome if he wanted to go shopping. She knew he would. "Of course I do," he replied. What's the occasion—new boyfriend?

Barbette had not told him she had agreed to have dinner with Carl. She felt too ashamed to tell him after he rescued her from the outburst of tears she had the other day in the office.

"Or did you make up with that man, Carl?"

Barbette wanted to lie, but she didn't. "Yes, I did," she said. "Well, I think I did. We're having dinner together tomorrow night."

Jerome looked at her with pity in his eyes. "It's okay baby, I've been there before, just enjoy the ride. Shall we start with Fredrick of Hollywood?" Jerome asked. Barbette started to laugh. Jerome was a true friend, she thought; he always knew what to say to make her smile.

When she got off the elevator, her father was standing at the reception desk talking to Peter, the IT specialist. "Hey Barbette, I need to talk to you," he said. Barbette walked up to him wondering what he needed. He ended his conversation with Peter and then turned his attention to her.

"Yes, Dad, I mean, Raymond." She tried to remember to call him Raymond around the office. It was more professional. She smiled as she pushed her hair off her face. She had worn it down with a part on the side that caused the un-parted side to fall in her eyes.

"I want you to join me and Rhonda for dinner, after work today. It's business," he said.

Rhonda had been Raymond's girlfriend of more than a year. She was only eight years older than Barbette. Barbette had not seen her in a couple of weeks and was surprised that they were still together. Rhonda had been working for BMA legal department for five years and the rumor was that she was not too good at what she was doing.

"What makes this dinner a business dinner?" Barbette asked still puzzled.

"We're meeting Gregory Moreland at Country Place at 6:30."

Barbette started to feel happy about seeing Gregory and was glad she had worn something sexy to work and did not have to go home to change. She loved teasing Gregory. He was a famous gospel singer who knew the Lord better than anyone she knew. Barbette attended two meetings in the conference room and went back to her office to make some calls. She knew that her dad would be late meeting Gregory for dinner. He was known to be late for all his dinner meetings, so she hurried to make sure she arrived on time to meet Gregory. It was 5:45. She stated to clean her desk off and headed for the bathroom to refresh her makeup.

She pulled into the parking deck, finding a parking space right next to the elevator that went up to the mall where the restaurant was located. On the ride up she brushed off her black, Ann Taylor suit with her hands. She thought about how lucky Gregory was that she had worn a short wrapped skirt that opened on the side, allowing a leg to show once she sat down and crossed them. She unbuttoned two buttons on her blouse to allow her breasts to be more visible. Country Place was pretty crowded. She spotted Gregory at the bar and she walked towards him, smiling.

He got up from his bar stool to greet her. "Well, well, well," he said, "I was hoping you would come."

"I was hoping you would be here," Barbette replied and quickly informed him of her dad's tardiness. Of course, he already knew that her father would be late.

"Would you like a drink?" he asked, as Barbette took the stool next to him.

"Sure would," she said. "I would like a Sex-on-the-Beach, please."

Gregory ordered her drink, laughing at the name of it. He was a very attractive 30-year-old man who claimed that he had not had sex since he had committed himself to the Lord. "So, when's the last time you've had sex?" she asked softly.

"Oh, here we go again!" Gregory always got a kick out of her trying to convert him.

"Tell me this, Gregory?" Barbette asked; "You're sitting on your bar stool looking so damn fine in that navy blue suit, talking to me in that strong masculine voice, showing those pretty ass teeth, and I'm checking you out, feeling horny as hell. Now, can you tell me that you can sit there and look at me, with this short ass skirt showing my legs, wearing shinny ruby red lipstick, breast falling all out of my blouse, hair looking good as hell, and you don't feel horny or the least bit turned on? Let's hear it Greg. What do you have to say, man?"

"Well, God knows that we will sometime lose control of our lust, but He said that if we pray He will help us maintain our control and remain true to Him," Gregory replied.

Barbette then got up from her stool, took her jacket off and placed it on the back of the seat and turned her back to Gregory. She dropped a quarter on the floor, then bend over allowing her ass to pop up in Gregory's direction. Her skirt rose up to show almost the crack of her ass. Gregory was trying hard to maintain his composure.

If she doesn't sit down, right now, I don't know what I might do but I do know it will be a sin, he thought,

He continued to watch Barbette picking up the quarter and then bring her body up slowly looking back at him in a lustful way. Once she was standing she turned around towards Gregory and sat down before asking, "Well, what did God just tell you baby?"

Gregory started to laugh. "Barbette, I'll tell you one thing, if I was going to give in, it would be with you. I love you, girl," he said in a soft and convincing tone.

"I love you too, Gregory. You know I believe in God, but I just don't understand how you can refrain from having sex. It's only been a week for me and I am about to die."

"Do you honestly think I don't crave it?" he asked. "I do crave it sometime; Barbette. Do you know that God will be there for you when you call His name? And I don't mean during a sexual act either," Gregory replied, and started laughing again.

Rhonda and Raymond walked in just in time. The host directed them to their table. Gregory allowed Barbette to walk in front of him and she put on a show for him, twisting all she had. Gregory just smiled. During dinner, Raymond and Gregory talked business. Rhonda was telling Barbette all about her brother, which she wanted her to meet. "He's a pilot," she said and "he is never home . . ."

I'm already home alone without a man in my life, what makes her think I want to be home alone with a man in my life, Barbette thought.

When dinner was over, Barbette got up to leave and Gregory offered to walk her to her car. She accepted. Gregory was of medium height with a very nice built. He was dating a very pretty young lady at one time, but he said she wasn't who he thought she was. Once they reached her car, Barbette turned to Gregory and said, "Thanks, man. As always, it's been a pleasure."

Gregory, came up close on her, bent his head to her and gave her a long gentle kiss on her lips. He had never done that before. Barbette's heart began beating at a fast rate.

41

"Gregory, man, what's up with you? You have never kissed me before," she said with surprise in her voice.

Gregory took a few steps back from her and said, "I think you turned me on a little bit too much tonight baby. Yes, I think you did. I'm going to have to go home and pray really hard. Go ahead and get in your car before I do it again, please."

Barbette didn't reply and he watched her get in her car. She took off without saying another word. All the way home, Barbette wondered how it would be to have sex with Gregory (not that fucking him had not crossed her mind before). They had been friends for three years and she did love him as a close friend. Once she arrived home, she got in bed and fell to sleep instantly.

Barbette decided to work from home on Friday. She got up made coffee and set up her laptop. There were only two items to address and she knew she could finish them in at least three hours.

She picked up the phone and called Ms. Ruby the Opera Singer. Ms. Ruby was about to marry a man who was thirteen years younger than her and had not demanded that he sign a pre-nuptial agreement. This was annoying Barbette badly. She knew all the love in the world could not prevent her from requesting that a pre-nuptial agreement be signed if she were to marry anyone. Not that Barbette had a whole lot of money. Her salary was only $85,000 a year but she had purchased certificates that were now worth at least one million dollars. Barbette's father was the rich one. Her father very seldom gave his children anything. He even made them pay their own way through law school. He always said, "This will help you appreciate what you have in life."

Ms. Ruby answered the phone in a happy voice; "Hello!"

"This is Barbette Jackson, Ms. Ruby; how are you doing today?"

"Oh just fine my dear—just fine."

"I just finished putting together your contract and wanted you to look it over for signature. Would you like me to send it to you by courier?" Barbette asked.

"Oh yes, please," she said, "but I'm still not sure if I will need it."

Barbette moved the phone from her ear and looked in to the receiver mouthing, *"Are you crazy lady?"* She put the phone back to her ear, "Okay, Ms. Ruby, I'll send it to you anyway, just in case you decided to have it signed." Barbette was pissed-off with Ms. Ruby, but could not do a darn thing about it. She completed the conversation and hung up the phone and thought, *who am I to tell someone what to do when it comes to a man. Look at me, I'm going over to a man house who don't even care about me because I, me, my crazy ass self, want to fuck him.* She continued working hoping to finish in time to make her hairdresser appointment.

She had been sitting under the dryer for an hour and was hoping her hair was dry. She hated sitting under the dryer, but that was the price she paid for curl and body. She had already taken her shower and had chosen to wear a flared black and white, flower skirt with black halter top and black sandals she had ordered from the Macy's catalog. The manicures rolled her table and chair over to where she was sitting and placed her hands into a bowl of warm water. Barbette had chosen clear finger nail polish this time. While her nails were being worked on, she started thinking about what Carl may have cooked and would he want her to spend the night. She chose not to take anything for granted after what had happened last Sunday.

She knew the street Carl lived on. She had a girl friend that lived on the same street. After finding the house number, she pulled into the driveway. Carl came out to meet her.

"Hey baby, did you get lost?"

"No, I'm pretty familiar with this area." She walked towards him and he met her with a hug.

"I hope you like fish," he said. Barbette walked with him into the house and was overwhelmed with the sight and smell of roses. Carl had placed yellow roses on every table in the house.

"Do you like it?" he said, "and by the way the roses are for you."

Barbette was so surprised; she held her mouth open so wide a fly could have flown in—no problem. She finally spoke. "Carl, they are beautiful, thank you!"

"You're welcome." He pulled her close to him and kissed her lips. His lips felt smooth as if he had just put Vaseline on them. Carl pulled his lips away and said in a lustful tone, "Don't worry, you will pay me for the flowers later."

The house was decorated in warm colors of beige, green and gold. A soft-cushion green sofa was placed in front of the living room windows. There were two matching chairs placed on both sides of the sofa and a lounge directly across from the sofa covered in a gold velvet material. The large living room entrance was dressed with pillars painted in the same cream color as the walls. The living room fireplace was made of red brick with a large mantel that reached from one end of the wall to the other. There were gold candles placed randomly across the mantel.

Carl seated her at the dining room table. The table base was made of iron that held a thick piece of glass on top. Barbette loved the high-back iron chairs that matched the table and thought the table and chairs must have been custom made for them. Carl had baked fish and steamed veggies.

"Would you like some wine," Carl asked.

Barbette knew that wine usually gave her a headache and it was the one drink she usually did not drink unless she wanted to get drunk fast. "Yes, please." Barbette did not want to worry about it.

"Where did you get this dining room set from?" she asked.

"We had it made." Dean knew a guy in Canada that made furniture, so I designed it on paper and the man made it for us."

Barbette was amazed and realized she really didn't know who Carl was.

"How's the fish?" Carl asked.

"Very good Carl, everything is wonderful."

"I wasn't sure if you liked wine or not."

"Oh, I do, but it sometimes does not agree with me."

"Oh really," Carl said in a concerned tone.

"Yes, most of the time it gets me drunk pretty quickly," Barbette confessed.

"Well; hell, let's drink up then," Carl said, laughing aloud.

Barbette was having a great time and decided this made up for him not calling her till yesterday.

After they finished eating, Carl cleared the dining room table and she followed him into the kitchen. The kitchen was a small area that consisted of a wood butler block table and two chairs. They had not replaced the original window cabinets allowing the view of very nice sets of dishes to show through the cabinet doors, which were painted the same beige color as the walls. *Very pretty*; she thought. They stacked the dishwasher and Carl escorted her into the living room and directed her to lie on the lounge and put her feet up and stretched out her body. Barbette laid back in the lounge feeling very comfortable. Carl put on some music, Old Isley

Brothers CD and stretched out on the couch. He shared the history of his old house and started talking about how their business was going to expand.

Carl adjusted himself on the sofa, lying on his back. "Hey Barbette, before we go in the bedroom, which I know we're going to go very soon, why don't you tell me what you like sexually. I need to know how freaky are you? He asked wearing a smile on his face.

Barbette smiled back, thinking; *this man really doesn't know me.*

"Oh, I don't know Carl. There are some things I will do and some things I've done and won't do again. Why don't you tell me what you want," she asked.

Carl sat up still smiling, ignoring her question and said, "I know, let's have desert."

Barbette had no idea what he meant. She watched Carl walk out of the living room and down the hall towards what she thought were the bedrooms. She lay there, waiting for him hoping that he would not mess up the evening by doing something crazy.

Carl came back into the living room with a stick of incense in his hand and walked over to the fireplace. After lighting it he placed it on an incense holder, pulled a joint out of his pocket and lit it. He took three puffs and walked over to Barbette and offered the joint to her.

"Here, Barbette," he said, I want you to loosen up and relax."

Barbette hesitated. She had not smoked marijuana in two years and did not know if she wanted to smoke again, especially with Carl.

"Don't be afraid. Trust me. I just want to relax you, so when we make love you will feel free to accept what I give you baby. That's all." His tone of voice was sensual and enticing. Barbette agreed to take two puffs and hand it back to Carl.

"Keep that one, I got my own," he said. Barbette knew she was going to get fucked up from smoking and fucked by Carl. She continued smoking until it was down to low. Carl took it from her and put it out in the ashtray.

She started to feel relaxed and horny as hell. She started to move her feet, sliding them up to her body causing her knees to bend, which allowed Carl to look under her dress at her bare ass. Barbette never wore underwear unless it was necessary. She started laughing at everything Carl was saying. She was turned on by his mere presence. He had raised his head up from the sofa to place another pillow under it to allow him to get a better view of Barbette's ass. He was getting so excited he wanted to fuck her, but decided to wait a little bit longer. "Barbette?"

"Yes b*aby*," she said.

Carl knew she was fucked up from the way she called him 'baby'. "Have you ever *experienced* anal sex?"

Barbette was fucked up but was not sure if she wanted to answer that question.

She gave Carl a serious look and replied. "Back in the day, I did a lot of drugs and things sexual that I don't care to talk about. I experimented, that's all." She waited for him to ask another question or continue talking.

"Carl," she said, "Have you ever been fucked from the back?"

She laughed so hard she started to cry; he laughed along with her.

"Hell no baby, I'm a real man. Don't you remember?" He sat up and started beating his chest. What's my mutherfucking name?"

Barbette responded in a loud lustful voice "CARL, CARL, OH, CARL."

"You're motherfucking right. I'm the man baby."

He then got up from the sofa and decided it was time to go drop his load.

"Hey baby," come on, let's go in my bedroom. He extended his hand to her and Barbette took it. Once Barbette stood up, she knew she had messed up. She felt like she wanted to throw up and her head began to hurt. "Oh man," she said, holding her head.

"What's wrong baby?" Carl asked, as they walked down the hall to his room.

"I feel sick. I knew I should have not had that wine." Barbette said. "Where's the bathroom?"

Carl pointed out the directions to his bathroom, which was located off his room and followed her in. "Hey man, I got to pee, you can stay if you want to," she added in a drunken tone.

"That's alright," Carl said. He stepped out of the bathroom and was hoping that Barbette would start feeling better so he could release his shit. After pulling the covers down on the bed, he thought it had taken long enough for her to pee so he walked back in the bathroom. Barbette was just getting off the stool and could not stand up. She was drunk. Carl lifted her up and sat her on the sink counter. He looked in his cabinet and pulled out a pack of Stand-Back powder. He thought; *this will help her.* He opened the pack up to expose the power that laid on a small piece of wax paper. "Here Barbette, take some of this," he said.

Barbette had her eyes closed. She opened them and looked at what Carl was offering her. "Hell no, Carl, you already got me fuck up from smoking that joint. "I'm not about to snort any coke."

Carl started to laugh, "No baby, this is not coke; it's *Stand-Back* headache powder, see . . ." He showed her the pack and Barbette agreed to take it. He carried her to his bed and laid her down.

She was out instantly. Carl wanted to make her more comfortable. He went to his drawer and pulled out a pajama set. He started to undress her and put his pajamas shirt on her. He took off her halter-top and then her skirt. He hurried to put his pajamas shirt on her, hoping she would not wake up and think he was trying to rape her. She was out cold.

Carl put on the bottoms that match the pajama's top Barbette was wearing and went in to the living room. He laid on the sofa and click on the flat screen TV, hoping to find something good to watch. He was considering leaving her to go over to Candice's house. She lived about two blocks away. Candice was a nurse and Carl loved to play doctor with her. He decided it wouldn't be right to do. Barbette might wake up. He hoped. After a couple of hours, he decided to go see if Barbette had awakened. She was out cold. He finally gave up and went in the kitchen; poured himself another glass of wine. He fired up a joint and watch movies until he fell asleep.

*　　*　　*

"Carl, Carl, man . . . its 11:00 a.m. man. What are you doing on the sofa and who car is that in our driveway?"

Carl woke up to the sound of Dean's voice. "Oh, hey, man." Dean was standing over him. "What are you doing out here, man?"

"That girl had too much to drink and fell out on me." Carl mumbled, trying to explain why he was on the sofa. Dean walked towards Carl's bathroom, which was located off his bedroom. He was going to retrieve some aspirin for him. He knew Carl had to have been drunk to sleep on the couch. Carl loved his bed too much. As he walked in the bedroom he realized Carl had company. He started to walk out of the room but stepped back realizing it was Barbette in Carl's bed. He didn't know if he was mad or disappointed. She was uncovered, wearing Carl blue silk pajama top. Her legs were curled up and her hair lay loose all over the pillow. *"She is beautiful,"* Dean said under his breath. He pulled the door slightly closed, leaving it cracked and walked back in the living room. Carl had not moved. He had pulled the cover over his head. Dean sat down on the lounge and could smell Barbette perfume confirming that she had sat there for a while.

"Carl, Carl," he said, the second time louder.

"What?" Carl replied, pulling the cover off his head and looking up at Dean.

"Please, don't forget we have a meeting with Barbette at 1:30, okay," he said quickly.

"You just meet us over her house man. We'll be there."

Dean had spend the night over his sister house. He had stayed up late working on some financial reports for their meeting with Barbette.

Dean walked out of the house and got in his car. He decided to go have breakfast and try not to think about want he just walked in on.

Barbette woke up realizing that she was in Carl's bed. She tried to sit up and her head started to spin. She decided to lie down a little longer. Carl had gotten up when Dean left and made some coffee. Barbette heard him talking on the phone. "Hey baby, what you doing later on. I'll be by about 7:30 and wear that black see-through night grown I brought you last week, okay?"

Barbette realized Carl was making a date with another woman. She thought, *this is a mistake. Carl only wanted to fuck her and every woman he could.* She heard him coming towards the bedroom. She closed her eyes and pretended to still be asleep. She heard him walk into his bathroom and turn on the shower, waiting a few minutes to make sure he did not come back, she got up and put her clothes on quickly and wrote a note.

SEE YOU AT THE MEETING.
Barbette

She laid the note on the dining room table and left.

Barbette was glad she had decided to stay at the condo, which cut her drive down to only a twenty-minute ride. She took a long bath and two Alka-Seltzers and lay in her bed. She let her mind go over what had happened last night. The evening was prefect until she got drunk. She should not have had so much wine. She knew the joint did not make her sick. As a matter of fact, she enjoyed the joint and wished she had one right now. She did not want to believe that Carl was such a dog, but what she heard this morning confirmed it. Carl fucked around too much for her. She got up to prepare for their arrival, cleaning up the mess she had left from the day before.

It was 1:30 on the dot when the intercom buzzer with off.

"Who is it?" Barbette asked.

"It me baby," Carl answered; "Dean is with me."

She unlocked the elevator to allow them to ride up and unlocked her door.

Carl walked in first and led over to kiss her. Barbette moved her head to the side so that he would miss her lips.

"Hey, what's wrong baby?" Carl asked. Barbette ignored him.

"Hi, Dean," she said.

"Hey, how you doing today, Barbette," he asked.

"Just fine . . ." Barbette asked them to follow her into the kitchen. She had already set up her laptop on the island. Everyone sat down on a stool. Carl chose the stool next to Barbette and Dean sat across from them. Carl opened his laptop and started setting it up. He was wondering what was wrong with Barbette, not wanting to kiss him. He felt that he should be the one pissed off if anyone should.

Dean passed three sheet of paper across to Barbette. "I printed these reports out. They show were we are financially, including profit and losses. Barbette started looking over the reports. From what she saw on the papers, their company was doing great. She asked them a few questions about long-term goals and their plans for the upcoming projects and events. Carl talked a lot about the expansion of their company and the employees they are in the process of hiring. After talking for two hours, Barbette updated them on the contacts she had made and informed them that she had set up a meeting with Mr. Peoples. Jim Peoples was a rich black man. He owned and invested in many music deals. He was part owner of one of the largest recording companies and he owed her a favor. She had turned him on to a girl-singing group and he has made millions on them. She went on to give them the date and time of the meeting. They agreed that they would be available to attend the meeting. Barbette then began serving the chicken salad sandwiches she had made for them while Carl and Dean cleaned off the island.

"Hey baby, what's wrong?" Carl asked as he closed up his laptop.

Barbette answered in a steady tone, "Nothing!"

"So, why did you turn away when I went to kiss you?" he asked.

Barbette saw that he was not going to leave it alone, so she walked over to where he was sitting, looked him straight in the eyes, and said, "Carl, you are not a one-lady-man and you're not willing to commit. You have to, need to, and want to fuck every woman you meet; I'm just not going to be one of those women anymore. Okay?"

Carl assumed that she had heard his conversation with Candice and was pissed off.

"Come on baby. You're just like me and you know it. You don't want a commitment either," Carl retorted.

Barbette walked back to the counter where she had been preparing the food. She turned around and said in the calculating tone. "Carl, I used to be like you but I grew up!"

"Maybe if you had given me a chance last night, I would have showed you how grown I am," Carl replied.

Dean sat there, checking them out hoping that they wouldn't get physical. He agreed with Barbette that Carl needed to grow up, but when you have been through what Carl had been through, it would take time—a lot of time.

Carl and Dean both thanked Barbette for helping them and were standing at the door saying their good bye's when Dean said, "Barbette, Carl and I were wondering if you would be interested in going on our payroll as a consultant/lawyer."

Barbette looked at Carl and Dean; she could not believe they were asking her to work for their company. She was surprised that Carl would even agree to it.

"Let me think about it, guys," she said. "But until I make my decision, I'm here for you."

"Thanks baby," Carl said

"Yes thanks, Barbette," Dean repeated after Carl.

"Well, I got to go," Carl said. "I have people to see and things to do."

"Sure," said Barbette. She opened the door so that they could leave.

As they walked to the car Dean was thinking, *what is going on with those two?* He got in the car with Carl and decided to find out if Carl was feeling Barbette or not.

"Hey, Carl, man . . . What's going on between you and Barbette, man?"

"Barbette ain't any different than these other women I fuck out here. Why, you wanted hit on that?" Carl asked, showing no feelings. Carl had noticed the way Dean had been watching her and he knew he was interested in getting together with her.

"Ya, man, I think she's cool and if you're not interested anymore, I would like to ask her out."

"Go ahead, man. You two might work out; cause she's not working out for me. She's not freaky enough," Carl said and started laughing.

"What happened with you guys last night, man?" Dean asked.

"Man, she got drunk and fell out on me. I didn't even get to fuck that bitch. I ain't with that, man. You know me. On Fridays I got to release."

"Ya, man. I know what you mean." Dean knew Carl better than anyone. Carl was his boy but he was so dam glad that he could now ask Barbette out on a date. Dean could hardly wait.

EPISODE FOUR

All about Dean

During the meeting Barbette realized that Carl was a very smart businessman, but a low down motherfucker when it came to his love life. It was still early and she decided to eat some Ben & Jerry and watch a Life Time movie. She lied across her bed and fell asleep while watching the movie. The ringing of the phone woke her up and she looked at the clock that read 5:30 PM.

"Hello."

"Hello, Barbette? Were you asleep?"

"Oh hey, Dean," she said, recognizing his voice. "Yes, but that's okay."

"How about joining me for a cup of coffee? I know this really nice place in Buckhead that sells the best coffee drinks in town."

"Why?" Barbette asked as she lifted her head from the bed and supported it with her hand.

"I would like to get to know you better since we are going to be working together."

"Hey now, I haven't made a decision yet, Dean," Barbette was quick to respond in a business tone.

"Well, maybe I can help you make a decision. Come on Barbette, it's just a cup of coffee."

Barbette was not sure if this was one of Carl's tricks or was Dean sincere.

"Hey, Barbette, I'm not playing games. I really would like to talk to you. Okay?" Dean continued in a more heartfelt tone.

"Okay then," Barbette replied.

"I'll be by to pick you up in fifteen minutes?" he said, now in a hurry to hang up before she changed her mind.

"All right," she said. "I'll meet you in front of my building."

"See you then . . ."

Dean hung up the phone, pleased that he was able to convince her to go out with him. He rubbed his hands together, now nerves. He wondered if he needed to change his shirt, but realized that he didn't have enough time. Dean grabbed his keys and practically ran out the door.

He pulled up and parked in front of Barbette's building. He was a few minutes early, but didn't mind waiting for her at all. Barbette walked out of the building wearing a pair of low waste jean that fitted tight around her thighs, black short-sleeves sweater that was cut high enough to allow her belly button to show, and a pair of black high-heel leather sandals. Her hair was parted on the side and flowing down her back with loose curls falling from the ends. Dean saw her coming towards his car and got out waiting for her to approach so that he could open the car door for her.

"Hey, pretty lady," he said wearing a smile.

"Hi, Dean," Barbette said as she admired his appearance. He was wearing the same jeans and a black short-sleeves collared shirt he had worn to the meeting. She loved his built. She noticed that he was taller than Carl and liked that. Dean held the car door opened for her and once she was settled comfortably in the passenger seat, he closed the door softly and walked over to the driver side. Once behind the wheel, he looked her over while she sat next to him and wanted to kiss her, but he didn't want to scare her off. He started the car saying nothing. He drove a black Lexus SC with cream leather interior. *Very nice*, Barbette thought.

Dean headed north on Peachtree towards the heart of Buckhead. The coffee shop was only about five blocks from Barbette's house. She sat quietly thinking about why she had agreed to go out with Dean and was hoping that she was not being played by Dean and Carl. She focused on the sights along the way since she never had a chance to do so; she was usually the driver and had to pay attention to the busy traffic.

They pulled into the parking space that Dean was lucky to find. It was a busy area filled with many storefronts, bars and restaurants. She started to get out of the car and Dean grabbed her arm. "No, Barbette let me do that for you," he said. He got out of the car and walked around to the passenger side and opened the door. Barbette stepped out and they walked, holding hands, to the Piper Coffee Shop that was located about three doors away. When they entered a young woman with pink hair approached them and asked if they wanted a booth or the area that was filled with couches and chairs, which she referred to as the 'living room area'. Dean looked at Barbette and asked her if the living room would be all right with her. She nodded. As they walked to the table Barbette looked around at the many pictures of different movie stars hanging on the walls. She also noticed that the tables were small allowing only two people per table. The colors of the wall were purple and orange to match the design of the floor. The hostess seated them on a couch that was covered in purple soft velvet. Dean asked Barbette if she had been here before.

"No," she replied, "but, I like it so far. Have you?" she asked.

"Yes, my sister used to work here while she was in graduate school."

"What would you like to order?"

"Why don't you order for the both of us since you've been here before?" Barbette replied.

"Sure."

The waitress took their order and came back quickly with two large cups of Spanish coffee. Dean had insisted that she tried it.

"So," Barbette said, "What should we talk about?"

"I thought we would play a game," Dean said

Barbette looked at him, wearing a worried look on her face and thought; *this is a game between him and Carl. "This is a fucking set up."* She was beginning to get upset.

Dean saw the look on her face and rubbed her back. "Barbette, I am talking about a game like you ask me a question and then I ask you question and so on. What did you think I meant when I said *game?*" he asked.

"Nothing," Barbette said. She didn't want him to know that Carl had even crossed her mind.

"OK my turn now," she said, "since you just asked me a question." She smiled.

Dean said, "Go right ahead; ask me anything you want. Don't hold back."

"OK, why did you ask me out? And please be honest."

Dean thought for a moment wondering if he should tell her the whole truth; that he thought he might be in love with her, or just half-truth.

"Well," Dean said as he laid his head back in the corner of the couch, resting his back against two large pillows. "I am attracted to you and wanted to get to know you better." Barbette took her sandals off and curled up on the couch making herself more comfortable. She thought about his answer and thought that she might be a little attracted to him too.

"OK, my turn," he said. "I know you have all the money in the world and everything you could possibly want, so what else could I give you to make you happy or happier?"

Barbette smiled. "First of all, I don't have all the money in the world, and everything I want. My dad has the money. I work for him. As a matter of fact, I paid my own way through law school."

Dean looked at Barbette in shock. "You worked your way through law school?" he asked.

Barbette said, "Yes, I did. I also helped my brother with his tuition."

She went on to explain that she worked as a stripper during her last year of college and her first year of law school so that she could pay her tuition for her first and second year of law school. She told him about the older rich man she met when she was in law school that invited her to live with him in exchange for sex and money. She explained how she even paid some of her brother's tuition and helped him sell drugs allowing them to have an income that would allow them not only to pay tuition but also to drive nice cars. She informed him that her dad did not know anything about her working as a stripper or any of the other stuff. Dean was astonished; he remembered what Carl had said about Barbette not being freaky enough for him. "*Well*, he thought, *Carl was dead wrong. If he only knew . . . .*" Barbette continued and told Dean that she had no idea what he could give her to make her happier than she was unless he gave her a good man, who was willing to make commitments, unlike Carl, and would be true to her for the rest of her life. Dean was speechless; he did not know what to say. He just knew, at that moment, he wanted her to be his lady.

"So," Barbette said, looking at Dean's expression, wondering what he was thinking. "May I ask you a question now?"

"Sure," Dean said

"What's going on with you and Dee?"

Dean thought, *I knew this was coming.*

He adjusted his pillows and looked at Barbette, peering into her eyes. He wanted to kiss her.

"Dee and I broke up. She decided to go back to her old boyfriend. I didn't have enough for her. Enough money, enough love, enough time." He went on to say that he and Dee had dated for ten months, but it had been a difficult relationship from the start. She wanted so much from him and did not understand the time he had to spend working on his business. Dean wanted to change the subject quickly. He looked at Barbette and wondered if she would want to go out with him later on that night.

"Barbette, do you like dancing?" Dean asked.

"Yes I do, very much."

"Well why don't we go dancing tonight?"

"Do you dance?" Barbette asked.

"Sure I do, I've taken lessons. I can get down, Baby," Dean said excitedly.

"Let's get out of here, so that we can get ready," Dean suggested.

He signaled for the waitress to pay the check and they left.

Dean dropped Barbette off at her condo and told her he would pick her up at 8:00 o'clock.

She agreed. She went into her apartment and rushed to find something sexy to wear. She had no idea where he was taking her but she was excited about dancing all night. She finally picked a black sleeveless, low cut, short dress that fit perfectly around her hips and flared at the bottom. She pulled out her black silk stockings and a pair of black leather high stiletto shoes. She tied up her hair, put on a shower cap and jumped in the shower to take a quick one. While drying off, she thought, what type of guy was Dean not to care about the relationship that she had with Carl, being that he and Carl were best friend.

Dean went home and took a shower. He was so excited that he had a date with Barbette that he could not think. Carl knocked on Dean's bedroom door.

"Come on in, man," Dean answered.

"Hey, man, where you going tonight," Carl asked, noticing that Dean was getting dressed.

"Out dancing with Barbette . . ."

"Dam, man you don't waste no time," Carl said with surprise in his voice. "I hope you get to fuck her, man, and whatever you do, don't let her drink any wine. She gets drunk when she drinks wine." Carl started to laugh.

"I'll remember," Dean said, laughing along with Carl

"Hey, man, can you let me borrow some of that 'Right-On-Man' cologne," Carl asked.

"Sure, man, it's on my dresser."

Carl walked over to the dresser and picked up the cologne and applied it to his neck. Placing the bottle back he turned around and looked at Dean who was now standing in front of the mirror wearing his black suit pants and a wife beater undershirt.

"Hey, man, have a good time," Carl said as he walked out of Dean's bedroom.

Carl walked into his bedroom wearing a smile. Carl knew Dean better than anyone else. He knew Dean liked Barbette a lot by the way he was acting. He also knew that meant that he had to back off from him and her and let them have their thing. Show them some respect, he said under his breath with a smile. Carl was going to meet Nurse Candice at AJ Sports bar for a couple of drinks and then they were going over to her house to play 'Dr. Feel Good' till the morning. *"God I love the weekends"* Carl said aloud.

Dean arrived at Barbette's house at 8:00 on the dot. He hated to be late for anything. When she opened her door, Dean felt his private getting hard. He wanted her so bad.

"Hello, Barbette, you look great baby," he said in a soft warm tone.

"Thank you. Where are we going?" she asked, wanting to make sure that this time she didn't end up in a place where she would run into old bed partners.

"Oh, it's a surprise," Dean said.

"Okay then—I'm ready."

Dean had let the top of his Lexus down and they hit the highway towards downtown Atlanta. She was enjoying the wind blowing though her hair. It was a warm night and having the top down allowed Barbette to appreciate the view of the sky. She looked over at Dean and smiled and he smiled back. Dean felt like a king who was with the finest woman in Atlanta.

Dean exited off the highway and made a left. Barbette was familiar with the area. She knew that the Butler Community Center was located two blocks down the road, but she didn't remember there being a club on this street. Finally, Dean came to a stop in front of the center. Teenagers were standing out in front and going in and out of the building. Barbette gave Dean a confused look. Dean just smiled.

"What's going on?" she asked.

"Surprised? I volunteer here once a week to teach hip-hop. Tonight they're having a Stay Drug Free Teen Party."

Barbette said, "I volunteered here too—once a month." She looked at him still confused and wondered if he knew she was involved in the center.

"I know. I saw you in some of the group pictures on the office wall and I know that your father has a lot to do with this center. I've been a volunteer for about a year and a half now."

"Come on let's go in," he said.

Barbette waited for Dean to come over to the passenger side of the car to open her door. She got out, took his hand and they walked into the center holding hands.

"Hey, Ms. Jackson," said three young girls approaching them. "Hello, Mr. Jenkins."

"Hello. You ladies acting like ladies," Dean asked.

"Yes sir," they replied in unison, giggling.

Dean took Barbette and led her to the dance floor, passing familiar faces, people greeting them and shaking Dean's hand.

"Come on baby, let's dance . . ."

The DJ was playing a P Diddy song. Dean and Barbette started to get down with it and Barbette was surprised at how easily Dean could keep up with her. Barbette had taken dance lessons for what seemed like all of her life and knew every type and style of dance there was. She was enjoying dancing with Dean, who moved his body very well. They dance as if they had danced together for years, anticipating each other movements. Barbette's dress moved to the music as she swayed her hips gracefully. Dean was into the music as well—he couldn't stop smiling.

Dean knew he had made an impression on Barbette and was almost in. She was starting to feel really comfortable with him and after a few drinks of punch, more dancing and conversations with the teenagers they knew, they said their goodbyes and moved on to an adult dance club not too far from the center. Barbette could not stop talking. She was comfortable with Dean and had loved his surprising her with going to the Community

Center. She was amazed feeling as if Dean didn't just want to fuck her. He carried himself like a gentleman and never spoke about sex.

Once at the club, Dean ordered Barbette and himself a double shot of cognac. There were no tables vacant, so they ended up at the bar with only one seat available at the end which Dean insisted Barbette take as he stood next to her. Barbette had never been in this club before and couldn't see much of the club with the club being so crowded and dark. She saw some familiar faces but not anyone she really knew. The music was so loud that Dean had to lean over and put his ear to her mouth so that he could hear whenever Barbette spoke. Just as he was about to say something to her, a man approached them. She looked up in shock; it was her brother, Lance.

"Hey man," he said to Dean in a loud voice over the music.

"What's going on Lance, man?" Dean said, shaking hands with Lance.

"This is Barb . . ."

Before he could get her name out of his mouth, Lance said, "Hey man that's my sister." He walked around Dean to give Barbette a kiss and a hug.

Dean said, "This is your sister, man?"

"Yep," Lance said with a proud look on his face.

A lady signaled for Lance to come to her, "Hey you guys, I'll see you later, got to go." Lance walked through the crowd to meet the lady and disappeared.

Man this day has been full of surprises, Dean thought.

Dean had no idea that Lance was Barbette's brother. He had met Lance through Carl who had taken him to a few parties giving by Lance. Carl and Lance were pretty good friends—they had known each other for at least a year. As a matter of fact, Lance gave them the party at the Peachtree hotel after the showcase party they gave last weekend. Dean was surprised.

"That was a surprise," she hollered in his ear over the music.

Dean nodded and took her hand. "Let's dance."

They danced straight through three songs, had another drink and left. Once in the car, Dean told Barbette how he came to know her brother and Barbette realized how Lance had come to know about her meeting with Carl. While listening to Dean talked about dancing and how he had been in several college musicals, Barbette thought about how different Dean was from the other men she had dated. She suddenly felt the urge to have sex with him.

Dean pulled into her parking garage and parked in the guest parking space next to Barbette's car. Since it was only 12:30, Barbette invited Dean in for another drink and once they were in the house, Barbette led Dean into the kitchen to begin preparing margaritas.

"Hey, let me help?" Dean said.

"That would be great. The glasses are in the cabinet on the right, second shelve and the salt is in the cabinet next to the glasses."

Dean pulled the items out of the cupboard not saying a word. He was checking her out as she poured some green stuff into the blender.

"Hey, Dean; can you get me more ice?" Barbette asked.

"Coming right up," he replied in a chipper tone. Dean loved the way Barbette said his name. He also loved the way she walked and the way she smiled at him. He wanted her but knew he had to wait. Once the drinks were made and poured, Barbette handed Dean his drink and said "Maybe we should toast."

"Okay, what should we toast to?"

"To a long friendship," Barbette replied.

Dean said, "That's cool, and smiled as he clicked her glass.

They tasted their drink and Dean nodded in satisfaction.

"This is good Barbette," he said.

Barbette smiled as she walked over to the counter and began cleaning up the mess she had made—Dean watched her walk. She still had on her black high heel shoes and sheer stockings, her dress swaying like a soft wind, showing muscles in her legs that were a sign that she was used to wearing high heels. *"Lord, help me, please,"* Dean whispered.

"Barbette," Dean said. She turned and peered at him. "I love your condo."

"This isn't really mine. My dad owns it. He purchased it as a tax right off."

"So where do you live then?"

"I live in the Alpharetta area, Monterey Heights Subdivision, with my dad and my brother."

Dean wondered if he knew where the subdivision was located and then remembered that the subdivision was one of the most expensive ones in that area. The houses sold into the millions. Barbette continued saying, "I own a summerhouse in Florida, which is rented-out most of the year."

Dean was amazed to hear that this independent, smart, young woman did not have a home of her own. "Why don't you consider purchasing a house?" Dean asked.

"Hey, I don't know. I've thought about it off and on but just never got around to it," Barbette said thoughtfully. "But, I do have to do something; I need a serious right off now that Dad has giving me a big raise or internal revenue will end up taking it all."

Dean sat his drink on the island and walked up to Barbette and pulling her into his arms, kissed her softly on the lips. When he started to pull away, Barbette would not let him go. She locked her lips on his and released her tongue between his lip and down his throat, letting out all the passion she had been holding inside her. She held his head with one of her hands enabling her to have more control of the kiss than he did. Dean went with it and put his hands on her ass, rubbing her cheeks in a circling motion. As she grinded up against him, Dean realized that she did not have on any underwear which caused him to develop an instant hard on. He moved one of his hands to the crack in her ass and started to move his finger up and down causing her dress to give her a wedge. Barbette started to moan. Dean wanted to taste her so badly it hurt, yet he knew it would be best for them to wait though he could hardly contain himself. He thought that what he had with Barbette was too special to mess up and they needed to go slow since Dean had just gotten out of a relationship with Dee and Barbette had just gotten out of a relationship with Carl—or maybe not. He was not sure.

Dean reached for Barbette's hand gently pulling it from behind his head as he pulled his lips away from hers. He held her close to him embracing her as if she was a teddy bear and he was a child. He held her for a while waiting for their heart rates to return to as normal a rate as possible and considered what he should say to her without making her feel rejected. Dean did not want to hurt Barbette's feeling by telling her Carl had given him permission to date her. He was not sure what to do. He did know that he did not want to make love to her, just not yet; he wanted them to be free of the past before starting a relationship with each other.

Dean pulled away from Barbette slowly and taking her by the hand, led her into the living room. He told her to have a seat on the sofa as he walked back into the kitchen to retrieve their drinks. Handing Barbette her glass and placing his on the table on the side of the sofa where Barbette was seated, Dean pulled an ottoman close to the sofa and sat on it facing

Barbette. He began to talk about the way he felt about her and his wanting to start a relationship with her.

Barbette asked, "So, what's wrong?"

Dean continued, "Nothing is wrong; everything is right. Barbette, I do want to say something to you, but I don't want you to get upset. I want you to hear me out before you say anything, okay?"

Barbette had no clue what Dean was about to say. She just nodded, took off her shoes and curled her legs under her. She looked into Dean's eyes and wondered, "What did I do?" Tears welled in her eyes as Dean resumed.

He spoke in a low caring tone. "As I was saying, I want you to know that I want you badly. Girl, you turn me on. I wanted you from the first time I met you but knew you were off-limits to me, because of Carl. I also want you to know that if and when we get together, I want it to be right. It is so very important," he said with compassion, "that we wait until all the old is cleared out of the way."

Barbette started to say something and Dean stopped her. "Let me finish," he said in a demanding tone. "Listen baby, I just ended a ten month relationship with Dee and you, I'm not sure . . . ," he looked into her eyes, "if you're still in a relationship or not. So, it would be best for use to step back and clear the air. You understand what I'm saying, Barbette?"

Barbette had started crying and could not speak. Dean gave her a napkin from the bunch that he had brought in with the drinks. He wondered if she was crying because she wanted Carl or because she wanted him. He decided not to tell her about the conversation he had with Carl about her, at least not yet. Barbette waved her hand, gesturing for Dean to come sat next to her on the sofa. She peered into his eyes and notices that they were filled with tears as well.

"You don't want me?"

Dean pulled her to him and held her in his arms. "No baby, you've got it wrong. I want you more than you can imagine. If you only knew how I have been holding myself back to keep from taking you in the bedroom and making love to you. But, I don't want to take Dee and Carl to bed with us."

Barbette managed to smile and continued to wipe her eyes.

Dean continued, "But, Barbette, don't think I'm Mr. Nice Guy. Back in the days, I would have fucked you, left, and gone over to another woman's house to fuck her too. But baby, that's not my thing anymore." Dean pulled Barbette close to him. "I am still a freak but not so much of a dog anymore. Now, I just choose to have one woman at a time unless that one woman doesn't know how to satisfy my sexual needs." He pulled Barlette close to him and in a softy sexy tone said, "Let's hope that the one woman does know how to satisfy my craving, okay?"

Barbette laid her head on Dean's lap and extended her body out on the sofa. They talked for hours about relationship, money, shared childhood stories and everything they could think of until Barbette finally fell asleep. Dean moved her head from his lap and placed it on a pillow and went in to her bedroom to find a blanket to put on top of her. While in her room he noticed that on Barbette nightstand was the book entitled <u>For Love, For Lust, For Friendship</u>. It was his favorite of all the books he had read this year. Dean smiled and thought, *I can't wait to fuck this woman.*

Barbette woke up and realized she was on the sofa. She wondered what time Dean had left and thought about how much she liked him. She went into her bedroom to check the time and realized that if she didn't hurry she would miss her Sunday Brunch date with her two girl friends.

Barbette had a standing date every other Sunday with Tee and Andrea since they had met. She met then about five years ago when she attended a birthday party, at Magic City Adult Entertainment club, for one of her other friends who was a bartender there. Tee and Andrea were strippers at the time but they now owned one of the most popular Day Spas in Atlanta. Barbette had loaned them the money to go into business two years ago and they had paid her back within a year's time. Most of the money they used to repay her came from Barbette's brother. Lance was sweet on them back then as he still was today.

Barbette checked the clock and found that it was only 9:00 o'clock. She decided that she had time to relax and take a long hot bath before getting dress. As, she went into the bathroom and started the water, pouring flower-smelling bath oil in the bathtub, she put on her new Lady Sharp CD. She walked into the kitchen and prepared a cup of tea to drink while she soaked in the tub and was about to get into it when she thought she better bring the phone in the bathroom just in case someone called. Sitting in the tub, she laid back to relax and began thinking about her date with Dean—she smiled. She wondered if Carl knew that they had gone out and if he even cared.

The music was sounding good and her favorite song was now playing, 'The Lust In You'. Barbette started singing along when suddenly she heard a knock at her door and wondered who it could be. She hadn't buzzed anyone in. She got out of the tub and wrapped a large towel around her, walked to the door dripping water from her body onto the floor.

"Who is it?" she asked.

"It's Dean," he said from the other side of the door.

Barbette flung the door opened.

"Dean!" she said, "Hey, how did you get in here?"

"I know the security guard," he replied with a smile.

"Sorry I got you out of the shower," he apologized quickly.

"Oh that's okay and I was in the tub."

Dean looked at Barbette with the towel wrapped around her, took her by the hand and escorted her back to the bathroom.

"Get back in," he said. "I'll just sit here on the stool and watch you."

Barbette smiled as she let the towel drop to the floor and got in the tub. Dean had never seen her naked and was very excited. He sat down on the stool watching her intently.

"So, why are you here?" she asked.

"I had to see you again. I missed you girl," he replied.

"Do you have plans for today?" he asked.

Barbette told him about her standing lunch date with her best friends when suddenly Dean got up from the stool got on his knees by the tub. He took Barbette washcloth from her, grabbed the bar of soap and rubbed the soap on the washcloth lathering it thoroughly, than he started rubbing her body. Barbette closed her eyes and let him take over. He started at her neck then moved to her breast. Not saying a word he continued down her legs, lifting them to able him to rub the back of them. Dean placed the cloth in the middle of her legs and began gently rubbing her private area in an up and down motion. Barbette was starting to get aroused. Dean asked her if it felt good. Barbette could barely speak. "Yes, oh Yes," she said, gasping with pleasure.

"Do you want me to continue?" he asked.

Barbette had now opened her legs wider and had begun to move in a sensual way.

"Oh yes," she said, "Oh yes, please don't stop." Barbette was about to cum. Dean continued to move the washcloth up and down adding pressure where he knew it would cause her to release.

"Talk to me baby," Dean whispered.

Barbette screamed out, "OH MY GOD, I'M CUMMING. FUCK, DAMN DEAN, DEAN DAMN!"

Dean eased up the bath cloth, bended over to kiss her and asked softly, "Was it good Baby?" Barbette could not talk. Her heart was beating so fast she could only lay there, waiting for her heart rate to return to normal and *wondering how in the hell could a man make a woman cum with a washcloth.* Dean kissed her softly on her lips and sat back on the stool. He knew that he must love her. He was about to burst, but was still willing to wait to have sex with her. He just wasn't sure how long he could wait.

Barbette finally spoke, "Dean, what was that about?"

"It was about me pleasing you. That's all baby" he replied.

Barbette was silent for a few minutes. She sat up in the tub and stretched her arm out for Dean to pull her up and help her out of the tub. Dean handed her the towel and walked into her bedroom leaving her alone for a few minutes. While sitting on the end of her bed waiting for her, Dean looked around and noticed that Barbette had a huge bedroom. It's very nice, he thought. He loved her king-size post-bed that sat midway against the far wall of the room and admired the tiger print lounge in the corner by the window. He wondered if Barbette had decorated this room or if her dad had, since he knew that the condo did not belong to her. Barbette came out of the bathroom with a towel wrapped around her.

"What time do you have to meet you friends?" Dean asked.

"11:30" Barbette replied. It was now 10:30. She only had an hour to get ready. She went in to her closet and pull out a pair of jeans, a white shirt and a pair of Gucci white sandals. Dean tried not to watch Barbette getting dressed. He wanted her to bad and couldn't handle the tease . . .

"Barbette, where are you meeting your friends?"

"Justin's; it's always Justin's," Barbette replied.

"Let me drop you off and pick you up, okay?"

Barbette didn't have a problem with that. Now she was free to drink as many Bloody-Mary as she wanted and not have to worry about driving home.

As they walked to his car, Barbette wondered if Dean was for real. She thought something had to be wrong with him. He was just too good to be true. She had taken Gregory's advise and prayed for a good man and wondered if God had send Dean.

On the way to Justin's, Barbette informed Dean she would be leaving the next day for a business trip and would be gone till Thursday or Friday. Even though he hated to see her go, Dean thought her going out of town might be good for the both of them. It would give them time to think about their relationship and if they wanted it to continue. Dean drove slowly, allowing him to have more time with Barbette while she continued talking about her friends and how they had met. When they finally reached Justin's, Dean told her to call him when she was ready to be picked up.

Barbette walked in to find her friends at the bar. "Hey you people," she exclaimed cheerfully.

"Hey, Barbette," Andrea said

Tee took a long look at her and said, "You look like you just got laid!"

Barbette screamed with laughter and said, "Something like that."

"Oh, girl, tell us all about it but wait till we get to our table." Andrea paid for the drinks and they headed to their table.

Once they had placed their orders, Tee demanded, "Okay, who is he, how does he look, and where does he work?"

"His name is Dean Jenkins."

"The Dean Jenkins of CD Production?" Andrea asked with excitement in her voice.

"Yes, do you know him?" Barbette asked.

"Who don't? He is fine and got some money too?" Andrea replied.

"How did you meet him?" Tee asked.

"Well . . . it's a long story."

Barbette filled them in about how she had met Carl and ended up with Dean. She shared her feeling for Dean with them and how much of a gentleman he had been.

"Is he good in bed?" Tee asked. "Because you know, girl, if he's not good in bed, all that money and looks don't mean a damn thing."

Barbette started to smile and said, "I have not fucked him yet."

"WHAT?" Tee burst out taken by surprise at hearing Barbette's statement.

Barbette told them what Dean had said about their relationship and also told them what he had done to her in the tub earlier. She informed them that she was excited about waiting to have sex with him because she knew that when she did do it, it would be the bomb.

Tee and Andrea looked at each other in shock. They knew Barbette and the Barbette they knew loved to fuck. She was a big freak. She had told them she had changed, but they had never believed it till this moment.

"I'm happy for you, sister," Tee said.

"Thanks," Barbette said lowering her eyes demurely.

Barbette turned the conversation to them. "So, who have you guys been fucking other than each other?" she asked. Andrea and Tee were very attractive young bi-sexual women. They both had small built frames. Andrea had long shoulder length hair that she wore in a bob, while Tee wore hers in a short cut with bangs with tapered sides and back. At one time they used to have sex with each other but now they were just friends.

"Andrea doesn't want me no more," Tee said, laughing aloud.

"You're damn right," Andrea replied, as she pulled her hair behind her ears.

Barbette order another drink after they had finished their meals and she sat a while longer listening to Andrea and Tee tell spa stories.

"When are you coming back in?" Andrea asked.

"Maybe the week after next, I have to go out of town on business this week," Barbette replied.

"Okay, call us and we'll schedule you. Bring your man with you," Tee said

"Okay. And I think it's time for us to go before we really get drunk up in here," Barbette suggested.

"I know what you mean," Andrea said. "You need a ride?"

"No, I just have to call Dean. He's coming to get me," Barbette explained.

"Do you want us to wait with you?" Tee asked.

"No. That's all right. You two go ahead."

Barbette called Dean on his cell phone as Tee and Andrea exited the restaurant. He answered right away.

"Dean, I'm ready," she said.

"Okay baby, I'll be there in 5 minutes."

Barbette wondered where he was that he could get to her in five minutes. She finished her drink, and then walked to the front door of the restaurant to wait for Dean's arrival. He was already there waiting. Barbette got into Dean's car, wondering if he had been waiting for her all that time; he was on his cell phone.

"Okay, man. We're going to need four microphones. Do me right now Jay, Okay?" Dean hung up the phone and leaned over, giving Barbette a long tongue in the mouth kiss.

"Hey baby," he said

"Hey Dean, tell me; where were you that you could get here so fast?"

"At the Cheese Cake Factory; I met some of my business associates over there for coffee."

The Cheese Cake Factory was up the street from Justin's. It happened to be one of Barbette's favorite places. She loved there cheesecake.

Dean stopped in front of Barbette's building.

"Barbette, would you like for me to come up?"

"Why are you asking now, Dean? You didn't ask earlier," Barbette said in a joking voice.

"Okay, then I won't ask. I'll just follow your ass up," he said with a teasing smile crossing his face.

He pulled into the parking garage, parked and followed Barbette up to her apartment.

He took a seat on sofa, picked up the Sunday paper and started leafing through the business section. Barbette took off her shoes and sat beside him on the sofa.

"Dean would you like to watch a movie with me?" she asked.

"Sure Barbette. What you got?"

"What's Love Got To Do With It, Love The One You're With and Janet Does The Navy."

Dean started to laugh; "Great selection, Barbette! Baby, I got a better idea."

"What's that?" Barbette asked.

Dean asked her to sit on his lap then he kissed her hard and long. She could feel his breathing enhance. He stopped kissing her, looked her body up and down, then threw his head back and closed his eyes.

"Hey, Dean, what's wrong?" Barbette asked with urgency.

Dean straightened up, opened his eyes and looked at her with real concern.

"OK Barbette, I can't take it any longer. I was trying hard, but I want to take you into your bedroom and make love to you so damn bad. I want you girl, but before I do, I have to ask you a question."

"What?" Barbette asked anxiously.

"Well, I know I won't be taking Dee to bed with me, but I need to know if you will be taking Carl to bed with you."

Barbette looked Dean in the eyes and said, "Hell no! It's only going to be me and you."

Barbette got up and extended her hand to Dean. He got up and took hold of her hand as she led him into her bedroom. She lay down on the bed and allowed Dean to undress her. He took off her blouse and started caressing her breasts, softy dancing his fingers on her nipples till Barbette started to moan. Then he pulled off her jeans, finding that she, as before, did not have on any underwear. He was about to explode. Dean kissed her body all over. When he reached her private area he whispered, "Barbette, open your legs baby."

Barbette opened her legs allowing him to place his mouth in her river of pleasure, extending his tongue to give her the up most pleasure. Barbette thought she was in heaven. Dean could tell Barbette loved how he was eating her by the way she was moving and arching her back. He could tell that she was about to cum and decided to postpone her pleasure. He wanted to take his clothes off. Barbette lay there patiently, watching him take off his shirt, pants and underwear. He stood in front of her naked allowing her to check out what he had to offer. He looked at her lying on the bed and said. "Are you sure it's just me and you, Barbette?"

Barbette said, "Yes, Dean, it's just us."

Dean continued where he had left off with his tongue down in her private area enjoying what he was doing for her. This time when she started to cum, he didn't stop. Barbette started to scream with pleasure, "OH DEAN, OH DEAN, YES, YES, YES, YES, FUCK, YES! Dean raised his head and climbed in between her legs to continue giving her pleasure. He brought his body down on top of her and entered her slowly, feeling the heat and the wetness from her release. He started to move in a rhythmic motion moving in and out of her body.

Barbette started to cry with pleasure. "Oh God Dean, why did we wait so long?" she said in a lustful tone.

Barbette had started to move to the same rhythm as Dean. "It is so dam good. Please, don't stop," she whispered. Dean started to move at a faster pace, hoping that Barbette would keep up with him. He started to breathe hard. He knew he was going to release any second.

Dean tried to hold back longer, not wanting their love making to end. "Barbette," he said in a shaky voice, "you are the only women in my life and as long as you can give it to me like this you will always be the only women in my motherfucking life. You hear me girl? You hear me? You're my Boo," he said.

Barbette could not speak. She was about to pop. Dean could not hold it any longer and released himself into Barbette. At the same time she came causing a river of wetness and joy.

"OH MY MY, OH SHIT!" Barbette screamed with pleasure.

They lay there, caressing each other, using their hands, mouths, and moans to communicate with each other.

"Barbette, let's get under the covers," Dean suggested.

They both got up and pulled down the covers and got into bed. Barbette position herself to lay in Dean's arms while he played with her hair. He was hoping that his body would allow him to get inside her again soon. Dean wondered if there was more she would want from him sexually and if he had pleased her.

"Barbette," Dean said tenderly as he ran his fingers through her hair.

"Yes, Dean," she answered softy.

"Is there anything else you need from me sexually and I need to know if I've pleased you."

Barbette had her eyes closed. She opened them to look at Dean's expression and closed them again. "Dean, you pleased the fuck out of me. There is nothing more I would ever ask of you sexually. Did I please you and is there anything sexual you need from me?" she asked.

"No," said Dean, "except . . ." he hesitated.

Barbette opened her eyes and looked at Dean. "Except what?" she asked puzzled.

"I do like a blow job every once in awhile. Would that be a problem?"

Barbette smiled at Dean and closed her eyes. "No problem, Dean. As a matter of fact, I'm pretty dam good at it."

Dean felt that everything was perfect. He knew he loved Barbette but he was scared. He felt that she was the one he would marry one day. He knew that he had not used protection for the first time in two years and did not know if she was on birth control or not. He decided it wasn't a good time to ask her.

Dean woke up with Barbette lying across him. He began rubbing her back. He thought, *I'm a happy man.* Barbette woke up and raised her head to look at him. "Hi baby," she said.

"Hi, Barbette; how do you feel?" Dean asked.

"I feel great," she said softy. "What time is it?"

Dean glanced at the clock on her nightstand. "9:00; what time does your flight leave?" he asked.

"1:45," Barbette replied. "But I still have to pack."

"So, how long do you think it will take you to pack?" He asked.

"If you help me, it might only take 20 minutes," Barbette said as she raised her body off of Deans and climbed out of bed.

"Where are you going?" he asked.

She walked towards the bathroom and looked back and said, "to pee. Want to come?"

Dean lay in bed smiling. He did not want Barbette to leave him. He thought that he would complete two up-coming projects during the time she was gone. He heard the shower running and wondered if Barbette had already gotten in. At that moment, she came out of the bathroom still naked and asked.

"Hey, you want to take a shower with me?" Excited, dean smiled as he got out of bed and walked into the bathroom. He got into the shower and began lathering up.

"Don't go anywhere—I'll be right back," Barbette said. Dean wondered where she had gone when suddenly, he heard her come back. Barbette stepped into the cubicle and began kissing Dean on his mouth and neck. As she backed him up against the shower wall, she began caressing his private area with her hands and at the same time, she started licking his nipples as if they were sucker. Dean was speechless as she went down on her knees, placed his cock into her mouth and began to give him a blowjob. Dean held on to the shower wall moaning. He realized that she was good. *As a matter of fact*, Dean thought, *she is first-rate.*

"Oh, Baby, Baby, Baby, go ahead do that shit," he slurred and moaned. He was about to shoot his load and did not know if she wanted him to come in her mouth or not, but he couldn't stop to ask. As he started to release, Barbette pulled his cock out of her month and began rubbing it on her breasts in an up and down motion as he released himself onto her. Dean's legs became limp. He was having a hard time standing and had to hold on to the walls of the shower. He leaned against the shower wall in a daze and watched her as she came up from her knees and began lathering up her body. He wondered what else she could and would do.

Dean stayed in the shower until Barbette had finished lathering and rinsing off her body, they both got out together.

"I'll be right back," she said as she wrapped her towel around her body and walked out. Dean continued drying off and, wondering where she had gone. He came out of the bathroom at the same time Barbette was walking back in with two cups of coffee in her hands.

"Hey, Dean; I made us some coffee."

"Thanks, Barbette," he said as he took a cup from her hand.

He placed his cup of coffee on the nightstand, wrapped a towel around his waist and took a seat on the bed. He observed Barbette while she was standing in front of the mirror towel-drying her hair

"Hey baby," he said. "That's a hell of a way to wake up a man."

Barbette smiled at him and said, "Did you like it?"

"Hell Ya," Dean replied, grinning from ear to ear.

Barbette went into her closet and started packing her suitcase. She knew she didn't have to take much with her since she had left several of her suits in Diane's closet. Diane Washington was Barbette's friend from law school and Barbette always stayed with her instead of in a hotel when she went to New York.

Dean walked into her closet; he had put on his pants and was sipping his coffee.

"Baby, where will you be staying in New York?" he asked.

"With my friend, Diane; I'll give you the phone number so that you can reach me there or on my cell—if you feel the need to talk to me."

"Oh, you know I'm going to want to talk to you," Dean replied.

Dean watched her zip up her carry on and wondered if she would be faithful to him while she was away. He had already made a promise to himself that he would never cheat on her—at least he was going to try to keep his promise.

Barbette pulled a navy blue suit and a white blouse off the closet rack. She walked over to the shoe shelves and picked up a pair of navy blue pumps and placed them on the floor.

"Barbette," Dean said wearing a dizzy look on his face.

"Yes?" she answered.

He pondered his words before finally speaking. "I think I'm falling in love with you."

Barbette passed Dean and walked back into the bedroom. She didn't say a word while she pulled her stocking and bra out of the underwear drawers and started putting them on.

Dean had followed her back into the room and was now standing in front of her.

"Did you hear me?" he said

"Yes, Dean," Barbette replied warmly.

"So what? You don't feel the same way, or what?" Dean asked in a demanding tone.

Barbette stopped dressing and looked up at Dean. "Dean," she said in a soft voice, tears in her eyes, "I know I love you; I'm just afraid."

"I am too," he said.

Dean went on to tell her that the few days that they would be apart would probably give them time to think about their relationship. He told her how scared he was about how fast everything had happened and he had not expected to feel this way so soon.

Barbette finished dressing while she listened to Dean. She wondered when he would address the matter of them not using protection during their love making session last night. After putting on her shoes, she walked over to her nightstand and opened the drawer. Pulling out a pad of paper, Barbette wrote down Diane's phone number and address and handed it to Dean as he finished his speech about their relationship.

Barbette said, "Call me, will you?"

"I will. Are you ready to go?" he asked as he turned towards her with his arms open.

"Yes, Dean," Barbette answered as she walked up to him and pressed her body against his kissing him in a lustful way. "I'm going to miss you this week," she said.

"Me too," Dean replied.

Dean dropped Barbette off in front of the airport. "Bye baby," he said as he waved and rode off. Barbette watched his car disappear into the traffic, adjusted her suit jacket and started towards the entrance of the airport. Walking through the hall she noticed the many improvements that had been made to the airport and how the security had been beefed up since the 9/11 incidents. She approached her gate just in time for loading. The flight attendant checked her out making sure that she only had one carry-on

EPISODE FIVE

My Sister, My Friend

Diane was a short, petite built, black, twenty-nine year old woman. She had been married when Barbette first met her in law school and had been divorced for 3 years now. Her son, Darrell, who was 15, lived with her in a large brown-stone in New York. Darrell recognized Barbette as his blood aunt, making sure he called her with his birthdays and Christmases' requests every year. Barbette loved him like a son. She could not wait to see them. They always made her trip to New York a pleasant one.

Barbette woke up as the plane was landing. She heard the pilot announce over the intercom, "It is now 2:10 and it's a sunny 85 degrees here in New York." Barbette was thankful she had worn a short-sleeve shirt under her suit jacket. She waited patiently in her seat for the other passengers to pull their luggage from the overhead storage bin before reaching for her own. Once in the airport's arrival lounge, Barbette moved towards the elevator that led to the exit. When she reached the ground floor she saw a man in a chauffeur's uniform holding a sign with her name written on it. She walked up to him and said, "I'm Barbette Jackson." He smiled and informed her that he was her limo driver.

"Please come this way," he said. Barbette got into the limo and made herself comfortable. The driver asked "Where to?"

Barbette replied, "1501 25th Street, Manhattan." As the limo pulled away from the curb and they were on their way to Diane's house Barbette thought about Dean. She wondered if he was with another woman already or if he was being faithful to her.

It was a long ride to Diane's house so Barbette decided to take another nap in the limo, knowing she and Diane had not seen each other in a long time and, they would probably stay up late talking. The driver pulled up in front of Diane's house and got out to open the door for Barbette. She went up to the door and rang the bell. Diane came out wearing a pink tank top, white slacks and white sandals. "Hey girl, it's been a long time," she said as she hugged Barbette long and hard.

"I've missed you sister," Diane said, taking Barbette's hand and leading her into her three-story home. The house was decorated in an Africa-décor. With every wall painted in pale yellow, accented with black art pictures or fixtures and furnished in leather and wicker. A black leather sofa sat in the middle of the living room with two matching chairs on either side. The back wall held book shelves from ceiling to floor and the wall opposite the fireplace was mirrored ceiling to floor. The dining room, which was located across from the living room, was separated from it by a hallway. It was decorated with high back petal chairs upholstered with African prints. The chairs surrounded a large round glass top table held up by a large cherry wood carved pedestal.

"Let me walk you up to your room girl so that you can put your things away," Diane offered. Barbette always slept in the same room on her visits. Diane and her son called it the "Lady Jackson' suite.

"So, girl, what's been going on?" Diane asked

"Nothing much, Diane," Barbette replied as she laid her carry-on on the bed and opened it.

"I know!" said Diane. "I'll make us some daiquiris and put some munchies together and we'll sit down and talk about old times, okay?" Barbette nodded in agreement.

Diane left the room and headed downstairs to her kitchen. Barbette checked the closet to find four suits that belonged to her, a navy, black, gray and cream. She had left them there on her last visit. Barbette wondered if Diane had a blouse she could borrow that would match the gray suit: she thought she would wear it to work tomorrow. Barbette washed her face and hands in the bathroom adjacent to the bedroom and headed downstairs. When she reached the kitchen Diane was standing in front of an open refrigerator bend over looking for items she needed to make the daiquiris. She opened the freezer part of the refrigerator and pulled out a tray of ice.

"Hey, Diane, can I help?" asked Barbette.

Diane closed the door of the freezer and walked up to the counter.

"No baby, I got it. You just sit down and relax. Matter of fact, you can start telling me about this new man in your life."

"I never said I had a new man in my life," Barbette replied.

"I see it all over you. Come on, girl, give it up, I've known you for a long time. I know your ass."

Barbette took a seat at the kitchen table and looked around. She wondered where Darrell was. "Diane where's my Darrell?"

"Oh, he's at the 'rec' center—basketball practices. He should be home in about an hour or so. You should see him! He has gotten so tall and he looks just like his father."

"By the way, since you brought him up, how is Donald doing?" Barbette asked.

"Please, don't ask. I hope he stays wherever he is. You know, that man was bad news and I hope he never comes around here. Anyway, we were talking about you, not me."

Diane continued preparing the daiquiris as she turned to look at Barbette. Barbette was sitting at the table crying.

"Barbette, what's wrong?" Diane put the spoon on the counter and walked over to Barbette.

"Hey, you want to talk?" She asked in a concerned voice.

"I think I'm in love," Barbette replied with tears flowing down her cheeks.

"So, what's wrong with that?" Diane said, smiling. "You should be happy!" Diane took Barbette's hand in hers and asked, "Who is this man?"

"His name is Dean, Dean Jenkins. He has his own music production business and he is too good to be true."

Diane stood up from her chair and walked over to the counter while keeping eye contact with Barbette. "Yes, go on"

Barbette told Diane how she had met Dean and all about their relationship. She smiled as she shared how she and Dean were lovers and told Diane about her fear that everything was going too fast.

Diane had finished making the drinks and begins pouring them into two very pretty glasses. She walked over and placed them on the table and sat down next to Barbette. "Barbette, I think that's great," she said. "But I only have one question . . ."

Barbette looked at her with concern. "What is it?" she asked as she wiped tears from her eyes.

"Is he saved? Does he know Jesus?"

Barbette smiled at her friend. She knew how serious Diane was about the Lord. She knew that she would not approve if Dean wasn't a churchgoer.

"I don't know," Barbette finally answered.

"Well, we'll just have to find out, wont we?" Diane replied in a stern tone. "And by the way, when was the last time you were in church?"

"About three Sundays ago," Barbette said, wanting to change the subject.

Diane took a sip of her drink and got up from her seat, walking to her cabinet to retrieve a bag of chips. "Want some chips, girl?"

"Yes, please, Ms. Diane," Barbette said with laughter in her voice.

They heard the door open. "Hey, Mom, is Barbette here yet?"

It was Darrell, Diane's son.

"Yes, we're in the kitchen."

Darrell walked in—he was as handsome as ever. He had grown about five inches since Barbette had last seen him. She stood up and walked towards him, meeting him with a hug. "Hey, boy," she said. She broke loose of the hug and stood back to look at him.

"Wild, you're so fine boy. You got a girl friend?"

Darrell smiled. "A lot of them.—don't you know I'm the Man' now?" He said with confidence.

Diane turned and looked at her son endearingly. "Come give your mother a kiss, boy," she said.

Darryl was now 15 and in his sophomore year of high school. He had always been an 'A' student and loved sports: he played football and basketball. His only memory of his father was of his father beating up his mother.

"Mom, I got homework; so, I'm going to make a sandwich and go up to my room, okay?"

"Sure baby," Diane replied.

Diane filled up both her and Barbette glass with more daiquiris and suggested they go into her living room and get comfortable. Barbette sat on the couch, curling her feet under her body while Diane sat in a big leather chair and put her feet up on a matching ottoman.

"Diane, why don't you have a man? Asked Barbette. You've been divorced for several years now. You mean to tell me you haven't met anyone yet?"

Diane looked at Barbette and started to chuckle.

"Hey, what's going on?" Barbette asked with laughter in her voice. Diane adjusted herself in her chair bringing her knees up to her breasts and hugging her legs. "Well, I have met somebody. Oh girl, he is something else."

"Where did you meet him? What is his name and what does he do for a living? Come on girl.

Tell me all about him," Barbette demanded with excitement.

Diane pulled her hair back from her face and began telling Barbette about her new boyfriend. She described him as a tall 40-year-old dark skin man with wavy hair. She had met him at church. He had visited her church with his cousin and ended up joining. Diane spoke with enthusiasm while she told Barbette that his name was Jimmy and that he worked for the New York police department as a lieutenant.

Barbette was impressed and very happy for her friend. "So, tell me," Barbette said with wildness in her eyes, "how long have you been dating this Jimmy man?"

"Three months."

"And you've never told me about him! Girl, you know I need the 411. So, tell me how is he in bed?" Barbette asked.

Diane stopped smiling and looked Barbette in her eyes.

"You know, I've been celibate for a year now and I am not going to have sex with anybody unless he's my husband. You know that, Barbette. We've already talked about my celibacy."

Barbette sat back on the sofa and thought, *how can Diane hold out from having sex.* "Diane I have a question."

"And what is that?"

"Is Jimmy aware that you're celibate?"

"We haven't talked about it"

"So you haven't told him?"

"No, he has not given me any reason to discuss it with him. I believe he respects me," Diane said with a little irritation in her tone.

"Diane!" Barbette screamed in frustration. "Do you even know if he is celibate or not?" Barbette stood up and started to pace back and forth. "Or maybe he's gay, since he has not tried to get with you sexually."

"What do you mean by that?" Diane was really pissed off by this time.

"I mean that a REAL MAN ain't going to wait three months before he makes an effort to tap that ass. OR, he's probably tapping on someone else's ass. That's what I mean."

Diane was very upset with Barbette suggesting that her man might be gay. "HE IS A REAL MAN, A GENTLEMEN, A KIND MAN AND I'M NOT WORRIED ABOUT HIM BEING WITH ANOTHER WOMAN," she hollered at Barbette.

"Okay, okay, Diane, then let's just say he did approach you with a request for sex—what are you going to tell him?"

"I'll tell him I prefer to wait till I'm married."

"Okay, but what if he says he's not planning to marry anytime soon? What then, Diane?"

"We will have to break up. I am not about to sleep around like you do." Diane tried to catch herself, but the words had already slipped out.

"Dam you, *Bitch*. You must be trying to call me a whore."

Diane sat up in her chair and looked at Barbette as if she was crazy. She knew she had pushed the wrong button. She stood up in a jerk and said, "Barbette, you're having sex with a man you've just met. Now, tell me this! What if he stayed around for, let us say, a year and then decides he's not interested in you anymore? Do you find another man and start having sex with him and so on and so on, until your body is all used up? And don't forget the chances you take in catching a HIV! Now you tell me Barbette—should I have sex or should I be celibate? You tell me, girl friend!"

Barbette was now standing in front of the fireplace with her back to Diane. She knew what Diane had said was true and she was upset *because* she had said it to her.

"Barbette, turn around and look at me," Diane demanded.

Barbette turned around slowly and Diane realized that she was crying.

"I'm sorry about what I said to you," Diane said, "but you have to stop sleeping around with every man you meet. It's wrong and you need to repent for your soul. You need to ask God for forgiveness and start to live your life the way God would want you to—in His name."

Barbette turned away from Diane, not wanting to hear anything else she had to say. She walked towards the staircase and turned around to look at Diane. "I think I should go to bed now."

Barbette walked into her bedroom and lay down across the bed, thinking about what Diane had said. She knew Diane was right, but wondered if she could stay celibate until she was married? She knew Dean would die if she told him she was not going to have sex with him anymore. She decided that she did not want to think about it for now and fell asleep without taking her clothes off.

Barbette woke up thinking she was in her own bed. She felt the sun coming in from the window touching her body and she loved the warmth. Realizing that she was still totally dressed, Barbette remembered her conversation with Diane. She hoped Diane wasn't angry with her and that what they had said to each other would be forgotten and forgiven.

Barbette looked at her watch that sent an alert that she was running late for work. She got up and walked into the bathroom to take a shower. Not having the time to do much with her hair, she pulled it into a ponytail, and wondering what blouse she would wear with the suite she had chosen since Diane had already left for work before she could ask about borrowing a blouse from her.

Diane worked for Ernest & Bailey Law firm—a firm that specialized in criminal cases. Before law school Diane had worked for the city. It was during that time that her ex-husband had started to abuse her. Diane had no idea that James was crazy—when she first met him as a city inspector. She was so excited about being in love. He brought her a three-carat diamond ring and they had gotten married a year after their first date. It didn't take long for Diane to find out how crazy the motherfucker was. When they finally got a divorce, Diane let him have everything—she just wanted out of the marriage.

Barbette found the keys to Diane's 2005 Volvo on the counter—she always drove Diane's Volvo when she was in town. Diane had decided not to trade it in when she purchased her new Mercedes so that Barbette would have a car available for whenever she visited.

Barbette arrived at the office and was greeted by Mr. Andrews.

"Hello, Ms. Jackson," he said.

"Hello, Mr. Andrews," she replied, wearing a smile.

"Let me escort you to our guest-office." Mr. Andrews walked in front of Barbette and lead her past a long line of offices. He finally stopped and turned in to an office located at the end of the hall.

"Here we are," he said as he walked over to the window and opened the blinds. Barbette looked around the office finding nothing in it but a desk and a chair. She hated it and wanted to complain but decided it would be best not to. Barbette thought that she could use the excuse of a bad cold as an opportunity to work from Diane's home office and just come in for meetings. Barbette finished her day with a meeting with the auditors. She was in a hurry to get back to Diane's house—she was sleepy and wanted to go to bed. She also was hoping that Dean would call her.

Barbette pulled up in the driveway and into the garage. Darrell was standing at the door to the house "Hey, Aunt Barbette. How was your day?" he asked.

"Oh, it was okay. Glad to be home though. Where's your mother?" Barbette asked.

"She's in her bedroom," the young man answered. Barbette walked in to the house, went straight upstairs and knocked on Diane's bedroom door.

"Come on in," Diane said. Barbette opened the door to find Diane lying on her bed with her eyes closed.

"What's wrong with you girl," Barbette asked.

"I got a headache that's all. How was your day?"

"It was okay. The auditor had nothing to say but good stuff and they think we'll be finished by Wednesday. Barbette took off her shoes, crawled up on Diane's bed and laid beside her. Diane opened her eyes and turned to look at Barbette. "You're going to wrinkle up your suit," she said.

"Oh, that's all right, I just wanted to be close to you and I just wanted to say that I'm sorry about what I said last night."

"Me too," Diane said. "But I meant what I said, Barbette. You need to get yourself together before something serious happens to you. By the way, do you use protection every time you have sex?"

Barbette was not about to tell Diane that she and Dean had unprotected sex.

"I always use protection. Do you think I'm crazy?" Barbette felt bad about lying to Diane, but she didn't want to get Diane all worked up, especially since she already had a headache.

"Well, that's good to know," Diane said with a nod of satisfaction

Barbette spent the rest of her visit with Diane, shopping, eating and sleeping.

The auditors were finished on Wednesday so Barbette made flight arrangements to leave Thursday evening. Barbette had gained four or five pounds since her visit with Diane but she was not the least bothered by the weight gain. She felt she was a little too 'light' for her height anyway.

"What time does your plane leave?" Darrell asked.

"8:52, why?" Barbette replied.

"I was getting ready to go to the library and wasn't sure if I'd be back in time to say good bye and it looks like I have to say my good-byes right now. I'm going to miss you, Aunt Barbette."

"No, I'm going to miss you more," Barbette said, hugging Darrell and kissing him on the cheek.

"You be good and look after your mother, okay?"

"OK. See you later."

Darrell left and Barbette headed upstairs to finish packing—she decided to leave the four suits she had previously left in Diane closet. Diane walked in and sat on the end of the bed, watching Barbette place a pair of shoes in her carry on.

"Hey, girl friend; I'm going to miss you," Diane said.

"Me too." Barbette stopped packing and sat down next to Diane, placing her arms around her shoulder. "Do you know that you're my sister and I love you?" she said with emotion. Diane reached over and hugged Barbette.

"I know," Diane replied with tears in her eyes.

"Remember, if you ever need me I'm just a phone call away," Diane said.

They finished their goodbyes and walked down the stairs together. The limo was already waiting for Barbette.

She got in and the limo dropped her off at the New York airport. The flight left on time and she was happy to be home. While walking through the airport she wondered why Dean had not called—she had decided not to call him to find out why. She thought the only thing Dean wanted was to fuck her and she was planning not to let that happen again. From the conversations she had with Diane, Barbette realized she had been abusing her body. Diane had given her some bible scripture to help her stay in the word and be true to herself. Barbette had decided not to have sex anymore and wait till she was married

Barbette reached the exit and walked out to the sidewalk in front of the airport. She had called her brother, Lance, yesterday and he had agreed to pick her up. Barbette was looking down towards the incoming traffic, looking for Lance's car to pull up any minute. After waiting for about 10 minutes, she saw Lance's Black Jaguar coming towards her. He pulled up and got out the car.

"Hey, Crazy Woman," he said as he opened his trunk and placed her carry-on into it while Barbette got into the car and adjusted her seat. Lance drove Barbette to the condo, where she had chosen to live for a while. "I think I'll stay the night, if it's alright with you?" Lance said.

"Sure," Barbette said.

Lance started talking about work and how busy he had been all week.

"How come you're back today? I thought you were supposed to be in New York till Friday," Lance asked.

"The auditors were finished yesterday, so I didn't see a need to stay any longer." Lance smiled, thinking that Barbette probably hurried back to see Dean. He had run into Dean Tuesday night at the Hard Rock Café. He was with a group of people, including two fine ass women. He had wondered if one of them was with him, but did not brother to ask.

"So, will you be seeing Dean tonight?" Lance asked

"No" Barbette replied, "I just want to go to bed. By myself."

Lance smiled and pulled up in the garage to the condo. As they walked to the elevator Barbette couldn't help but noticed that her brother had been working out with weights; his muscles imprint came through his gray silk shirt. Barbette commented on it and Lance put on a pleased smile.

Barbette opened the door and walked in as Lance followed her in going straight to the kitchen.

"Hey, what do you got to eat in here?" he asked.

Barbette ignored him and headed to her bedroom. She laid the carry-on on the floor and started taking off her clothes—. Her skirt and then her top, letting them fall to the floor. Looking through her bottom dresser drawer she found her favorite nightgown and put it on. Barbette pulled back the covers on her bed and got in. Once in bed, Barbette closed her eyes and started thinking about Dean. She could still smell his cologne in the sheets and pillowcase.

Lance walked in to her room and laid at the bottom of her bed. Barbette did not move nor did she open her eyes.

"Hey, Barbette . . ."

"Yes, Lance"

"Are you going to work tomorrow?"

"No. I think I'll work from home. Are you?" she asked.

"Got to; I have two meetings tomorrow."

Lance laid there in silent for a while. He wondered about Barbette and Dean's relationship and why Dean wasn't coming over tonight. Barbette usually shared her relationship updates with him, but she had not once mentioned the relationship between her and Dean.

"Barbette, can I asked you a question?" Lance adjusted himself on the bed, laying his hands behind his head to raise it and allow his body to stretch out in front of him.

"Yes, Lance, what is it?" Barbette's voice was soft expecting her brother's question.

"What's going on with you and Dean? Is he your man or what?" Lance asked.

Barbette opened her eyes and adjusted her pillows, allowing her to sit up in bed. She looked at Lance stretched out at the foot of her bed and remembered how when they were small, he would come into her room when he couldn't sleep and make her stay up all night talking to him.

"Lance, I thought Dean was my man; at least that's what I thought when I left for New York—but when he finds out that I have chosen to be celibate until I get married, he probably won't want to be bothered with me."

Lance sat up, looked at Barbette and started to laugh uncontrollably. "Barbette, you mean to tell me that you are going to tell that man that you're not planning to have sex with him anymore? He is going to die." Lance could not stop laughing. Barbette waited patiently for Lance to get control of himself.

"I'm sorry, Sis. But please tell me, what brought this on?"

Barbette rolled her eyes at Lance then began telling him about her visit with Diane. Lance looked at his sister with his mouth wide open and put his hand out in front of him.

"Please, don't say any more. I suppose she got you reading the scriptures too?" Lance was laughing so hard, that tears were coming out of his eyes.

"As a matter of fact, she did give me some to read," Barbette replied.

Lance got up from Barbette's bed and walked towards the door, still laughing.

"Hey, I'm going to leave you in here by yourself to think about what you just said to me."

Barbette lay there wondering if this whole thing about being celibate was a crazy idea. She knew what Diane had said to her was true, but she just didn't know if she could refrain from having sex. Finally, she fell asleep.

Lance had gone into the other bedroom. He got into bed and called Whitney, his latest girl friend. Lance relationships never lasted more than a few months. He was the type of man who chased every fine woman he saw, and once the chase was over, he had no interest in the woman.

Informing Whitney that he had a busy day ahead of him tomorrow, he talked with her for only fifteen minutes before hanging up and calling Damika, his old girl friend. Lance loved Damika. Even though they no longer dated, he considered her one of his best friends and still called her at least twice a week. Lance stayed on the phone for an hour before he hung up. He fell asleep while letting his mind run through the information that his sister had shared with him about being celibate.

The next morning, Barbette walked out of her bedroom at the same time Lance was leaving for work. "See you later girl," he said. Barbette waved him good-bye and walked into the kitchen. She made coffee and poured it in a cup. She sat down on a stool at the island-counter and sipped her coffee while allowing her mind to think about Dean and the fact that he had not called. She finally decided that thinking about Dean was not her priority and retrieved her laptop out of her carry-on. Walking into her bedroom while carrying her coffee, she wondered why she had not gotten her period and realized that she had better check her calendar for her start date.

Lance's ten-o'clock meeting was cancelled so he decided that he would go by CD Production to see Carl and Dean. He wanted to let Dean know that Barbette was back, since he didn't expect her till that evening. Lance could not stop smiling as he thought about what Barbette had told him the previous night. He pulled in the parking lot and took the elevator up to the top floor of the building.

Walking in to CD Production he was greeted by a receptionist. "Hello, what can I do for you, Lance?" she said. Lance smiled at Jade as he approached her desk. Lance had introduced Jade to Carl and Carl had given her a job after Jade gave Carl something in return.

"You know what you can do for me—but not right now." Lance smiled at her. "Is Carl around?" he added as he adjusted his tie.

She looked down at the five line phone and said, "Yes, but he's on the phone right now. Would you mind waiting?"

"Not at all."

He sat there for five minutes reading a magazine when Dean walked through the doors. Lance stood up to greet him.

"Hey, man, aren't you late for work?"

"Oh, man, I had a long night," Dean said.

"Where were you, man? I know you weren't at Barbette's because I was there."

"She's back!" Dean asked with a surprised look on his face.

"You didn't know, man?"

"No, I didn't. I thought she wouldn't be back until tonight," Dean said with a puzzle look on his face.

"Well, she's back."

Dean wondered if she was mad at him for not calling her. He had been busy working on a showcase, which was to open that very same evening. He also wanted to give her some time to think about their relationship while she was gone.

"Did she go to work today?" Dean asked.

"No, man. She was at the condo when I left. Are you going to call her?" Lance asked, wearing a smile on his face wondering if she would tell him about her celibacy over the phone.

"Yea, man," Dean said

Carl came out of his office wearing a pair of jean and a New York Nicks jersey.

"Hey, people, what's up?" Carl said as he walked towards Lance and grabbed his hand to shake. "What are you doing here this early?" he asked.

"Hey, boy, I came to check on you and the progress of the showcase for tonight."

"It's on, man. It's going to be the bomb. Tell him, Dean, Man . . ."

"Hell yea, it's going to be hot, man."

They stood around talking for a few more minutes about sports and business.

"Well, I got a lot of work to do, so I got to go. See you later at the party?" Dean said, directing his good-bye to Lance.

"Yea, man, I'll try to be there," Lance, responded.

Dean walked into his office and opened his laptop. He pulled the blinds up and stood in front of the window viewing the buildings and sky around him. He wondered if he should call Barbette now or wait till later. At that same moment Carl knocked at the door before entering Dean's office and interrupting his partner's thoughts.

"Hey, man, I thought you were going to be here at 8:00?" Carl said.

"I was, man, but I got tied up," Dean answered.

"With ropes?" Carl asked with a smile on his face.

"I wish," Dean answered while packing up his laptop and placing it in his carrying case.

Carl asked, "Where you going man?"

"I got to go see Barbette."

"She's back?" Carl asked.

"Yeah, man."

"Okay, man. I'll see you at the club by 7:30, right?"

"I'll be there," Dean answered as he walked out the door.

Carl went back in his office and sat down behind his desk and thought.—*Man, I think Dean is strung out over Barbette.* He wondered how long their relationship was going to last and smiled.

Dean arrived at Barbette condo at 10:00. On his drive there he had been thinking about the last time he had been with her and was starting to get aroused. He was excited about seeing her again. He pulled into the parking garage and spotted his security guard friend.

"Hey, man, can you let me in?" Dean asked.

"Sure, man. Going to see that girl again?" the man asked.

"Yea, man; and she's not that girl—she's *my lady* man," Dean said in a joking tone. The security guard chuckled.

"See you later, man," he said.

Dean got on the elevator and pushed the top floor button. He was hoping Barbette was still in bed so that he could jump in with her. As he approached her door he heard music and was hoping she would hear his knock.

Barbette heard a knock at the door. She turned the music down and walked towards the door. She was hoping that it was Dean. She had wanted to see him bad.

"Who is it?" she asked.

"It's me, Dean."

Barbette opened the door so fast she felt a gust of wind going through her hair. Dean walked in looking so good. He was wearing a soft baby-blue shirt and a pair of jeans. He dropped his carrying bag on the floor and grabbed Barbette around her waist, pulling her to him and began rubbing her back enjoying the softness of her terry-cloth robe. He placed his hand on her chin, pulling her head up to force her lips to meet his. Barbette could not move. She wanted him so bad. Dean pulled away from her and looked her in the eyes.

"Hey baby, are you mad at me."

"No. I missed you, Dean," she said.

"I missed you too baby. I've been busy working; but never stopped thinking about you," he replied.

Barbette leads Dean into the kitchen where she had been sitting at the island, working on her laptop. She walked around the counter to place a plate in the sink then turned towards Dean who was now standing behind her.

"Would you like something to eat?" Barbette asked

Dean had gotten so aroused he was about to burst. He picked her up and sat her on the edge of the sink

"Of course I do," he replied. Then he opened her robe to view her naked body. Dean began kissing her on the lips and caressing her breasts, paying much attention to her nipples. Barbette had been caught by surprise with Dean placing her up on the sink, but loved the spontaneous move he had made—she wanted him so badly. Dean continued kissing and feeling her up and down her body until he touched her wetness and it was on. He pulled her legs apart and drove his tongue into her very wet pussy, moving it in an up and down motion, concentrating on her clitoris knowing that it would cause her to cum right away. Barbette held on to his shoulder to brace herself. She was really enjoying it when she suddenly remembered that she was supposed to be celibate.

"Stop, please stop, Dean," she shouted, pushing Dean away from her. Barbette jumped down from the sink and ran into her bedroom—closing and locking the door behind her. Dean followed her only to find that Barbette had locked herself in her room.

"Hey baby, what's wrong?" Dean asked, talking to her from the other side of the door. Barbette didn't answer. She was lying across her bed wondering how she was going to tell Dean she had chosen to be celibate.

"Come on, Barbette, open the door and tell me what's going on with you," Dean shouted.

Barbette got up, unlocked and opened the bedroom door. Dean came in slowly approaching her. She sat down on the side of the bed.

"What's wrong?" he asked in disbelief.

Barbette didn't speak. She was wondering if she would lose him if she told him what she had to tell him.

"Dean, I have something to tell you?"

Dean's first thought was she must be pregnant.

"What baby?" he asked as he slid down on the bed next to her.

"I have chosen to be celibate—not to have sex, until I get married," she ventured, looking away from him.

Dean smiled, relieved to hear that she was not pregnant. He took her in his arms and hugged her.

"Barbette, baby, hey that's fine. If you don't want to have sex anymore that's fine. But tell me what am I suppose to do? I'm not celibate and don't want to go without sex at any time in my life. Hell, if I had my way, I would be fucking five times a day, every day. So, tell me what I'm supposed to do while you're closing your legs to me and my dick is getting hard?" His tone was sarcastic.

Barbette broke away from his hug and looked at him.

"I'll tell you what to do. You do what you want to Dean," she said as she stood up and walked over to her dresser, Barbette opening a drawer and pulling out a pack of cigarettes and a lighter. She took a cigarette out of the pack and lit it. Dean was shocked.

"Barbette, when did you start smoking?"

Barbette blew the smoke out of her mouth.

"I only smoke when I'm upset. It's not a habit."

Dean smiled.

"Give me one."

"Dean, you don't smoke," Barbette said.

"Only when I'm upset," Dean retorted with laughter. He lit up his cigarette and laid back on Barbette's bed, looking at her standing by the dresser. He began asking her more about this celibacy thing.

"So, Barbette, baby, does this mean that I can't kiss, hug or touch your body anymore? Baby, does this mean I can't eat your pussy and finger fuck you or suck your breasts?" Dean took another puff and sat up looking for an ashtray. Barbette realized that he needed one and passed him an empty one she had on her dresser.

"I don't know, Dean."

"What do you mean, you don't know? Haven't you done your research on this thing before committing to it?" Dean asked as he lay back again.

Barbette had put out her cigarette and walked back to the bed. She looked down at Dean as he lay on her bed and wondered if she would be able to handle not making love to this man.

"So, do I get an answer to my questions or what?" he asked.

"I'm afraid if you do all those things to me you will want to have sex and it would not be fair to you to please me without me pleasing you," Barbette explained.

"Hey baby, I can handle it. The question is can you handle it?" Dean said, while thinking he knew Barbette well enough to know that she couldn't.

"Yes, I think I can handle it," Barbette said as she relaxed and smiled at Dean. She was feeling good about Dean respecting her decision but wasn't sure if his request was in the bible. She had not read all of the bible verses Diane had given her and wondered if any of them even addressed what celibacy really meant.

"Come here baby and lay on me," Dean said.

Barbette lay on top of Dean and started to kiss him on the neck.

"Yes, baby, that feels good," Dean said. He began to rub and squeeze her ass allowing her body to push into him, causing him to develop a hard on.

"You know I love you, girl," Dean said in a lustful tone. He then rolled her over and climbed on top of her placing her legs between his.

He opened her robe and began sucking her breasts as if they were baby bottles.

"Come on baby, open your legs so I can play with that hot pussy." Dean pleaded.

Barbette opened her legs as Dean moved his body down enabling him to place his hand between her legs. He slowly slid his two fingers inside her hot wetness causing her juices to overflow. Barbette moaned.

"Oh yes, Dean. That shit feels so dam good," Barbette purred. Dean toyed with her for a while and then decided it was time to pop that pussy. He began with licking and kissing her thigh, teasing her out of her mind. Barbette could not stand the pleasure that he was bestowing on her. Dean heard her begging for what she wanted and got so turned on he went for the pussy full force, licking and sucking as if it was his last super. Barbette started moving—rotating her hips. She had placed her hands on Dean's head and pushed it down to cause Dean to lick and suck her harder and faster.

"Yes, Yes. Eat my pussy baby. OH HELL YEAH I'm Cumming," Barbette hollered with pleasure as her pussy exploded. Dean knew what turned her on and he loved the way she reacted to him when he was pleasing her.

Dean raised his head from between Barbette's legs and got up to go to the bathroom to wipe off his mouth. He came back into the bedroom holding a wet bath cloth and placed it between Barbette's thighs so she could clean herself off. Barbette was lying there with her eyes closed, thinking about how good Dean was at eating her pussy.

"Barbette?"

"Yes," Barbette mumbled.

"How do you feel baby?" Dean asked as he sat on the side of the bed.

"Great, I feel really great," Barbette said as she lay there with her eyes closed.

"Baby, I just thought about something," Dean said.

"And what is that?" Barbette asked, not opening her eyes

"Well, you were concerned about me pleasing you and it not being fair that I wouldn't be pleased too."

"Yes," Barbette said, thinking that she knew he would not be able to handle it.

"You can please me baby," Dean said.

"What Dean . . . I knew you couldn't handle it," she said, feeling somewhat disturbed by his statement.

"You can give me a blowjob if it's not going to break the rules of celibacy. So, what do you think, baby?" Dean asked with the hopes that she would comply with his needs.

"Okay," Barbette said, "Where do you want to do it? Here on the bed? In the bathroom? In the chair? You name it and I'll blow you?"

Dean started to laugh and lay down beside her on the bed. Barbette rose from the bed placing her body on top of Dean's. She began kissing him. She slid her body down to allow her to adjust the zipper on Dean's jeans. Dean assists her in unzipping his pants. Barbette placed her hand into his jeans, pulling out his penis. Dean was already hard as a brick. Barbette started to gently rub his rod up and down.

Dean started to moan. "Yes baby, that's what I want. Go ahead baby. Suck my shit baby. Put my cock in your motherfucking mouth and suck it, baby." Dean was hot. He was ready to burst. Barbette bent over placing his rod in her mouth. She began moving her mouth in an up-and-down motion while watching Dean. He had closed his eyes and was breathing through his teeth.

"Oh shit. That's it. Please don't you even stop," Dean surged out. Barbette started to work his cock, using her hands at the shaft and working her mouth, allowing his cock to go down her throat. He couldn't hold back any longer. His body jerked and out it came. After swallowing some of his cum, Barbette took his penis out of her mouth allowing the warm liquid to shot out on her breast, dripping down her stomach.

Dean lay with his eyes closed—unable to move. Barbette reached for the bath cloth that Dean had brought in and wiped off her body. Then she climbed off the bed to go in the bathroom to finish cleaning herself up. Dean still didn't move—he lay back thinking about how good she was at giving him head. He thought about the sex he had with Tammy, three times, while Barbette was in New York. Dean was glad he had since Barbette had made a decision to not have sex with him. Barbette came back in the bedroom and lay down next to Dean.

"You all right?" she asked.

"Hell Yeah," Dean replied with a smile on his face. They lay together, talking about work, their relationship, and Barbette told Dean about her time in New York. Suddenly Dean got up, zipped up his pants and said,

"I got to go, Barbette. I have some work to do." Barbette continued to lay back fully relaxed, watching him rushing to put his self back together.

"I want you to be ready at 7:00. I'll be back to pick you up," Dean said in a demanding tone.

"Where are we going?" she asked.

"To the showcase party, the event I've been working on since you've been gone."

"Oh, okay. What should I wear?"

"Something funky, cut out, and short," Dean replied. Barbette started to laugh as she placed several pillows behind her head.

"I'll see my own self out," Dean said. "Since you've gotten comfortable on your bed, I would hate to ask you to move. I'll see you later baby," he added with a smile.

"Okay, Dean."

She heard the door closed and closed her eyes. She knew she loved Dean more than any other man she had ever loved. Barbette wondered if she would end up getting married to Dean or she wondered would he leave her for another woman who was not celibate. Barbette fell asleep and dreamed about her wedding.

Dean got into his car and headed back to the office. He was feeling pretty good thinking about Barbette blowing him off' He hoped that she would not be able to stand not having sex for more than a weeks.

He pulled into the parking lot and got out of his car. In the elevator, he adjusted his pants and shirt that had been wrinkled while lying on Barbette's bed. As he entered the office receptionist area, Carl was coming out of his office.

"Hey man—everything alright?" Carl asked.

"Yeah, man; just have to finish up a couple of contracts and then I will be heading to the house to get dressed."

"Did you see Barbette, man?" Carl asked, wearing a smile and checking out Dean's wrinkled clothes.

"Yeah, man. Matter of fact she will be coming with me tonight."

"Cool, man. I'll see you later then." Carl walked towards the exit and out the door. He knew something had happened. He felt a little jealous and decided to call his newest lady, Tara the stripper, to make arrangement to meet her for sex before he started his evening. It was now 2:00pm and

Carl realized that he didn't have much time. He pulled out his cell phone and dialed Tara's number.

"Hello!"

"Hey, do you think I can come by for a minute. I need to see your ass," Carl said.

"Sure baby," Tara replied. Come on over and make sure you bring some condom with you. Carl started to laugh. He liked Tara. She was straight and always said what was on her mind. Carl got in his car and headed to Tara's house.

EPISODE SIX

Show Case Party

Dean arrived at Barbette house at 6:45. He was dressed in a black suit accessorized with a white shirt and a black and white Harry Mood, design tie. He was sitting on Barbette's sofa, wondering how much longer she was going to be. He had been waiting for her for fifteen minutes. Barbette finally came out of the bedroom wearing a black Channel fitted suit, jacket with a skirt so short that if she leaned over to touch her knees, you would be able to see her naked behind. She had chosen a red bra type top that allowed her stomach to show and, on her feet, she wore four-inch strappy black sandals.

Dean's mouth dropped open with surprise. "Baby you look good enough to eat," he said with excitement. "Damn girl! Don't you forget that you're my women while you're out there tonight?"

"Oh, I won't and don't you forget it either," Barbette replied, batting her long eyelashes.

On the way to Dean's car, they walked together holding hands. Dean was parked in his usual spot—next to Barbette's car in the guest parking space. Dean opened the car door for Barbette, and then went around to the driver side to let his self in. As he was driving out of the garage he waved at the security guard.

"So, that's how you've been getting in," Barbette said.

"Yes, that's my man," Dean rejoined, laughing out loud.

On the way to Club Atlanta, Dean talked about the groups that would be appearing that night and talked about their being signed up with Motown's and how he and Carl had built a relationship with Motown

Talent Division. Barbette listened to Dean, holding on to every word he was saying. She wondered if Dean felt the same for her as he did before she left for New York or was he just bullshitting her.

"Dean, I have to ask you this," she said.

"What is it Barbette?" Dean asked with concern.

"Do you still love me?"

Dean was silent for a moment. He was not sure if he wanted to tell her how he felt, but he knew that there was no need to play games with her.

"Yes, I do love you," he said, "and I believe I told you that the first time we were intimate."

Barbette did not speak; she just wanted to repeat what Dean had said to her over and over in her mind.

When they arrived, people were already lined up outside of the club. Dean parked at the back and they walked to the back door where Dean rang the doorbell.

A big tall man opened it and said, "Come on in man."

Dean never let go of Barbette hand as they walked down a long hall and entered a large room filled with people that, from the way they were dressed, she thought were the 'entertainment' for the night.

"Hey, Dean," several people shouted.

"Hey, what's going on? You guys ready?" Dean asked.

A couple of people hollered in response; "Yeah, man. We're cool."

Dean took Barbette's hand and led her out of the room. They walked through doors that led to the club. Tables were everywhere. The balcony that overlooked the stage was set up with table along the edge and each table in the club had a lit candle placed in the center of it. The walls were black and the carpet was purple. There were studio lights everywhere and there was a long bar on the left side of the room that ran from the front to the back of the club. Barbette had passed this club many times but had never seen the inside of it. She was impressed. Dean escorted her over to the bar area and directed her to take a seat at the end of it.

"I'll be running around, but I'll keep coming back to check on you," Dean said.

He then told the bartender that he would be running a tab and he should give Barbette whatever she wanted.

"They're about to open the doors so I have to go, but I'll be back," Dean added as he leaned over to kiss Barbette on her lips. Barbette smiled at him—she was very excited to see him work. She thought as he walked away, how talented he was and how proud she was of him.

The crowd entered in the club with people everywhere; trying to find the best seats, ordering drinks and socializing and within twenty minutes, the club bar and tables were full—leaving standing room only. People kept coming in and the waitresses were running back-and-forth, from the bar to table, serving drinks. Barbette had ordered a treble shot of cognac with a glass of water on the side. She had drunk most of it and was starting to feel really good. Dean had been gone for about thirty minutes and she had not missed him; she was too busy watching the people in the club. A man approached her and asked if he could buy her a drink. Barbette declined and told him she was with somebody. The man smiled and said, "I thought so, 'cause you are just too fine to be here by yourself." He then walked away.

The show was about to begin. The music started to play. The stage lit up and a voice came from somewhere other than the stage, introducing the announcer. Then as a man came onto the stage, everyone started to applaud while some people screamed. Barbette felt excited. The announcer was the radio DJ that worked for the station that she listened to all the time—V103. He hollered out; "Hello people" and everyone started screaming louder. She was so into the announcer that she did not see Dean come back and stand by her. Dean looked down at Barbette and smiling, ordered both of them a drink, as the DJ announced the first group. The curtain opened and the band started to play as five young men came out of both sides of the stage and started to sing and dance—they were great. Dean stayed at Barbette side for the first half of the show. During intermission, the DJ played recorded music that was low enough to allow people to talk to each other.

Dean turned her bar stool towards him and asked, "So, how did you like the first half?"

Barbette smiled and replied, "It was great, and I'm really enjoying myself." By now Barbette had drunk six shots of cognac and was feeling better than 'good'.

"Baby, you want another drink?" Dean asked.

"If I do, I would probably be drunk," she said

"Don't worry, I'll take care of you," Dean said as he thought *maybe she'll let me fuck her if she has one more drink*. He smiled and asked the bartender to give her a double shot, then leaned over and kissed her.

A man walked up behind Dean. "Hey man, where's Carl?" he asked.

"He's back stage working out some last minute details," Dean answered.

"Oh, Barbette, this is Carl's brother, Marty. Marty this is my lady, Barbette."

"Hello, nice to meet you." Marty extended his hand and Barbette took it and shook it.

"Hello, it's nice to meet you also," she said.

Marty smiled and excused himself as he walked towards the stage.

The second part of the show was better than the first, Barbette thought, and felt that the girl's group was the best group, based on the crowd's reaction. Dean left her to go back-stage to check on thing. He stayed gone until the very end of the show. As people started to leave Barbette could hear them talking about how good the show was and commenting on what groups they liked the best. She was proud of Dean.

She saw Dean approaching her. "Hey baby, come with me." He said. Barbette got down from the bar stool and Dean took her hand and led her back-stage. People where lined up waiting for Carl to pay them for their services.

"Hey, Barbette," Carl said.

"Hi, Carl."

"Did you enjoy the show?"

"Yes, I did, very much so."

Carl continued handing over money and writing checks. There were two people left to pay and Carl paid them with cash and put the rest of the money in his briefcase.

"Okay, I'm ready," he said. As two off duty policemen approached him, he said—"I'll see you guys later. Got to go to the night-deposit and then I'm heading over Tammy's house."

Barbette assumed that Tammy was Carl new lady.

"Carl, man, be careful and call me later to let me know you're all right, okay?" Dean said.

"Don't worry, man. The police are going to follow me to the night-deposit box and the bank is only one block away but; I'll still call you, man."

"Hey, great party," Dean added.

"Yeah, man," Carl said, "we did it again." Carl had a smile on his face as he said his goodbyes and walked towards the back door of the club with the police on his heels.

Dean checked on a few band members who had almost finished loading up their equipment and asked Barbette to have a seat in a fold up chair and wait for him. While waiting in the hall, Barbette was approached by a young attractive lady.

"You're Dean's woman?" she asked.

Barbette wasn't sure if she should answer yes or no. "Why are you asking?" she decided to ask.

"Because, I'm interested in him," answered the girl. Barbette smiled at the lady and said, "Yes, we are dating and he is my man." The young lady turned to walk away and then turned back to look at Barbette and said, "He might not be your man for long. You better be careful, I might have to take him from you."

Barbette decided not to address her statement. She just continued smiling.

Dean walked up to her and said, "Come on baby, let's go." Barbette followed him to the back door where a security guard stood watching them until they got in their car and pulled off.

"CD Production has done it again," Dean said with excitement. His cell phone rang interrupting him. It was Carl telling him that their profit was now in the night-deposit and everything had gone well. He also told him he was on his way to Tammy's and that he'd call him once he was there. Dean ended the conversation and smiled again. As he stopped at a red light, he glanced over at Barbette. He noticed that she had laid her seat back allowing her partly to lie down. He rubbed her thigh.

"Baby, are you all right?" She looked at him and thought that maybe she shouldn't tell him she was tipsy and feeling good. She didn't want him to take advantage of her. "I'm okay. I'm just relaxing"

Dean knew she was a little drunk but wasn't sure how drunk she really was. He also knew that Barbette never wore underwear, so he decided to reach up under her skirt. Once Dean's hand reached her wetness, Barbette started to moan instantly, "Feel good, don't it, Baby?" Barbette was so turned-on and Dean was causing her to become wetter than she already was.

"Oh man, Dean. Shit man, you got to stop," Barbette purred out. Dean loved turning her on. He could tell Barbette loved to fuck, but wasn't sure if it was at the level that he was accustomed to.

"Come on baby, just relax. I'll take care of you, I promise."

Barbette moved his hand away and readjusted her car-seat. "No Dean!" she said in an argumentative tone.

Dean stayed silent for a long while wondering when he would be able to make love to her again. He knew he wanted her and that he didn't want to go somewhere else to satisfy his needs.

He thought about how different it was making love to Barbette than having sex with other women and wondered if it was because he truly loved her. Dean decided they needed a vacation together. "Hey baby, you want to go to Marco Island with me?" He asked unexpectedly.

Barbette looked at him and wondered where did that come from?

"Marco Island? Florida?" she asked puzzled.

"That's the one."

"Sure, when are we going?"

"How bout we leave next Thursday and stay till Sunday."

"That sounds good," Barbette said. "But, tell me, how did you come up with this idea?

"I just wanted to take my lady on a trip, so that we can spend some quality time together."

"Okay," Barbette said all smiles.

Dean pulled up into Barbette parking garage and parked. Once they were in the elevator, Dean pinned her up in the corner and started kissing her on the neck. The elevator stopped and they got off and entered the condo. Barbette headed to her bedroom and sat on the edge of the bed to take off her shoes. Dean followed her carrying an ashtray that he had picked up from one of her end tables.

"Barbette, do you have any incenses around here?" he asked. Barbette looked at Dean with raised eyebrows.

"Dean, you smoke marijuana?"

"Yes, but only when I'm excited," he said and started to laugh. Barbette laughed along with him.

"Look in my closet, first shoe box on the left bottom shelf. It's a white box." Dean walked into her closet and picked up the white box. He opened it to find a pack of incense, two holders and what looked like a half pound of marijuana. He walked out of the closet holding the box in his hand.

"Barbette, did you know there was about half a pound of grass in this box."

Barbette looked surprised. "Oh really? My brother must have put it in there. I'll have to tell him to move it. I don't want to get busted for his shit.' Dean put the box back and lit the incense placing it in a holder as he stood by Barbette dresser, watching her undress. He inhaled the joint and held it in for a few seconds before blowing out the smoke.

"Hey baby, why don't you have a puff?" he asked. Barbette had just slipped on her navy blue silk robe and was tying the belt around her waist. She walked over to him and Dean handed the joint to her. She inhaled and immediately began coughing. Dean started to laugh at her.

"Barbette how often do you smoke weed?" he asked.

She wondered if she should tell him about how she and Carl had gotten high and decided that it wouldn't be a good idea. "I hadn't smoked for few years, till recently, when I smoked a joint about four weeks ago. How often do you smoke?"

Dean loosened his tie and stepped out of his shoes. "Once in a while," he replied. Barbette pulled back the covers and lay down on her bed.

"Are you staying the night?" she asked.

"Yea, baby, if it's all right with you?"

"Sure, it's all right with me," she said as she adjusted her pillow and pulled her hair back off her face. Dean began to undress down to his boxer shorts. He walked over to the bed and sat down on the side where she was laying.

"Barbette . . . ," he said, "I am going to try to respect your decision on being celibate as long as I can, but I want you to know, this is not easy for me. A blowjob is great but there is nothing greater than entering you, girl. Making love with you is a different feeling to me than with any other women I've been with and I think it's because I love you, girl. I just hope we can work this out soon." Dean climbed over Barbette and got into bed pulling the covers over the both of them. He slid her back against him and held her around her waist. Barbette had started to cry. She didn't know what to say to him about what he had just said so she just lay there very still. Dean knew she was crying but decided not to say anything. He was tired and wanted to go to sleep.

Dean woke up with a hard on and wondered if he could get Barbette to help him out by giving him a blowjob. Barbette was knocked out, so, he didn't brother to wake her. He just lay there, thinking how much he loved her. He had dated many women, but this one was something special. He knew he would have to marry her. He closed his eyes and fell back to sleep. The sound of Dean's cell phone ringing woke Barbette. She gently pushed him.

"Wake up Dean, your phone is ringing."

Dean got up mechanically and walked over to his jacket that was lying across a chair. He pulled his cell phone out of his pocket and answered.

"Hello." It was Carl.

"Hey man how you doing this morning?" Dean rubbed his eyes and sat down in the chair where he had thrown his clothes the previous night.

"Man, anything wrong?" Dean asked

"No, just wanted to let you know that I'm still over Tammy's. I forgot to call you last night and I didn't want you to be worried."

"Okay, man. I got to go," Dean said

"Where are you, man?"

"I'm over Barbette's."

"Okay, man, I'll talk to you later then," Carl said and hung up.

Dean got back in bed and moved close to Barbette. She was naked and the heat from her body turned him on.

"Anything wrong?" she asked.

"No baby that was Carl. He just wanted me to know he was over Tammy's," Dean replied. He raised his head up and looked down at Barbette.

"Hey baby, were you naked when you got in bed last night or did you just take your robe off?" Dean asked.

"I've been naked all night," she replied.

Dean layed down and felt disappointed knowing that he could not make love to her. He couldn't take it anymore.

He got up and started putting his clothes on. Barbette lay there, wondering where he was going in such a hurry.

"Hey baby, I got to go. I have to take care of some business, but I'll be back. Okay?"

Barbette wondered what type of business needed to be taken care of at 10:00 in the morning on a Saturday, but decided not to ask.

Dean had finished dressing and was now sitting on the chair putting on his shoes. "Barbette would you like to meet my sister?" he asked.

Barbette was honored that he would want to introduce her to anyone in his family.

"I sure would," she said.

"Be ready about 6:00. I'll pick you up and we'll go over for dinner," he said.

"All right, I'll be ready." Dean kissed her on the lips and let himself out. Barbette lay in bed, wondering why he had to leave all of a sudden.

Dean had pulled out of Barbette parking garage and was driving towards the north side of Atlanta. He called Kathy on his cell phone and told her he was on his way over. She had just woken up and was still in bed and he had requested that she stay right where she was. While driving, he thought about what he was doing and knew it was wrong, but he also knew he wanted to fuck.

Barbette got up, made coffee, and lay on the sofa to watch a Christian program that had caught her eye. The show was about relationships. They were talking about when a women or a man cheats on his or her partner. She wondered if God was trying to tell her something. Dean had left her without really saying what he had to do and she knew that she wasn't accommodating his sexual needs. She watched the program to the end and then pulled out the verses that Diane had given her to read.

Kathy and Dean had been friends for about five years. She was a very attractive white woman with long blond hair. Kathy had a boy friend, who was out of town on business fairly often allowing her to spend time with Dean, whenever he called. Kathy went to school part-time and worked as a secretary for an accounting firm.

Dean had just finish having sex with Kathy and as they were lying in each other's arms, Kathy felt that Dean had not performed as well as he usually did—she wondered what was wrong with him.

"Dean, you want to tell me about it?" She asked.

"It's Barbette." Dean had told Kathy all about Barbette and how special she was to him.

"Man, I believe you love that girl," Kathy said.

"I do."

"So, why don't you marry her?" she asked.

"I think I will," Dean replied and moved his arm from around Kathy's neck. He got out of bed and sat on the edge of it. "Kathy, she doesn't want to have sex anymore. She's celibate and wants to wait till she's married." Dean looked confused.

"Man, you're strung out, aren't you?" Tammy said as she adjusted her body to get more comfortable under the covers. "You have enough money, you can afford to get married and it's time for you to get married. You're in the prime of your life, man. Just do it."

Dean turned around to look at her lying in bed with the covers pulled tightly around her body.

"You're right? I'll buy a ring for her and ask her next week while we're in Florida . . ." Dean got up and started to get dressed.

"Oh, you guys going to Florida?" she asked

"Yeah, I thought if I got her away from here she would relax and want to fuck. I asked her last night and she agreed to go."

Kathy was smiling now. She knew the day was coming when their relationship would come to an end and she had no regrets.

"Hey Dean, just leave my money on the dresser," Kathy said as she smiled at her friend. Dean would give her money to help her out with school tuition. Dean put five one hundred dollar bills on her dresser, more than he usually gave her, just because he appreciated her friendship and her advice about his relationship with Barbette.

EPISODE SEVEN

My boyfriend, his sister

Dean and Barbette arrived at Dean's sister's house at 6:30 on the dot. Barbette was excited about this meeting, and Dean was happy that it was finally going to happen—since Dean had talked about Barbette every day since he had met her.

Dean used his key to open the door. "Come on in," he said as—Barbette walked in ahead of him. He directed her to a red leather chair in the living room. "Have a seat baby. I'll go find out where she is."

"Donna! Hey, Donna," Dean shouted as Donna walked into the living room.

"Hey, man, why are you hollering?" Donna laughed.

"Donna, this is Barbette," Dean said as he pulled Barbette from her seat.

"Glad to finally meet you, girl" Donna said embracing Barbette.

"It's nice to meet you also, Barbette replied.

"Come on, Barbette, I'm getting ready to set the table and I can use your help," Donna said. Barbette followed Donna through a house that couldn't be more than two years old. There was a very large living room that had been decorated with contemporary furnishings and a dining room that was equally large with an iron table and chair set similar to the one she had seen in Carl and Dean's house. Once they reached the kitchen, Donna gave Barbette another hug and asked her to have a seat. The medium sized kitchen had a wooden table and chair set that was placed near a large bay window.

"My brother talks about you all the time, girl. I can tell you, he is crazy about you!" Donna said.

Barbette could see the resemblance between sister and brother. Donna and Dean looked alike except Donna had lighter complexion and fuller lips, similar to Barbette's own. Donna was a petite young lady with shoulder length hair that was styled in an attractive bob. Barbette assisted in setting up the table while Donna placed the food in the middle of it. She had made collard greens, potato salad, baked sweet potatoes, and baked chicken.

"Look at all this food." Barbette said. "You must have been cooking all day?" Donna just laughed and continued bringing the food from the kitchen to the dining room.

"Have a seat," Donna said as they all sat down at the table. When Dean blessed the table, Barbette found that she was impressed.

During dinner, Donna spoke about Dean when he was little and spoke of how proud she was of him.

"Dean and I are very close. You do know that?" Donna asked.

"Yes, he told me," Barbette replied.

"Our mom and dad died in a car accident when we were young and our uncle and aunt raise us, so really, all we had was each other."

Dean smiled at his sister and Barbette as he ate his food.

"The food is wonderful, Donna," Barbette said.

"Thanks girl." Donna replied.

Barbette was so excited about being there with Dean and his sister that she could hardly eat her food.

After dinner, they retired to the living room where Donna served cocktails.

There was a knock at the door and Donna asked her brother to answer the door. Dean opened the door to a short black man, with a head full of locks, who followed him into the living room.

"Barbette, this is Donna's man, Jeff," Dean said by way of introduction.

"Hello," Barbette said as the man pressed his lips to her hand.

"Damn, Dean, she is fine," Jeff said as he looked Barbette up and down. Dean couldn't help but laugh.

"Did you think I would have an ugly woman, or what, man?" Dean said, still laughing.

Donna leaned over to kiss Jeff and handed him a glass of wine as they all sat down. They are good people, Barbette thought as she listened to Jeff and Donna share stories about their relationship while Dean jumped in every now and then. Barbette was enjoying their company.

On the way home, Barbette told Dean how much she enjoyed meeting his sister.

"Barbette?" Dean interrupted her in mid-sentence.

"Yes, Dean?"

"I wish you could have met my parents. They would have loved you as much as I love you," Dean said with a straight face. He kept his eyes on the road and never once looked in her direction as he said these words. Barbette was overwhelmed.

"Thank you, Dean," Barbette said and noticed that Dean was not going in the direction of her condo.

"Where are we going?"

"I thought we would spend the night at my place tonight. Is that alright with you?"

"Sure, but you're going to have to give me something to sleep in," Barbette responded with a smile.

"I'm not giving you nothing. There is a rule at my house."

"And what is the rule?"

"You sleep naked." Dean laughed as he turned up in his driveway.

Once in the house, Dean escorted Barbette to his bedroom.

"Let's get in bed and watch TV," he suggested.

Barbette looked around the room and liked what she saw. Dean had a king size iron post-bed covered with a white eiderdown comforter and she watched him as he walked around the bed to fold back the comforter allowing the soft grey cotton sheets to show. Dean clicked on the flat screen TV that hung on a wall directly in front of the bed and surf the channels finally stopping at what seemed to be an action movie.

"Barbette, do you want to watch this?" he asked pulling off his shirt.

"I don't care, Dean; whatever you want to watch will be fine with me."

Barbette was sitting in a chair taking off her sandals. As Dean watched her struggle to unbuckle her shoes, he walked over to Barbette, got down on his knees and assisted her. Barbette watched as Dean took off both of her shoes and started to rub her feet. He took one of her feet and placing the big toe in his month and began sucking it. Barbette felt a sensation go through her body. He took the toe out of his mouth and looking up at Barbette, asked in a lustful tone, "You liked that, didn't you?" Dean asked in a lustful tone.

"Yes," answered Barbette, "no one has done that to me before." Barbette began unbuttoning her blouse while keeping her eyes on Dean.

"Baby, there is a lot I want to do to you when you'll allow me," he said as he got up from his knees, and took the rest of his clothing off. Dean reached into his drawer and pulled out a pair of gray and white striped; drawstring cotton pajama pants. He pulled the matching pajama top out and placed it across the bed and said, "Baby, I got you something to put on."

In the meantime, Barbette had completely undressed. She picked up the shirt Dean placed on the bed, looked at it and then at Deans matching pants and started to smile at the idea of them sharing an outfit. She put the top on and got into the bed.

"I'm going to get us something to drink. I'll be right back," Dean said.

He walked out of the bedroom and down the hall. As he entered the dining room area, Carl was walking in the door.

"Hey, man," Carl said.

"How you doing?" answered Dean

"Just fine—just left Candice's house, man."

Dean walked into the kitchen and pulled the cognac and two cognac snifters out of the cabinet. Carl walked in the kitchen just as he was pouring the drinks. "Dean, you got company?" Carl asked.

"Yeah man, Barbette's over." Dean replied.

"So things between you two must be going good," Carl said, wearing a smile.

"Yeah man. Listen, I have to tell you something, but I don't want this to go any further. I don't even want you to tell any of your women," Dean said, wearing a serious look.

"Okay, man, I promise I won't tell anyone. So, what is it?" Carl asked in an excited voice.

Dean pulled out another class and poured Carl a drink and handed it to him.

"You're going to need this," he said. Carl drank the content of the glass in one swallow. "Okay what is it?"

"Carl, I am going to ask Barbette to marry me," Dean announced with excitement in his voice.

"WHAT!" Carl was in shock. He could not believe that his main boy was going to become a married man. "When did you decide this?" he asked.

"When I met her, I knew I loved her, man. She's different from the other women I've dated," Dean confessed. He turned to Carl.

"Man, I need you to be my best man."

Carl hugged Dean right away. "Hell yeah, man. I'm here for you, dog; you're my man."

Dean picked up Barbette and his drink and as he started out of the kitchen Carl turned to Dean and said, "Dean, man, I love you, man, like a brother."

Dean smiled. "I know you do, man."

Dean entered his bedroom and placed Barbette's drink on the nightstand closest to her and sat down at his computer desk and placed his drink on it.

"Barbette, we need to talk," Dean said. Barbette had changed her position in bed while Dean was gone and sat watching an old Sanford and Son rerun.

"Yes?" she answered, looking at Dean, thinking how fine he was with his chocolate self.

"Do you remember that on our way to the airport, we talking about being tested for HIV after the first and ONLY time we made love and didn't use protection?"

"Yes I do, and I scheduled my test for Monday after work. What about you?" she asked.

'I had it done while you were gone."

"Everything OK?" she asked.

"Sure baby; but there's something else . . ."

"Okay, what now Dean." Barbette was starting to become concerned.

"I need to know if you use any type of birth control." Barbette was wondering when this would come up.

"No, I don't."

Dean lay back in his chair and reached for his glass. He felt that he needed a drink before asking the next question.

"So, when do you expect your period or do you even keep up with that?" Dean asked. Barbette knew Dean probably wouldn't want to hear her answer but she was not going to lie to him.

"No, not really," Barbette said softly, "but I remember the last time I had a period and I think we're safe," Dean thought to himself that he wouldn't mind if she was with child. After all he was going to marry her anyway.

"That's cool baby. We'll deal with it as it comes." Barbette looked at Dean and smiled as he returned her smile.

"Carl's here and will probably have company later on tonight. It gets a little noisy with him and his lady, so be prepared," Dean said wearing a sheepish grin. Barbette thought about the first time she had met Carl and how he had got her into bed. She was glad that Carl had been civil about her relationship with Dean and the two of them were on speaking terms.

Dean turned to his computer desk and opened up his laptop. Barbette wondered what he was doing.

"Baby, we are still going to Marco Island Thursday, right?" Dean asked. Barbette had forgotten about Dean inviting her to go to Marco Island.

"Sure," she answered with excitement.

"What time can you leave?" He asked, turning around to look at her.

"Any time, I'm not going to work Thursday."

Dean completed their flight reservations and swung his chair around to face her.

"I made the flight reservation for 8:00 a.m.," "What about the hotels? Shall we stay at the Marco Island Inn, or the Hilton?"

"It doesn't make any difference to me." She replied.

Dean turned back to his laptop and hitting keys, entering the information for the reservations at the Hilton. "It will be the Hilton," he said without turning around. Dean checked his messages and signed off.

"Baby, I promise you, we are going to have a good ass time." Barbette wanted to jump up and down, but was able to control herself.

Dean got up and walked over to the bed and got in lying on his side that allowed him to face Barbette. "So, you want to make love, kiss, or what?" he asked, laughing at the expression on her face.

"No, I just want to be with you." Barbette said. "See, I knew you couldn't handle it,"

"Hey, believe me, I can handle it but one day, you'll be begging me to make love to you and I am going to pay you back for making me wait," Dean said.

Barbette started to laugh and gave Dean an endearing hug. They watched two DVD movies and talked about their trip before finally falling asleep in each other arms.

The next morning Barbette woke up feeling like she needed to go to church. She wondered if Dean would want to go with her but seeing that he was still asleep decided not to wake him yet.

Barbette got out of the bed and headed towards the bathroom. After starting the shower she pulled a bath cloth and a towel off the rack and stepped into the cubicle. Dean woke up to the sound of running water and remembered that Barbette had spent the night. He lay there, playing with the idea of joining her, but decided that he would respect her privacy. Anyway, he was too tired. The week had been a busy one and this was the first day he could sleep as long as he wanted. Dean turned on the radio on the nightstand; the gospel hour was on. Memories came flooding to his mind as he remembered when he and his mother, father and sister used to go to church together, then he began to pray. He thanked God for his success and for meeting a nice young lady. He prayed for his safety and asked for forgiveness for sleeping with so many women. He was feeling good.

As Barbette walked into the bedroom with a towel wrapped around her, Dean looked at her and screamed out, "Thank you, Jesus."

Barbette looked at him like he was crazy. "What's wrong with you, man?" she asked.

"Nothing baby, I'm just happy to see you," he said.

"Hey, Dean, want to go to church with me," she asked.

"I don't know. I was planning to lie in bed till at least noon. I'm tired from my busy week," Dean answered.

Barbette started to get dressed and asked, "Well, can you take me home so that I can get ready for church?" Dean sat up in bed and watched her as she stepped into her shirt and pulled it up.

"I might as well go to church, if I got to get up to take you home," he said.

Barbette smiled as Dean rolled out of bed and headed to the bathroom. She had finished dressing and laid across the bed, waiting for him.

*   *   *

As Barbette and Dean entered the church, Dean was greeted by a young woman.

"Hey, Dean," she said smiling. "What are you doing here? I didn't know you went to my church."

Dean smiled back at her and said, "I'm visiting with my lady."

Barbette took Dean by the hand and led him into the church. They took a seat at the back as the service had already begun. The preacher was preaching about faith and Barbette thought Dean was enjoying the sermon. As the choir started to sing, Dean sang along with them when another young lady, who was sitting in front of them, happened to turn around and noticed Dean. She smiled and gave him a little wave and Barbette wondered who she was. The singing stopped and the preacher invited people to join the church. Several people walked down the aisle to go up front to join.

Service lasted about an hour and a half and as they walked out of the church another woman approached Dean, threw her arms around him and planted a big kiss on his cheek. "Dean, Baby. How you been doing?" Barbette noticed the nervous smile on Dean's face.

"Hey; how have you been doing?" he responded.

"I've been just fine and how is Carl?" she asked.

Barbette assumed this woman must know Dean pretty well since she had kissed him and also knew Carl.

"Carl is doing great. Hey, let me introduced you to someone," he said.

The woman turned towards Barbette, who was now standing at the bottom of the church stairs and as the woman and Dean started towards her he said, "Barbette this is Rhonda."

"Nice to meet you," Barbette said.

The woman looked at Barbette expressing approval and finally spoke, "Nice to meet you too," as she turned her gaze back to Dean.

"I got to go. I'll see you around," she said curtly as she walked away.

Barbette wondered who that rude woman was but decided to save her questions for another time. On the way home, Dean told Barbette how much he had enjoyed the service and how he often thought about the times when he and his family would get up on Sunday mornings, have breakfast, and go to the morning service. Barbette was thankful that Dean knew the Lord and couldn't wait to share this news with Diane.

I've never been to that church before Barbette. Are you a member?" Dean asked.

"Yes." Barbette replied.

Dean wondered if they would end up getting married in that church. Barbette realized that Dean was not going to offer any information about the women he spoke to at church and decided she wouldn't say anything either. She knew that when men are in situations where they need to provide an explanation, they try to plan in advance, what they are going to say, so that they're prepared when questions like, who is that? And where do you know her from? And why did she kiss you? Therefore, Barbette decided to wait until later and catch him off-guard before questioning him about the women in the church.

Dean took Barbette home then went back home and got into the bed. Barbette was glad to be home and decided that she would hang around the condo all day. She had some work to do and she needed time to herself. The phone rang to disturbing the quiet . . .

"Hello."

"Hey, this is Lance. Where you been?" he asked.

"Church. How come I didn't see you there?" she asked.

"Hey, I was lying in the bed with my woman. Listen, I just called to see if you'll be working every day this week?"

"Yes, everyday but Thursday and Friday. Dean and I are leaving for Florida on Thursday. And why do you ask?" Barbette knew Lance was going to ask her to do something for him.

"You and Dean going out of town together? I guess you're not celibate anymore," he said and started to laugh.

Barbette decided not to reply to Lance's statement.

"What do you want, boy?" she asked in a mean tone.

"Would you mind sitting in on the Johnson meeting for me on Tuesday?" Lance asked.

"Sure, I'll do that for you. Just send me your notes with the information I'll need."

"Okay then, I'll do that," Lance said. "And, thanks a lot Sis; I owe you."

"Yes you do, and by the way, get that shit out of my closet. I'm not going to jail for you."

Lance knew right away what she was talking about. "Oh Yeah, I'm sorry. I forgot it was even there. Don't worry. I'll take care of it." He chuckled.

Lance hung up and Barbette walked into her bedroom closet to pull out outfits she thought would be appropriate for the trip. As she pulled a black evening dress off the rack, she wondered if Dean would expect her to have sex while they were in Florida. They had not talked about it. Barbette sat on the floor and started pulling shoes out of boxes, as she tried to decide which ones would best match the evening dress. She selected a pair of black toe-out sandals—strip around the ankle with a diamond buckle.

She then selected nightgowns and robe sets choosing a peach and white short gown set and a black long gown set. Barbette smiled thinking about Dean's reaction to seeing her in them. Barbette spent the rest of the evening selecting clothes for the trip, paying her bills online and working on contracts she knew had to be completed by the end of the week. She began to get tired as she sat at the island in the kitchen, and decided to go to bed. While lying in bed, she wondered where Dean was and decided to call him on his cell. Dean answered.

"Hello, Barbette." He knew it was her from the number showing on his caller ID. Barbette could hear music and people talking in the background.

"Where are you, Dean?" she asked.

"I'm at Sambuca with Carl. Are you all right Baby?"

"Yes. I just wanted to hear your voice before I went to sleep."

Dean and Carl always tried to hang out together at least once a week—It was a man thing between them. Carl always picked up women while Dean socialized with the women but no one could tell if he tried to pick them up or not. Dean had always been private about his personal relationships and he was very picky.

"I was going to call you to say good night baby, and to ask if you would have lunch with me tomorrow."

"Sure, I would love to."

"Okay, I'll call you at work in the morning to set a time and a place."

"Okay Dean. I'll talk to you later." Barbette had to practically shout into the phone over the background noise as she hung up.

EPISODE EIGHT

Another Week

On the way up in the elevator, Barbette shared a brief conversation with Ms. Star who spoke about her weekend in Miami and the condo she owned on the beach that she often loaned out to her clients. Barbette exited the elevator and walked towards her office.

"Good Morning, Ms. Jackson," Sonia, her dad's administrative support representative said, as Barbette passed her desk.

"Good morning Sonia, I love your hair style." Sonia was a very attractive Mexican woman and a divorcee with two children. Her father could not make it through the day without her.

Barbette walked into her office, sat down and began looking through her messages that where left for her on Friday.

"Hey, Bar," her brother shouted from the door to her office.

"Hello, Lance. How was your weekend? Make any babies?" she asked in a smart-ass tone.

"Hell naw! I always use a raincoat, girl. However, I did meet a very special woman. She is fine, and guess what?"

"What?" Barbette asked.

"She's a lawyer for the Buff D. Production Company."

"Wow! She must be awesome."

"Hell, yea. I'm taking her to dinner tonight."

"That's great." Barbette was impressed. Buff D. owned one of the biggest Production companies headquartered in California with divisions located in Atlanta and Chicago. Mr. Buff ran a tight staff and only hired the best. *Lance's new woman must be a bad as bitch, at least when it comes to the law,* Barbette reflected.

Lance went on to tell his sister how this woman was different from the others or maybe he was just getting older and was starting to look at women as wife material instead of fucking material. Barbette listened, thrilled for her brother and hoping he was thinking about settling down

"Her name is Nicole. Nicole Nelson," he said with excitement in his voice.

"Well, I am happy for you, Lance. But, I have work to do before lunch. I have a lunch date with Dean."

"Dean? Hey you guys must be hitting it off pretty good."

Barbette nodded a smile at Lance as he started towards the door. Turning around to face Barbette, and while trying to keep a straight face, he asked, "Hey, Barbette; how's Dean handling you not giving it up?"

"Just fine, thanks for asking. And now get the hell out of my office." Lance burst out laughing as he reached the door.

Barbette's phone rang as Lance walked out of the office.

"Barbette Jackson," she answered.

"Hello baby! How are you feeling today?"

"Just fine, Dean," she replied.

"How about I pick you up for lunch at 1:30, or is that too late?"

"No, that will be fine. I can't wait to see you," she said

"Me neither baby. I missed your ass."

Barbette began to laugh at Dean's remark.

"Hey baby, let me hang up so that I can finish up this report and make some calls. I'll be in front of your building at 1:30, okay?"

"Okay, Dean. See you later."

Dean hung up and Barbette tried to stay focus on her work and not him. She wanted to concentrate on finishing up her work since not only did she have a lunch date, but she also had a doctor's appointment at 4:00.

Barbette was so engrossed in her work that she lost track of time and glancing at her watch, realized it was time to meet Dean. On her way down in the elevator she adjusted her suit and ran her fingers through her hair. Losing track of time had not allowed her to refresh her lipstick, but she was sure Dean would not even notice.

Barbette walked through the glass door and spotted Dean's car at the curb in front of the building. As she approached him, Dean got out and walked around to the passenger side to open the door for her, while holding a cell phone to his ear.

"Hey baby," he said as he pulled her in his arms and give her a gentle kiss.

"Hey, Dean," she replied.

Once settled in the car, Dean pulled out into the traffic. "I know this place that serves the best Chinese food in Atlanta and it's not that far from here. Do you like Chinese food?" he asked

"Sure, I do."

Barbette was checking out Dean's appearance. He wore a camel colored suit with a light tan shirt that brought out the rust, brown and camel colors of his tie, which was perfectly tied around his shirt collar.

"So, are you ready for our trip?" he asked.

`"Am I ready? I can't wait—and I'm already packed," Barbette said with giddies in her voice.

"Me neither, girl. I can't wait to get you alone." Dean stopped at a light and looked at Barbette to check her expression. He wondered if she was planning to have sex with him or what.

As they walked into the restaurant Dean informed her that he had reserved a table for them at the back in a corner. The hostess escorted them to their booth where Barbette slid in first followed by Dean. He leaned over and kissed her on her neck. "Damn baby, you smell so good."

"You do too, Dean," she replied.

Dean placed the order for the both of them. Once the server had walked away, he placed his hand on her thigh and said, "Baby, I have to ask you a question."

"What?" Barbette asked as she poured them both some tea into the little Chinese cups.

"Do you think we're moving too fast? I mean, we just met and I feel like I've known you all my life and that shit is scary."

"I know what you mean. I really don't know what to tell you, but I know I love you and that the simple truth," she said earnestly.

"Girl, I love you too," Dean replied and thought, *Man, I am about to ask this woman to marry me and I've only known for two weeks.*

"Barbette, why does it seem like I've known you longer than I have?"

"I don't know Dean. Maybe we're soul mates," Barbette responded as she took a sip of her tea.

Dean started rubbing her thigh and ran his hand over her garter hook.

"Baby, Baby, Baby; please don't tell me that you have on a garter belt?" Dean stated with excitement in his voice. Yes, I like wearing silk stocking sometimes."

Dean moved his hand from her leg. He didn't want to lose control. He couldn't stop picturing her fine body standing in front of him dressed in a garter belt, stockings and high heels. The food came just in time to interrupt his thoughts.

As they ate their lunches, they talked about work, family, and children. Dean asked Barbette if she thought she was ready for motherhood and told her that he felt that she would be a great mother. Barbette informed him that she would want to wait till she was married to have children.

"Oh, so I have to wait till we get married to have sex, wait till we're married to have children. What else do I have to wait for?" Dean asked with laughter. Barbette made a face as if she was thinking about his question.

"I think that's it," she said joining in with her own laughter.

They continued their conversation and two hours later, Dean dropped Barbette off in front of her office building. On the way back to his office, he spent most of the time thinking about their conversation. He just couldn't get over how fast he had fallen in love with Barbette and remembered his uncle saying, "You'll know when she's the one and you know when you're in love." Dean chuckled to himself, placed his earpiece on and dialed Barbette's office.

"Barbette Jackson," she answered.

"Hey, Baby, it's me."

"Hey, didn't we just leave each other?" she asked as she leaned back in her chair, feeling excitement flow through her body.

"Yes, this is the man that just left you, but I was wondering if you would like some company later on tonight."

"I would love to see you. What time are you coming?" she asked.

"I hope soon. Matter of fact, I've been trying to CUM for a long time." Dean laughed and continued—

"Not sure, what time I'll be there. I have some things to do first, but it won't be too late, okay?"

"Okay," Barbette answered and hung up.

"Damn, I love that man," she said out loud. She looked in her purse and pulled out the verses that Diane had giving her to help her stay celibate. She had looked them up and typed the verses on a sheet of paper so that when she didn't have her bible at hand, she would still have access to them. She began to read them when the phone rang again.

"Barbette Jackson," she answered.

"Hello Ms. Jackson, this is Jerome." Barbette was surprised that Jerome was calling her. His account was, and always had been handled by Kerry so she decided it must be a personal call. Barbette had not seen or heard from him since she and her dad had met him for dinner two weeks ago.

"Hey, Jerome is this personal or business?" she asked.

"It's personal, Barbette."

"How can I help you?" she replied, wondering what he might want.

"I called to invite you to my birthday party next Saturday. I've already sent you an invitation, but I guess you haven't received it yet." Jerome went on to explain that it was going to be held at his house located off Bells Ferry.

"Wow!" Barbette replied.

"So, will you be able to attend?" he asked.

"I'll try. Would it be okay if I brought a date?"

"Yeah, that will be fine even though I was hoping you would be my date," he said and started to laugh.

"Don't worry, Jerome, since it will be your birthday we're celebrating, I'll be sure to give you a lot of attention," Barbette said with a smile in her voice.

Jerome was saying his goodbyes then remembered that he forgot to tell Barbette something. "Oh, Barbette, one last thing . . ."

"What is it, Jerome?" she asked.

"Wear something short and sexy for me?"

"Jerome, you know I will—for you baby, just for you," Barbette replied wearing a smile on her face.

Suddenly, Jerome was silent.

"Anything else, Jerome?"

"No, I just want to say that you are a wonderful women and I want to thank you for being my friend."

"Oh, you are wonderful too Jerome, and thank you for being my friend. I'll try to make the party, okay?"

"Alright, see you later then." Jerome hung up.

Barbette hung up and worked fast to finish her work. She didn't want to miss her HIV testing appointment

With the HIV testing completed and feeling good about the results, Barbette wanted to make a nice dinner for Dean. She stopped at the grocery store to pick up some items to make a salad than went to the wine section and wondered if she should purchase wine for the evening. Remembering how wine had affected her the last time she was with Carl, Barbette decided to skip the wine and continued on to the ice cream freezer placing two quarts of Ben-and-Jerry in the buggy instead. It had started to rain and Barbette hurried to her car, walking fast and trying to watch her step. She was wearing her four inch high heels and didn't want to slip and fall on the wet parking lot ground.

The drive was wet and messy but she was able to make it home in one piece. Once the groceries were put away, she prepared hot tea hoping that it would relax her. The rain was coming down so hard; she could hear the drops hitting the windows. She lay down on the couch and placed a throw pillow under her head. While listening to the rain she thought about her relationship with Dean and asked herself if—maybe they were moving too fast. She also wondered if Dean really loved her or if he was just playing her. As she adjusted her pillow, she wondered if Carl was even having a problem with her dating Dean at all.

Dean was on his way out the door when Carl walked in. "Hey, man," Dean said.

Carl pulled off his wet shirt and walked towards the bathroom to retrieve a towel. He came back to the front room, wearing the towel over his head and gave Dean a strange look.

Dean was putting on his London Fog raincoat. "Man, you're going out in that mess?" Carl asked.

"Yea, man; I'm going over Barbette's for the evening."

"You better be careful, man, it's bad out there."

"Okay, man. I'll see you in the office about 9:30," Dean said as he walked out the door.

Carl went to his bedroom, undressed and put on a pair of cotton pajama pants and a sweat shirt. He could feel himself coming down with a cold. He checked his bathroom cabinet for cold medication but didn't have any, so he went into to the kitchen to make some hot tea with lemon and honey. As he walked towards the living room with his cup of tea the door bell rang. Carl knew he hadn't invited anyone over and he knew he had trained his women not to come over without calling first. He wondered who it could be. As he walked to the door and peeked out the peephole he saw that it was Dee, Dean use-to-be girl friend.

"Hey, girl," Carl said as he answered the door.

"Hello, Mr. Carl. What's going on tonight? And what are you doing home?" she asked as she walked into the house towards the living room. Carl wondered why she was there and what she wanted.

"I'm not feeling well. I think I'm coming down with a cold or the flu." Carl replied as Dee removed her coat and sat down on the lounge across from the couch. Carl walked over to the couch and lay down.

"So, what are you doing here?" he asked as he placed a pillow under his head.

"I had to go pick up a prescription at CVS Drug store off Ponce De Leon and thought I might stop by to check on you guys." Dee looked around the room before continuing.

"To tell you the truth, I was hoping Dean was home. Damn, Carl, I miss that man," she replied and reclined on the chair, making herself more comfortable. Carl had met Dee through a lady friend and he had introduced her to Dean.

"Girl, Dean is over his lady's house," Carl replied.

"What!" Fuck, he didn't waste no time; did he?"

"Matter of fact, he has been with her ever since you two broke up," Carl said. Not caring to spare her feeling.

"Who is this bitch?" Dee asked.

"Barbette Jackson."

"Barbette Jackson? Isn't that the woman you use to date? The one that was with you that Sunday night we were out together at the jazz club?"

"Yep! That's the one," Carl said, smiling at the expression on Dee's face.

"Oh, so you two trade off women now; or what?"

"She wasn't my type and Dean was interested in her the first time he met her," Carl explained.

"Shit, that bitch is a whore," Dee replied.

"No, the bitch is not a whore, the bitch's got dough and she's a nice woman; at least, that's what Dean said," Carl said.

Carl started to cough. "Man, I think I have a fever," he said in a shaky tone.

Dee looked over at Carl lying on the couch.

"Hey, man, you need to sweat that cold out of you and I got just what you need," she said.

"Dee, baby, I don't want to fuck you; I'm too damn sick anyway," Carl said, wondering at the same time if she would be any good in bed.

"Motherfucker, I don't want to fuck you either. I picked up some cough syrup when I was at the drug store and I was just going to share some with you to help with your cough and maybe sweat some of that cold out of you." Dee got up and walked into Carl's kitchen to retrieve a tablespoon. On her way back she picked up her purse and pulled the syrup out.

"Here you go," she said as she handed the syrup and spoon to Carl. She plopped herself down in the chair once again and said, "So tell me, Carl, what does the bitch have that I don't have?"

Carl finished taking the cough syrup and placed the bottle and spoon on the table. Lying back down he looked directly at Dee and said, "Only one thing."

Dee gave Carl a serious look.

"What?"

"She has a lot of money. Her daddy owns one of the top three entertainment law firms in the US," Carl answered.

"Oh, a rich bitch?" Dee said.

"Yep," Carl agreed with a nod.

Carl turned on the TV and began to surf the channels with his remote. He was ready for Dee to leave so that he could go to sleep. He realized that he was really feeling bad and wanted to be alone. Dee noticed that Carl had closed his eyes and knew the medication was getting ready to take him out. She stood up and put on her coat.

"Carl, I'm going to let you go to sleep now. I'll call to check on you tomorrow, okay?" she said, as she headed towards the door.

"Okay. Thanks for coming by and I definitely appreciate the cough syrup. Do you mind seeing yourself out?" he asked.

"No, not at all; I will lock you in." Carl dropped off to sleep soon after Dee's departure.

* * *

Barbette had fallen asleep when she heard a knock at the door. She knew it was Dean and got up to opened the door.

"Hey Baby."

"Hey, Dean, I fell asleep," Barbette said.

"You can go back to sleep if you want to."

"No, I'm alright; I just needed a little nap," she replied.

"Want something to drink?"

"Yes, that would be nice."

"Why don't you take a seat, I can do it," Dean suggested.

He knew from his previous visit to the condo, where the liquor and glasses were located and pulled out a bottle of Patron and two shot glasses and salt then walked over to the refrigerator to retrieve a lime. As he walked back towards the counter, he stopped to kiss Barbette on the forehead.

"Baby, you were knocked out, huh?" He lifted her chin up gently and looked at her. Her eyes were still half closed and her hair was a mess.

Dean started to laugh. "I guess I must be seeing the real you?"

Dean continued to the counter, began cutting up the lime and placed the slices on the paper towel. He carried the shot glass, tequila and limes, over to the island. Barbette smiled at him as he looked at her and sat down next to her. Okay baby, let's see if you're a women or a girl. We're going to do two shots back to back. I bet you a hundred dollars that you can't handle it," Dean said as he poured the first shots in the shot glasses.

Barbette started to laugh aloud. Her eyes were wide-open now and she had managed to brush her hair down with her hands to make it more presentable.

"Okay, Dean. We'll see if you are man or boy," she replied as she picked up her shot glass.

"Let's toast," Dean said.

"Okay, you make the toast," Barbette replied.

"Okay, here's my toast. To a very long relationship," he said

Barbette smiled as she licked the salt that was on her hand and drank her shot. Dean followed the same steps. Barbette frowned, picked up a lime wedge and began sucking it. Dean poured another shot in the glasses.

"Barbette, baby, I believe that you're a bad ass woman. You drank that down like a pro. Come on baby let's do it again."

Barbette picked up her shot glass and said, "I want to do this toast."

"Okay."

"May you have wealth and good health," Barbette said and downed her drink. Dean finished his before she did and started to laugh. Dean leaned over and kissed Barbette on the lips. He placed his tongue in her mouth and kissed her hard and long.

Barbette pulled back and looked him in the eyes. "Dean, you know I still can't have sex with you," she said

"Yes baby, I remember—you're celibate," Dean replied with a warm smile on his face. Barbette got up and placed the slices of lime in the refrigerator. Following her, Dean gently pushed her up against the refrigerator door, pressed his body against hers, and kissed her gently.

"Damn, Barbette, you make me hard just looking at you. Man Baby, you got whip appeal," he said and started to laugh. Barbette laughed along with him. Dean untied the drawstring at the waist of her soft cotton pajama pants and looked her in the eyes as he placed his hand in her pants. Reaching her pussy, he was happy to find that she was wet. He gently rubbed his fingers, allowing them to dance in her wetness. He maintained eye contact with her, watching her as she slowly closed her eyes and parted her lips. She was holding her breath.

Dean leaned over and whispered in her ear. "Come on baby, breathe. Let it out. I know it feels good." Suddenly, Barbette exhaled and tears started flowing out of her eyes. She began to move her body. Dean was having a hard time controlling himself. He wanted to pull her pants down and enter her. He was trying hard not to disrespect her commitment to remain celibate.

He knew if he didn't stop there would be no turning back. "Damn baby, you are so damn wet. Girl, I want you," he said as he pulled his hand out of her pants, leaned up against her and kissed her on her forehead.

Barbette was crying. "Dean, I'm so sorry, but I am trying so hard to . . ."

Dean interrupted her. "It's all right baby. Come on let's go to bed. We both have to get up early for work." As they walked towards to the bedroom, Dean asked Barbette if she was ready for their trip to Marco Island. He was filling her in on the agenda for the trip and informing her of his excitement of sharing a few days with her alone without interruptions. Dean had Carl design a ring for him. A jeweler friend of theirs made it and Dean was to pick it up the next day. He was planning to give it to Barbette once they arrived in Florida.

Barbette fell asleep as soon as her head hit the pillow and Dean watched her sleep wondering again, if he was moving too fast. But he knew he loved her and he felt it was the right thing to do. Dean had many conversations with his uncle about Barbette over the past two-weeks and it was his uncle who reminded him that love sometimes came when you least expected it. His uncle shared his story of how he met his wife, Aunt Mildred, and how they married two months later. Talking to his uncle helped Dean realize that he wasn't crazy. Carl had no opinion or advices. He just told Dean, "Better you than me and good luck, my brother."

Tuesday and Wednesday were busy for both Dean and Barbette. Barbette had to close some outstanding deals and Dean had to do both his and Carl's job. Carl's cold had caused him to stay in bed for two days and Dean was hoping that Carl would feel better by Thursday so Carl would be able to handle everything while he was away on vacation.

Wednesday evening Barbette stopped at the mall to purchase two new swimming suits and a pair of sandals. She got home late and was tired but knew she had to have everything packed and ready by morning. She was just completing her packing when the phone rang. She was hoping it was Dean. She wanted to tell him how excited she was about the trip.

"Hello."

"Hey baby," Dean said in a low tone.

Barbette could tell by his tone that something was wrong.

"Dean, are you sick?" she asked.

"No baby, it's not me, it's my uncle. He had a heart attack and I'm on my way to the hospital. Barbette, he's not doing too well," Dean replied.

Barbette was silent for a few moments as she tried, to digest what Dean had just told her.

"Dean, I am so sorry. What can I do for you?" she asked.

"Not be mad. We will have to postpone our trip," Dean replied.

"Mad! Dean he is the man that raised you; like a father. Why would I be mad? I'm here for you so just let me know if you need me. Now, do you want me to meet you at the hospital?"

"No baby, I'll be all right. I'll call you later tonight to let you know how everything is going.

"Sure baby, I'll be up late so just call me. Love you," she said.

"I love you too, Barbette," Dean said and hung up.

Barbette sat down on the bed and bowed her head in prayer. She prayed that God wouldn't take Dean's uncle now and would allow Dean to have more time with him. She also prayed that Dean and his family would be strong.

*   *   *

Dean and his sister Donna arrived at the hospital and were greeted by their Aunt Mildred who was crying uncontrollably.

"It will be okay," Dean said as he hugged her close.

"What did the doctor say?"

"That it doesn't look too good," she replied between sobs.

Dean's sister walked over to the nurse's station and asked if they could see their uncle. The nurse told her to wait one minute and she would check.

They took a seat in the waiting room.

"Are you his niece, Donna," the nurse asked as she approached them with her eyes on Donna.

"Yes, I am," Donna answered.

"He wants to see you," the nurse said.

Dean and his aunt looked at each other, wondering why he had asked to see Donna alone.

Donna walked into her uncle's room apprehensively. When she saw him connected to tubes everywhere she began to cry. She walked over to his bed and looked down at him as he opened his eyes and managed a smile.

"Hey, Baby girl. I don't think I have much time, so I have to tell you something."

"What is it you have to tell me Uncle Milton?" she asked.

"The truth," he said softly.

"What are you talking about?" Donna asked.

"I want to tell you who your real father is," he said.

"My father died in a car accident. What are you talking about?"

"Your mother had an affair with a friend of mine and got pregnant. Your mother never told the man, you considered your father about the affair and he always thought you were his daughter. When he found out he wasn't your father and your mother had had an affair, he lost his mind."

"Stop! Stop, you're talking crazy. You're sick and talking out of your head," Donna cried.

"No, Baby. This is the truth, please just listen to me," he said,

"They were not in a car accident. Your father went mad when he found out the truth. He shot your mother in the head and drove their car off a cliff killing both of them," he said as he closed his eyes with tears flowing onto his cheeks.

"No! No! You're wrong, right?" Donna screamed.

"Baby girl, your father's name is Raymond Jackson. He owns a big law firm and lives here in the Atlanta area."

Donna was now crying hysterically. She knew who Raymond Jackson was and she was in shock. She didn't understand. As she tried to pull herself together she asked, "Uncle Milton? Does Mr. Jackson know that I'm his daughter?"

"Yes, he does. He has been taking care of you and your brother financially every since you've been living with me. The year that you and Dean came to live with us, my daughter, Deanne, was killed on her way to school; she was a college student at that time. Raymond and some of his friends opened the Deanna Carter Community Center in her name and I was the director of that center the first two years you and Dean lived with me. Believe me Donna, he is a good man," he said.

Donna laid her head on the side of the bed and her uncle began to gently caress her hair.

"It's alright baby. Nobody knows this but me, you and Raymond; not even your aunt knows that Raymond is your father." As Donna started for the door, she turned as her uncle called her name gently. "Donna," he said. She walked back to his bed.

"Yes, Uncle Milton . . ."

"I don't think Dean should know about this just yet. I know he loves Raymond's daughter Barbette, and he will probably marry her." Donna looked at her uncle with a surprised look on her face.

"Yes Donna, Dean and I have had many discussions—what you might call, man to man talks, and her name came up often. Donna, don't tell him. This might be too much for him. Okay, promise?" Donna was crying hard now.

"Yes, Uncle Milton. I promise. I won't tell him."

Uncle Milton closed his eyes and told her to send Dean in to see him right away.

Dean and his Aunt Mildred wondered what was going on. Finally, after 45 minutes, Donna walked out of the room, still crying. Dean got up to meet her.

"Donna, what did he say? What's wrong?" Dean asked.

"Nothing. He was, just talking about how he loved me," Donna said, still crying. "He wants to see you now.

Dean walked into the room and approaching the bed, looked down at his uncle.

"Hey boy—what you looking at?" said Uncle Milton, trying to smile.

Dean returned the smile. "Uncle you got to get well so we can take you home," Dean said, tears welling to the rim of his eyes.

"I know boy, but just in case I don't make it home, I need you to take care of some things for me."

"Come on, Uncle Milt, you'll be home by next week," Dean said in what he hoped was a cheerful voice.

"Okay, sure, whatever you say. But, do me a favor. If I don't make it home. I need you to look in my bottom dresser drawer on the left, under my old bible and you will find an envelope with a key in it. It's the key to my safe deposit box." Dean started to say something but his uncle cut him off.

"Shut up and listen boy," he said as he began to cough. "You'll find a lot of money in the box. I want you to split it with your sister and there is an envelope that will give you some instructions that I need you to follow. Do you understand?" he asked.

"Yes, Uncle Milton." Dean was now crying. He was scared and he could tell by the way his uncle was looking that he would probably not make it through the night.

"Dean, go on and get out of here and send my pretty wife in here to see me," he said, speaking at a slower pace.

Dean kissed his uncle on the lips and walked out of the hospital room. Aunt Mildred met him at the door. "He wants to see you now," he said.

His aunt went into the room to hear what her husband had to say; what Dean had accepted as his goodbye.

Dean sat next to his sister who she was still crying. He thought she was in bad shape and wondered what he had told her. Dean took Donna's hand into his and held it tight. Suddenly, Dean saw a nurse run into his uncle room. He got up to follow her but when he reached the door; the nurse was holding up his aunt and helping her out of the room. The doctor ran into the room, along with two other nurses. Dean knew it was over. He tried to hold himself together for his sister and aunt's sake. When he finally got his aunt to sit down in the waiting room, his sister, who had been sitting, watching what was going on, fainted. Dean caught her before she fell out of her chair and picking her up, laid her gently on a cushioned bench on the other side of the waiting room.

"Nurse! Nurse! Please help my sister!" Dean hollered. A nurse rushed over to assist allowing Dean to comfort his aunt who was screaming and crying. Just then the doctor came out of his uncle hospital room and walking over to Dean asked,

"Are you his nephew?"

"Yes," Dean replied.

"He's gone. I'm sorry."

Dean started to cry as he hugged his now hysterical aunt. Blessedly, a nurse came to his aid and as Dean stood in the middle of the waiting room watching his sister and aunt fall apart, he knew that he was in no shape to help them. Thankfully, nurses were everywhere as Dean closed his eye and began to pray.

$$* \quad * \quad *$$

Dean called Barbette the next day and told her about his uncle's death. He explained that he was obligated to see his family through their loss and would be in touch with her as soon as everything was in order. Barbette was very sympathetic and deeply worried about Dean.

Uncle Milton's funeral was held at the New Hope Baptist church were his Aunt Mildred and Uncle Milton had been members of the church for as long as Dean could remember. Uncle Milton's younger brothers, Uncle John and Uncle Ben, both flew in from Chicago. The place was teeming with people—cousins and friends from Atlanta and other places came bearing flowers and food.

Dean sat down in his uncle's office going through his papers and found that his uncle had left him two rental properties and over 200,000 dollars to be shared with his sister Donna. Uncle Milton had also left his wife 500,000 dollars and the house. He had also left her several shares of Raymond Jackson's company stocks. That confused him and he wondered if his uncle knew Mr. Jackson or if he was just gambling on a stock purchase. He decided to ask his aunt about it later.

The house was filled with people and Dean decided to stay locked up in his uncle's office for a little while longer. He leaned back in the chair and closing his eyes, tried to think about happier things; as Barbette crossed his mind. Dean had seen her at the funeral earlier and had talked to her briefly. He also remembered that her dad was also there. He opened his eyes and wondered what Raymond Jackson was doing at his uncle's funeral. He decided to call Barbette. As he went to pick up the phone to dial her number, someone knocked on the door.

"Who is it?" Dean asked.

"It's me, Barbette," she said.

Dean hurried to open the door. Barbette walked in the office wearing a black suit with a white shirt, shear black stocking and black patent leather high heels. Her hair was combed back off her face, and hung straight down her back.

"Hey Dean, how are you holding up?" Barbette asked as she walked into the office. Dean closed and locked the door and turned towards Barbette.

"Hey baby, I'm okay," he said, reaching for a chair and pulling it up to the desk. Dean invited Barbette to have a seat. He then walked to the other side of the desk and sat in his chair.

"Barbette, I need to know something," he began.

"What is it?" Barbette replied quizzically.

"I saw your father at my uncle's funeral. How does he know my uncle?"

"I was surprised too and I asked him the same question you just asked me. I had no idea that he knew your uncle. He said, he used to be a director at the community center and they had been friends back in the day."

Dean didn't say a word. He just sat there wearing a blank look on his face.

"Dean, did you hear what I just said?" Barbette asked.

"Yes, I did." Dean felt that there was more to the story and knew he would have to ask his aunt about it later.

"Barbette, I don't feel like company right now. I'm sorry, but would you mind leaving me alone?" Barbette got up, walked quietly to the door and unlocked it, walked out closing the door behind her.

She was not sure what was going on but she was upset that he did not want her around him. She walked through the crowd of people, looking for Dean's sister finally spotting her in a chair by the living room window. Barbette walked over to her.

"Hey Donna. Is there anything you need me to do?" she asked.

"No, everything has been done," Donna answered while looking at Barbette's facial features and wondering if they looked alike in any way.

"Well, I got to go, but if you need me, call me, okay?" Barbette said.

"Okay, Barbette."

Barbette started towards the door and heard Donna call her name. She turned around and spotted Donna coming towards her.

"Give me a hug, sister. I love you, girl," Donna said with tears in her eyes.

"I love you too."

Barbette walked out of the house and started towards her car. As she was walking down the sidewalk, she noticed Carl coming towards her. He greeted her with a hug.

"Hey girl, are you all right? You look upset," Carl said. Barbette adjusted her suit while turning her back to Carl.

"Hey, girl, what's wrong?" He could tell she was crying and he knew it wasn't about Dean's uncle.

"It's Dean," she said as she broke down into tears.

Carl turned her around towards him placing his arm around her waist. "Come on, girl; let's sit in my car for a while and you can tell me all about it. Carl opened his car door to help her in then walked to the other side of the car and got in.

"Barbette, would you like a cigarette or a joint or something?" he asked as he looked at her, wondering what had happened.

"No, thank you."

"Okay then, what's wrong?" Carl asked with concern.

"I just left Dean in his uncle's office. He asked me to leave him alone—he doesn't want me around him. Oh God, I knew it was just a matter of time for me to see the real Dean," Barbette said, crying so hard she could hardly breathe.

Carl knew Dean and he knew that Dean loved Barbette. He also realized that Dean was having a hard time right now.

"Barbette, Dean's uncle was like a father to him. He's having a hard time trying to keep things in order. Please don't take what he says or does personally. He loves you, girl, and I know this for a fact. Just be patient. He will come around and everything will be alright," Carl explained. Barbette had managed to stop crying and had focused her attention on Carl. He was wearing a dark navy blue suit, cream shirt and a cream, wine and blue tie. She had never seen the caring side of Carl and was happy that they were able to be friends.

"You must be right," Barbette said

"I am baby. I know Dean better than anyone so just give him some time and whatever you do, don't walk out on him, okay?"

"Okay, I'll be patient. I love him too, you know?"

"I know, girl, and I know that everything will be alright."

Carl got out of his car and walked around to the passenger side to open the door for Barbette and walked her to her car giving her a hug.

"If you need anything or just want to talk, just call me, okay?" Carl said.

"Okay, Carl. Thanks."

Barbette got into her car and headed home.

Once home, she decided to call her dad. Barbette wanted to find out if there was something that she needed to know about his relationship with Dean's uncle but first she wanted to get comfortable. She went to her bedroom, took off her clothes put on a cotton nightgown. Then she went to the kitchen and made herself a cup of tea before heading back to her room. Once in bed, Barbette picked up her phone to speed dial her dad.

"Hello."

"Hey, Dad, how are you doing?" she asked.

"Oh, I'm doing okay. What about you?"

"Just worried about Dean," she said

"Oh yeah, Lance told me you were dating a young man who owned a Production Company, but I had no idea that your young man's uncle was Milton Andrew."

"Dad, how long had you known Dean's uncle?" she asked

"I knew him before I even started my business. Milton and I used to hang out together, gambling, picking up women, everything. Then we both got married at about the same time. Your mother and I started having kids and I started my business while, Milton married the mother of his five-year-old daughter and opened a clothing store in the hood with some money he picked up from gambling. He invested a lot of money and was lucky and he helped me get my business off the ground. I'll tell you one thing; we remained friends until he died. We didn't keep in touch much but he was my friend and a great guy."

Barbette's father sounded as if he might have been crying. She had no idea that her father had any close friends.

"I'm sorry, Dad, I didn't realize that you and Mr. Andrew were that close. Would you like me to come home and be with you?"

"No baby, you stay there in the condo I've been thinking and I've decided to give you the condo since you spend most of your time there," Raymond said. Barbette was surprised. Raymond never gave anybody anything.

"Dad! That would be great. Thank you."

"I love you, daughter," he said

"I love you too, Dad."

"I got to go. I've got a long day tomorrow. Are you coming into the office?" he asked.

"No, Dad, I'll be working from home, if it's alright with you."

"Sure. Tell that crazy brother of yours to call me if you see him tonight."

"Okay, Dad, I will. Good night," she replied

"Good night."

Raymond hung up the phone and lay down in his bed. He knew he would have to tell his children about his daughter Donna, eventually, but he didn't know the when and the how. He felt ashamed that he had let so much time pass without mentioning her. When he saw her at the funeral he felt his heart drop and he wondered if she knew that he was her father. To Raymond, Donna looked just like her mother—the only women he had ever loved. For the first time in a long time, Raymond felt old.

Raymond knew he had to call Barbette's mother to tell her about Milton's death. He had not spoken to her in a year and that was at another funeral of another old friend of theirs. He positioned himself on the edge of his bed and dialed her number.

"Hello."

"Hello, Rita. This is Raymond," he said

"Hello, Raymond. It's been a long time. To what do I owe this pleasure?"

"I have bad news," he said.

"Oh no! This isn't about any of my children is it?" Rita asked anxiously.

"No. I just called to tell you that Milton died," Raymond said softly.

"Milton? You mean Milton Andrew?"

"Yes, he died Thursday. They had the funeral today."

"OH NO!" She said in a high pitch tone. I am so sorry to hear that. How is his wife doing?" Rita asked.

"She's hanging in there, as far as I know."

"Rita, I saw her," he said softly.

"You saw Donna?" Rita said, knowing right away who he was talking about. Rita found out the news about Donna the same time the husband of Donna's mother found out and that was the reason she had left Raymond. Raymond had always fooled around on her, but when she learned that Donna's mother, Pearl, was pregnant by Raymond, she couldn't and wouldn't take it anymore. Rita had tried to take her kids with her, but Raymond fought her for them and he knew so many important people, he was able to win. Rita had moved to Chicago and remarried. Raymond allowed her to see the kids once a year. Back in the day, Raymond had been a cruel and heartless man. They had only started talking again two years ago, when she saw him at the wedding of her younger brother's son. Barbette and Lance had come to Chicago with him and had stayed for a while in order to spend a few days with her. The children had never asked her why she left and she really didn't know what they knew about the situation.

"Did you talk to her?" Rita asked.

"No more than 'how are you.' Rita, there is a problem," Raymond said.

"What? What do you mean, there is a problem?" she asked.

"Our daughter is dating Donna's brother, Dean."

"What? How and when did that happen?" Rita asked.

"He owns a Production Company and she met him at one of the events that he and his partner were giving. At least that's what Lance tells me."

"Well, Raymond, are you going to tell them about Donna?"

"I plan to, but I just don't know how to tell them and I want to choose the right time," Raymond replied.

"I don't know what to tell you, Raymond. I'll pray that the children will forgive you as well as God. You did some crazy things back then and I always knew that they would catch up with you one day."

"I know, Rita, and I would like to tell you how sorry I am for what I've done to you back then. You were a wonderful wife and I ran you off. I am so, so, sorry."

"I am too," Rita replied and added, "Raymond, if you need me to help you tell the children, just let me know and I'll come, okay?"

"Okay, Rita, thanks and I'll talk to you soon."

"Alright. Goodbye, Raymond . . ."

"Good bye."

Raymond hung up the phone and walked to the kitchen. He opened a small cabinet where he kept his liquor and pulled out a bottle of scotch and a small glass—and poured about a fourth of a glass of scotch drinking it down in one gulp.

Barbette spent the next two weeks working at the community center. She was hoping Dean would show up, but he never did. She had not seen or heard from him since the day of the funeral and although she had tried calling him several times and had left messages, he has not returned her calls.

It was Saturday and Barbette felt lonely and sad. She missed Dean and didn't know where their relationship was going. Also she had not started her period, but had gone to the doctor for a pregnancy test that came out negative—Barbette was relieved.

Barbette lay across her bed, trying to decide if she should go out somewhere or just stay home. She was thinking about spending some time with her dad but dreaded the drive, and decided that she would spend the night if she went to see him. She picked up the phone and called him.

"Hey baby." He knew it was her by viewing her phone number on the caller ID.

"Hello, Daddy. I was thinking about coming out to spend some time with you. Have you made plans for the evening?" she asked.

"No, Baby. I'll be home. I can't wait to see you, Baby girl."

"Okay, Dad. I'll be there in about an hour and a half."

Barbette got up and walked into her closet to find something to wear. She chose a pair of black jean and a new white top that still had the tags on it. She had started to dress just as the phone began to ring. She walked towards the phone; hoping that it would be Dean on the other end.

"Hello."

"Hello. Barbette?" the person on the phone asked.

"Yes, who is this?" Barbette asked.

"This is Donna."

Barbette had to think about who Donna was for a minute and finally realized that it was Dean's sister.

"Oh, hey, Donna, how have you been doing?" Barbette asked.

"Oh, okay, Barbette," she answered with a sigh. Barbette expressed her sympathy about her uncle Milton's passing once again and finally worked up the nerve to ask about Dean.

"Donna, how is Dean doing?"

"You haven't talked to him?"

"No. Not since the day of the funeral," Barbette replied.

"I saw him yesterday and he seemed okay. He's been busy finalizing Uncle Milton's financial situation, but other than that; I believe he's doing fine."

Donna was surprised that Dean had not seen Barbette and wondered if there was something wrong between them.

"Did you two have a fight?"

"No," Barbette answered. "To be honest with you, I don't know what's going on with him. Donna, I love him," Barbette confessed.

"I know you do. Just be patient and everything will be okay," Donna said, as she made a mental note to talk to Dean on Barbette's behalf.

"Hey, Barbette, would you like to meet for brunch tomorrow," Donna asked.

"Sure, where would you like to meet?"

"Dean tells me Justin's is one of your favorite places. How about we meet there, at about 11:30?"

"Okay," Barbette said.

After she finished talking to Donna, Barbette hurried to finish dressing. She arrived at her dad's house 6:30 and as she drove up she noticed Lance's car parked at the end of the driveway. She pulled her car alongside his and used her key to let herself in.

"Hello everybody," she shouted as she entered the house.

"Hey baby girl," her dad said as he approached her. He wrapped his arms around her and gave her a big hug.

"Daddy, where's Lance? I saw his car out front."

"Oh, he's out by the pool." Raymond took Barbette by the hand and walked with her towards the sunroom at pool-side.

"Barbette, would you like a drink," Raymond asked.

"Yes, Daddy, please. I'll take a beer."

"A beer? Since when did you start drinking beer?" he asked.

"Since today." Barbette smiled at her father and noticed that he seemed to have aged since the last time she had seen him.

"Dad, is everything okay?" She looked him in the eyes as he left her side to walk towards the bar in the sunroom.

"Yes, why do you ask?"

"You look a little tired."

"Just not getting much sleep lately, but I'll be alright," he replied.

They walked out of the sunroom to the pool where Lance was sitting in a lounge chair and she was surprise to find Carl sitting next to him, separated by a small table where they had placed their drinks.

"Hey, Barbette," they both said. Carl stood up and embraced her with a warm hug.

"Hey, Barbette, girl, you look good as hell. Where are you going tonight?" Carl asked.

"Over here," Barbette answered. She glanced over at Lance then back at Carl and said teasingly,

"What are you two doing here? How come you guys aren't out picking up women?"

"I got a woman and she'll be here about 10:00 tonight to take care of her man. Don't you know I am the man?" Lance said with a smirk on his face

"Lance, don't tell me you're still dating that girl that works for the production company?" she said.

"Yes I am," Lance said, wearing a proud look on his face.

"And what about you, Carl" Where's your woman?"

"I still don't have one baby. I'm waiting for you. Didn't you know that?" he said, laughing, as he sat back down on the lounge chair.

"Sure, Carl," Barbette said. She pulled a folded up chair in front of Lance, took a seat and began drinking her beer.

"Barbette, when's the last time you talked with Dean?" Lance asked.

"I haven't," she said and glanced over to check Carl's expression.

"Hey, don't look at me. I've only seen him twice this week. He's has been working from home and by the time I get home he's asleep or gone," Carl explained as he pulled out a cigarette.

"Would anyone like a smoke?" he asked.

"No, man, I'm trying to quit, but I'm still having trouble with the cravings after I have sex." Lance said and laughed.

"I'll take one," Barbette said. She stood up and leaned over to retrieve a cigarette from Carl's opened pack.

"You guys want to hear some music," Raymond yelled from the sunroom.

"Yeah, Dad, Throw on some of that old school stuff you like," Lance said while smiling in his dad's direction.

Carl watched Barbette as she took a drag on her cigarette and wondered if it would be out of line for him to invite her to go with him to Ben Samson's party tonight. He knew she was Dean's woman, but he felt that they were beginning to become very good friends.

"Barbette, why don't you do me a favor?" Carl asked.

"And what is that?" she replied with a puzzled look on her face.

"Ben Samson, the football player—do you know him?"

"Everybody knows him," Barbette said as she reached for her beer that was sitting on the ground near her chair.

"Well," Carl said as he cleared his throat, "he's giving a party tonight and I had not planned on taking any of my women with me because there are always so many bad ass babes up in his parties and you know me . . . ," Carl said, snickering.

Barbette had already figured out that he was trying to ask her to attend the party with him. "Yes, Carl, go on," she said

"Well, I'm not taking any of my ladies and I thought it would be nice to take a friend especially since taking you will help me out on the action I'll be getting from the babes. You know what I mean?"

"Oh yes I do. If a man is with a woman, especially an attractive woman, women want him, if only for the game of being able to take him from the woman. If he's not with a woman, he still gets action, but some women feel that he must not have much to offer."

"Yes, that's it. So, you want to play with me?" Carl asked, wearing a smile. "I mean, do you want to play this game with me by going to the party?" Carl asked.

Lance looked at the both of them with a bewildered look on his face.

"Hey, hey, Carl man, Barbette is Dean's woman—your friend, your partner's lady. Remember?" Lance shouted.

Carl looked in Lance's direction. "Man, it isn't about me and her. I just need her to help me pick up women. And this will give her an opportunity to get out of the house and meet people." Carl had stood up and turned towards Barbette. "And I thought instead of sitting in the house waiting for Dean to call, you could have a little fun."

Barbette lowered her head. She felt sad and knew Carl was right. She needed to get out of the house.

"Okay, Carl. What time? What should I wear? How should I wear my hair? And don't you think it would be better if I met you there? You might meet someone and you wouldn't have to worry about taking me home and stuff like that," Barbette said. She walked over to the pool and looked in at the water.

Barbette was feeling a little excited about getting out and meeting people. She missed Dean but wondered if this was his way of saying their relationship was over.

Carl sat back down and reclining in his lounge chair, watched Barbette as she walked towards her chair. "Barbette, are you alright?" he asked.

"Oh yes," she replied. She had gotten very quiet.

"Well, I think meeting me there would be a good idea," Carl said while also thinking, *then no one can say, "he took Dean's lady to a party."* "And just look sexy," he added, as he pulled another cigarette out of the pack.

Lance was lying there, laughing at the two of them.

"Man, Carl, you need to find you a good woman. Man aren't you getting tired of these games?" Lance asked, still laughing.

"Hell yeah, but I just haven't found that special one yet man and until I do, I got to keep going to the store, buying candy," Carl said, laughing out loud with Lance.

Barbette got up from her chair and walking towards to sunroom—turned towards Lance and Carl who were still laughing and said,

"Hey, Carl, why don't you write down the address and directions? By the way, what time shall we meet?" she asked.

"Let's say 10:45, at his front door," Carl replied.

"Okay. I'm going to talk to Dad and I'll be leaving here in about fifteen minutes. Bring me the information before I leave," she said as she turned around.

Barbette walked through the sunroom to reach the family room where her dad was sitting on the couch reading.

He looked up over the rim of his glasses and said, "Barbette, come over here. I have some papers for you to sign."

Barbette sat down next to him on the couch. He handed her the folder, which was filled with legal document informing her that the Buckhead condominium was now her property. She looked at him and smiled.

"I told you that you could have that condo," Raymond said. "Now, just sign here . . . ."

Barbette did not know what to say. Raymond had never just giving her anything. They always had to earn whatever he would give them. He had always been hard on them about making their own way in life.

Barbette signed the papers and gave Raymond a big hug and a kiss. "Thank you, Daddy," she said. Once she pulled away from him, she realized that she was smiling but he wasn't.

"Hey, what's wrong, Daddy?" she asked.

"Nothing baby, I just wanted to talk to you about Dean," he replied. Barbette was not sure what he could want to say about Dean.

"What about Dean, Dad?" she asked. Raymond put his face in his hands and rubbed it. He then turned to look at his daughter.

"Barbette, I know you love Dean," he said. "Lance has told me all about your relationship with him, you being celibate, also. I'm familiar with the love you feel for him and I know he feels it for you."

Barbette was in shock that her dad knew her personal business. He continued, "So, I think you should find him and sit down and talk to him. He's going through a bad time right now and Carl tells me that he works from home most of the time. He's also told me that he hasn't shaved or dressed and hasn't been eating."

Barbette sat in shock. She had no idea that Dean was in such bad shape and wondered why Carl hadn't told her about Dean.

"I know you're wondering why Carl didn't tell you this but, Carl asked me to tell you about Dean instead. It's been hard for Carl to deal with Dean and Dean asked Carl not to talk to you about him. Since Carl promised that he wouldn't talk to you, he asked me to relay the information to you. He didn't want to break his promise." Raymond stood up and walked to the other side of the room and turned to find his daughter crying uncontrollably. He knew there was nothing he could do for her—she would have to work it out.

Raymond left Barbette and went into the kitchen and placing two glassed on a tray with a container of ice cubes and poured a double shot of Hennessy into the glasses. He walked back into the room just as Barbette was blowing her noise.

"Here baby, I made us a drink," Raymond said, as he handed a glass to her. "So, what are your plans, Baby girl?" he asked.

"I have to see him and make him talk to me," Barbette said.

Barbette was wiping the tears from her eyes, when Lance and Carl walked in. They could tell by the quietness of the room, and the tears in Barbette eyes, that something had happened. Carl looked at Raymond and asked, "You told her?"

"Yes, I did," Raymond said.

"So, I guess you won't be meeting me at the party tonight, right?" Carl asked as he sat down next to her and placed his arm around her. He knew that she would want to go check on Dean right away. Carl felt relieved that Barbette knew about Dean and felt that she was the only one that could help Dean.

"Can I borrow the keys to your house, Carl?" Barbette asked, standing up and adjusting her clothes.

Carl pulled his keys out of his pocket and said, "I hope you can help him," as he handed the key ring to her.

Barbette left immediately to see Dean, arriving at the house at about 10:45. Using one of the keys that Carl had given her, she let herself in locking the door behind her. She could hear the sound of the TV coming from the direction of Dean's bedroom. Barbette started down the hall towards the sounds. As she approached his room, she noticed that the door was open and the only light in the room was from the TV screen. She walked in and to her surprise sitting on the bed was a woman with red hair. This was the same woman that Carl had stopped to talk to at the Jazz Club the night she was out with Dean, Carl and Dee. The woman was wearing a red dress and her hand was rubbing Dean's private parts. Dean was lying on the bed as she leaned over to kiss his neck and whispered in his ear. Barbette could hear her saying,

"How do you want it? Do you want a blow job or sex, baby?"

Neither one of them noticed that Barbette was standing in the doorway or that she had walked into the room and was standing at the foot of the bed. When Dean looked up, he was shocked to see Barbette standing there.

"Hey baby," he said. "Let me . . ."

"Explain?" Barbette finished the sentence for him.

The red headed woman stood up. "I think I better go," she said as she walked past Barbette and picked up her purse on the dresser on the way out of the bedroom.

Barbette did not move. She looked at Dean lying on the bed, wearing a pair of gold silk pajamas. Dean also did not move. He seemed to be afraid to move or say anything.

"How long have you been wearing those pajamas," Barbette asked.

"About two weeks," Dean answered in a rusted voice.

"And when's the last time you been outside?" Barbette asked.

"I'm not sure. I think about two weeks."

"Dean, get up and take those pajamas off and go into the bathroom and take a shower," Barbette ordered.

"Dean moved slowly, but was able to do as he was told. As his pajamas dropped to the floor, Barbette noticed Dean's body. It seemed to her that he had lost at least 20 pounds. He walked past her into the bathroom and started the shower. Barbette still had not moved. As she looked around the room she noticed glasses on the dresser and newspapers lying everywhere. She wondered when Dean had last changed the sheets.

Meanwhile, Dean had gotten into the shower. He assumed that Carl had sent Barbette over to check on him because he was worried about him. As Dean lathered his body and washed his hair, he thought about the two weeks he had spent in isolation and realized that he wasn't crazy, but just might be experiencing some type of depression. He rinsed off his body and hair, stepped out of the shower and grabbing a towel to dry off, wrapped the towel around his waist and walked back into the bedroom where Barbette was pulling the sheets off the bed.

"Dean, where do you keep the clean sheets?" she asked.

Dean walked over to a closet and pulled out a set of gray sheets with matching pillow cases. He began helping Barbette put the clean sheets on the bed. Once they had finished making the bed, Dean walked to his closet and pulled out a pair of jeans and a shirt. Walking over to his dresser drawer, he pulled out underwear, socks and a tee shirt. During this entire time neither he nor Barbette had said a word. Barbette sat in a chair on the opposite side of the room and watched him dress.

"What?" Dean asked.

"What do you mean what?" Barbette questioned.

"Why are you looking at me like that?" he asked.

"Dean, I just want to know why you haven't returned my calls. What's been going on with you? And who the hell was that red headed woman who just left?" Barbette was pissed off but was trying to hold back her anger until she could figure out Dean's state of mine.

"She's just a friend and I just haven't felt like being around you," Dean replied.

"What do you mean you haven't felt like being around me? I thought you and I had something special. I thought you loved me, you bastard," said Barbette. "Tell me, Dean, what happened to us?" Barbette was nearly in tears, but was trying hard to hold them back. Dean was not even looking at her. Instead he was looking around on his dresser for his watch. "Barbette, I love your ass and that's why I don't want to be around you. I love you so much and I want to make love to you. You don't know how I've been feeling! I fuck around because my lady doesn't want to have sex with me." Dean raised his hand up to the sky and looked up to the ceiling. "My woman is waiting for us to get married first. That is some dumb ass shit. Remember, I said that you had whip appeal? Remember?" Dean spoke loudly.

Barbette watched Dean strode back and forth waving his hands and screaming at her.

"Yes, I remember," she managed to say in a low tone.

"Well I meant that shit. You see, Barbette, your pussy is like a drug. I got to have it, and if I can't have it, I go looking for another woman to please me and if she doesn't make me feel like you do, I go to another bitch. Trying to get that same motherfucking feeling you give me. Your pussy is like crack and, yes, I am sick. I'm sick, because I can't have you Girl and I'm fucking every bitch that comes my way trying to get what I want from your ass."

Barbette was still sitting in the chair across the room. She didn't know what to say or do. She hadn't realized how strongly being celibate had affected Dean and their relationship. Barbette also felt the death of Dean's uncle had played a part in his reaction towards her. Barbette thought how strange it was that she had never considered the fact that Dean would sleep around on her. After all he was not celibate, she was.

"Dean, I love you and I want this relationship to work," Barbette said in a shaky tone. "I'm sorry that I didn't realize that my being celibate was affecting you this way."

"Sure, Barbette," he said in a smart-ass tone. Dean walked to the bedroom door turning towards Barbette, looked at her without showing any feeling.

"Barbette, I can't bear to look your ass. Every time I look at you, I want you. My dick gets hard and baby, it hurts like hell. So, you need to leave and don't call me unless you're ready to be my woman totally. No, don't call me till you're ready to FUCK period!

Barbette stood up and walked past Dean and walked out of his bedroom into the hall. When she reached the outside door, she turned around and looking at Dean who had followed her to the door and said, "Dean, I wish the *real* Dean would come back to me, because, I don't know who the hell you are anymore. FUCK YOU DEAN! She hollered as she stormed out the door.

Dean sat on his bed and wondered if he had lost his mind after all. He had just let the love of his life walk out of his house and, as a matter of fact, he had put her out. He realized that he didn't know what he was doing anymore and decided that he needed to apologize to Barbette. Dean jumped up and grabbing his jacket and keys, and rushed out of the house. As he got in his car, he thought about what he had just done and he knew that he loved and wanted Barbette like he had never wanted a woman before in his life.

Dean was still sitting in his car when Carl drove up and parked his car next to his. He got out of his car and knocked on Dean's window. Dean let the window down. "Hey, Carl," he said.

"Hey Dean, why are you sitting our here? Are you going somewhere?" Carl asked.

"Yeah, man. I'm going over Barbette's," he said in a gloomy tone.

"Dean, man, how long have you been sitting in your car?" Carl looked at Dean's facial expression. He looked as if he had just woken up from a deep sleep.

"Man, what time is it? Dean asked. Carl looked at his watch.

"It's 1:00 in the morning, man. Come on in the house."

Without a word, Dean opened his car door and got out. Carl took the keys out of the ignition, locked the car door and walked with Dean to the house. Once he was in the house, Dean sat down at the dining room table and started to cry. Carl rushed over to his friend and placed his arm around his shoulder.

"Hey, man, you want to tell me about it? What's wrong, man?"

Dean told Carl about what he had said to Barbette. He talked about how much he loved her and how guilty he felt about sleeping around on her. He shared his feelings about his uncle's passing and told Carl that he had found some old police reports in his uncle stuff and that he now knew that his father had killed his mother, but didn't know why and that he did not want to hurt his sister by telling her the truth. Carl listened to Dean talk till he was talked out and was finally ready for the bed at 4:00 in the morning.

Dean's phone rang at 9:30. He reached for it on the nightstand, while managing to keep his eye closed.

"Hello"

"Hey, brother; I love you this morning. It was Donna.

"Hello, Donna. I love you too. Is everything alright?"

"Yep, but I wanted to talk to you about something."

"And what is that?"

"What's going on with you and Barbette? I talked to her yesterday and she told me that she had not talked to you since Uncle Milton funeral," Donna said.

"I talked to her yesterday," he said. "Now, can I go back to sleep?"

"So, you two are all right now?" Donna asked.

"No, not really," Dean replied. "Come on, Donna, I need to go back to sleep. Can we talk about Barbette later?"

"No, because I'm going to meet her for brunch at Justin's at 11:30 and I want to know what's going on with you two before I get there and start running my mouth?"

"You're going to meet Barbette for brunch?" Dean said, sitting up in bed, rubbing his eyes.

"Yep."

Suddenly, Dean had an idea.

"Hey, Donna would you mind if I met her instead. I said some things to her last night that I need to apologize for. I really need to talk to her."

"Okay, Dean, I'll call her and let her know that you will be meeting her instead of me.

"NO! I need it to be a surprise, okay?" Dean replied.

"Okay, but call me after you guys meet and let me know what happened," Donna said.

They finished their conversation then Dean hurried to take a shower and get dressed. He walked over to his dresser drawer and pulled out the jersey box that held the ring he was supposed to give to her on their trip to Marco Island. As he opened the box to check it out, Carl knocked on the half-opened door then walked in.

"Hey, man, where are you going?" Carl asked.

Dean smiled at him and said, "I'm going to meet Barbette for brunch and I'm going to give her this ring and ask her to marry me. He showed Carl the ring.

"Wild, man—, I didn't realize Lou had finished making it. That's a motherfucking rock, ain't it?"

"Yep, its five carats platinum, man," Dean said. "Hey, Carl, do you think she'll say yes?"

"I would! Shit, ask me, man; I'll marry your ass," Carl said, laughing aloud.

Dean sounded like an excited kid as he went on to explain to Carl, how Donna was supposed to meet Barbette, but that he was going in her place instead.

"Well, I got to go. I have to meet her at 11:30."

"Well, good luck, man!" Carl said as he embraced his friend, Dean.

"Thanks, man."

It took Dean thirty minutes to reach Justin's. He parked and went in through the side door of the restaurant and spotted Barbette at the bar, looking towards the front door for Donna. Dean walked up behind her.

"Hello, Barbette!" Barbette turned to look straight into Dean's eye.

"Dean? Hello—I mean why are you here? Did something happen to Donna?" she asked, giving him a strange look.

"Donna is not coming, Barbette. I asked her if I could come instead. Barbette, I owe you an apology. I'm so sorry for the things I said to you last night and I'm asking you to please forgive me. And before you say anything else, I have something to ask you."

Dean was standing next to Barbette, sweating. He reached into his pocket and brought out a small white box. "Barbette," he said with shaking hands as he held out the little satin box. "Would you marry me?"

Barbette was in shock—she didn't know what to say. Dean opened the box to expose a beautiful five carat diamond ring. Barbette started to cry. She was speechless.

"Barbette, please marry me. I love you baby," Dean said as he started to cry also. The people in the restaurant had stopped talking and eating to watch them as they waited to hear her answer. Barbette stood up and placing her arms around Dean's neck half screamed and half sobbed, "Yes, Oh Yes, I will marry you." They kissed a long hard kiss and the people in the restaurant started to clap and cheer. Dean took the ring out of the box and placed it on Barbette ring finger. It fit perfectly. Barbette hugged Dean and whispered in his ear, "Let's get out of here."

Since they had both driven their own cars, Dean followed Barbette back to the condo. Dean was feeling good about himself and was anxious about getting to the condo. He was about to marry the only woman he had ever loved.

Once they were at the condo, Dean followed Barbette into the kitchen and began preparing drinks for them. He pulled out the Patron and retrieved a lime from the refrigerator, sliced it up and placed the salt shaker on a tray. Barbette had gone to the bathroom and had just entered the kitchen. She stood at the island and held her hand out in front of her to check out her ring.

"Damn Dean, this is a bad ass ring baby! You did good!"

Dean was standing at the counter pouring liquor into their glass and turned in her direction.

"Only the best for you girl."

"Now, let's do three shots this time," he said.

Dean could not stop looking at Barbette. He felt there was a magic between them that would last forever.

"Come on over here and stand by your man," he said, wearing a smile from ear to ear. Barbette walked over to Dean and sat down on the barstool. Dean remained standing.

"Let's toast!" he said.

Barbette sprinkled salt on her hand, picked up her shot glass and said, "To my first and last marriage." They both drank their shot of tequila and picked a slice of lime to chase it. Barbette waited patiently while Dean poured another shot.

"Dean, it's your turn to make a toast," Barbette said.

"Okay baby."

"To our happiness!" he said. They downed the shot and smiled at each other. Dean poured their third shot but before he could make another toast, Barbette had picked up her glass and downed her drink. Dean downed his and stood by Barbette looking at her as if she was the most beautiful woman he had ever seen in his life. He knew he was in love.

"Barbette, I'm so sorry for what I've put you through. I've been going through a lot of changes with, Uncle Milton's death and to add to the stress, I just recently found out that my dad shot my mother and ran their car off a cliff, a double suicide. I have no idea why my father would have done something like that.

"Oh my God!" Barbette exclaimed astonished. "I am so, so sorry to hear that!" She was astonished and went over to put her arms around Dean. She didn't know what to say to him and she finally understood that he probably hadn't been thinking straight for a while.

They stood in the kitchen talking, hugging and kissing for about 45 minutes before Dean looked at her and asked, "So what do you want to do now?"

"This is your day." he said. "We can do anything you want to do."

Barbette looked into Dean's eyes and spoke in a child like tone.

"Dean, I don't want to made love because we've already done that and I know how that feels."

Dean looked puzzled but hung onto her every word. He couldn't help feeling a little disappointed that he still might not have the opportunity to get her into bed. It had been a long time since they'd make love and he was hoping that they could indulge in more than foreplay. He wanted her body more than anything. Barbette leaned over slowly and whispered into Dean's ear.

"But, baby I would love to fuck,"

Barbette took Dean by the hand and led him into her bedroom. She pushed him causing him to fall back onto the bed. Dean watched as she stood in front of him and began to undress. Once she was naked, Barbette walked over to Dean and he placed his arm around the lower part of her body allowing him to squeeze her ass. Dean slid his hand between her legs and started to play in Barbette's already moist private area as Barbette moaned her pleasure—she could hardly wait to have him in her.

Barbette reached for the buttons on Dean's shirt to unbutton them as Dean stopped moving his hand to look at her and say, "Baby, let me get undress and why don't you get into bed?" Barbette followed his instructions and got under the covers as Dean finished undressing and got into the bed next to her.

"Baby, tell me what you need," he said as he continued playing with her wetness. "Tell me baby. Come on talk to me baby," Dean said.

"I want you in me. I can't wait. I'm so ready," Barbette replied breathlessly.

Dean pulled back the cover exposing their bodies. He got on his knees in front of Barbette, lusting at her body movements. He knew she wanted him as badly as he wanted her; but decided to compose himself and make her wait.

He pulled her legs open.—He wanted to taste the sweetness of her juices before he entered her. Barbette started to moan with pleasure.

"YES, OH YES,' she screamed. Please, Dean, I want you in me. Please Dean, fuck me now. PLEASE, PLEASE, PLEASE," Barbette yelled. Dean had waited a long time for this and he was trying hard to prolong it. He didn't want to let Barbette's plead take him to the point of explosion. He didn't want to stop, but knew he had to give her what she wanted. Dean entered Barbette slowly at first, pulling her legs up to enable him to go deep inside of her. As he began moving in and out, harder and harder with every thrust, he felt her muscle expand and wanted to cum. Dean was trying not to release himself—at least not yet. He continued entering her deeper and deeper and noticed that Barbette's breathing had increased as she began to reach her climax

"OH FUCK, I'M GETTING READY TO CUM. OH SHIT," Barbette screamed.

"Go ahead, Baby, and let Dean feel the wetness. Come on Baby. Give it to your man."

Barbette felt herself released and went crazy. She screamed and twisted, turned and jerked her body all over the place, causing Dean to release before he wanted to.

"Sh—it, Baby. Shit! You got the shit," Dean said as he released. Barbette finally calmed down and stopped moving about. She laid there wondering why and how she had not allowed herself to have sex with this man. Dean raised his body up from Barbette's and laid beside his fiancée. Her eyes were closed and she was lying very still.

"Hey, Baby, are you all right?" Dean asked. Barbette nodded. She was still breathing hard. Dean realized that, again he had not used protection, but felt it didn't matter. He wanted to wait to have children, but if it happened earlier than he wanted, it would be okay.

"Dean?" Barbette said as she turned her body on her side to face him.

"What, Baby?"

"You pleased the fuck out of me," she said with a smile.

Dean started to laugh. "And you pleased me too, Baby."

They spend the rest of the day in bed, making love, talking, touching, making love, talking and touching.

Suddenly, Dean's cell phone came to life, interrupting their afternoon blissful interlude. He reached for it on the nightstand.

"Hello"

"So, tell me what happened?" Donna said expectantly.

"Donna, everything is fine." Dean laughed—Matter of fact, we're engaged and right now we're trying to get some sleep. We'll talk to you in the morning. Bye Donna." Dean hung up the phone before she could respond and moved up close behind Barbette, placing his arms around her waist and went back to sleep.

EPISODE NINE

The wedding

The makeup artist had just finished applying Barbette's make up and was packing up her stuff to leave as Barbette turned towards the mirror to check herself out. She was delighted with her looks and was now ready to slip into her dress. Donna and her oldest brother's wife Sylvia retrieved her wedding dress from a coat rack placed in the corner of the room.

"Okay, Barbette, let's do this," Donna said as they walked towards her carrying the very long white dress. The dress was a Bob Maxon Design that was beaded and designed on a roaring twenties style. Barbette stood up as they approached.

"Okay, let's be careful not to get make up on this dress," Donna said.

Donna and Sylvia took the dress off the hanger and assisted Barbette in slipping on the gown being careful to avoid straining it. Once fitted, Sylvia placed the matching headpiece on Barbette's head then they stood back to get the full effect and looked in awe at the beautiful bride standing before them.

"Girl, you look so damn good," Donna said as. Sylvia who had started to cry said, "Barbette, you look absolutely beautiful."

"Please stop crying before you make me cry too," Barbette said as she turned towards a full-length mirror to admire herself. She adjusted her headpiece then turned towards Donna and Sylvia.

"Finally, after all these months of waiting—Thank you both for helping me with everything," she said in a sincere tone.

Just as they were about to do a group hug, there was a knock at the door.

"I'll see who it is," Diane said. She had been sitting in the room touching up her nails the entire time.

The door opened and the rest of the bridesmaids entered. They had come to check out the bride in her gown after first dressing in their purple velvet vintage gowns. They buzzed around the bride like excited bees.

"Barbette, girl you look good," Marlene and Sue wailed with excitement. Marlene and Sue were her old friends from boarding school and they all had vowed that they would be bridesmaids at each other's wedding. Barbette was the first to go down the aisle.

"Girl, I saw your man and he's looking dam good," Sue said. Barbette smiled remembering how Sue would steal a man from anybody, if she wanted him.

"Keep your hands off, and this time I mean it!" They all started to laugh and stopped when they heard another knock at the door.

"Yes," Diane said as she walked towards the door being careful not to mess up her nails.

"It's me!" Barbette's mother had taken a late flight in and had just arrived. She walked through the door and instantly extended her arms towards her daughter. "My Baby! My Baby is getting married."

Barbette embraced her mother. She had not seen her in over a year and was relieved that she could make the wedding. She had been traveling the world promoting her new religious book, Speak and It Shall Be Done. "Hey, Mom, I'm so glad you could make it."

"Oh, I wouldn't have missed it for the world. My daughter's wedding? No, I wouldn't miss that."

But you could miss my graduation from high school, college and law school. And don't forget the birthdays, school plays, mother and daughter Girl Scout camping trip, Barbette thought to herself.

Barbette knew she had to pull herself together and focus on the present not the past.

Her mother had pulled back from the embrace and looked Barbette up and down. "Baby, you are a beautiful bride."

"Thank you, Mom," she said.

Another knock at the door and a voice on the other side said, "Three minutes."

It was time. Everyone and everything was in place and ready. The groom's men had lined up at the back door of the church and the music had started to play. Barbette's bridesmaids all hugged and kissed her as they joined with their groomsmen. Barbette stood up and for the first time since all of the wedding preparations had begun, felt extremely nervous. As she stood there, she was trying hard not to cry and decided to placed her thoughts on something funny instead of thinking about her future with Dean, like the time she poured a bucket of water over Lance when he wouldn't get up for school. She started to laugh as the dressing room's door opened slowly and turned to find her father standing in the doorway wearing a black tail tuxedo. She thought he looked so handsome. She smiled at him as he walked up to her and gave her a big hug.

"Hey baby, you all right?" he asked.

"Yes, Daddy, I'm fine."

"You're beautiful," he said as he stood back to look her up and down.

"Thank you, Daddy. You look great too."

"Well, Barbette, I just need to ask you one question."

"And what is that?" Barbette asked curiously

Raymond walked over to a chair and sat down. He watched his daughter as she approached him and stood in front of him.

"Baby, I need to know if you have any doubts. If so, we can call this off right now."

"No, Daddy, I have no doubts. I know with all my heart that I love Dean very much and I'm ready to get married to him," she said as she extended her hands out to her father. Raymond stood up and took her hands in his. "Okay baby, then let's go walk down that aisle then."

The wedding party, including Carl, who was best man, had walked down the aisle and were all in position. The flower girl was just finishing spreading rose petals down the aisle when Barbette and her father approached the entrance to the church.

The wedding march started and everyone stood. The church was full. Raymond had invited several famous and wealthy clients and friends. Dean had done the same. The church was beautifully decorated with a chandelier hanging from the ceiling that lit up like candles reflecting happily the cut-glass windows surrounding the nave and apse of the church.

Barbette father looked at her. "You're ready?" he asked.

"Yes," she said as they began walking down the aisle. Barbette could see Dean waiting for her at the altar and she never took her eyes off him. As she got closer she realized that he was smiling—he seemed to be relaxed and sure of himself.

Once they reached the altar—the minister asked "Who gives this woman away?" and Barbette's father answered "I do." Barbette turned to her father and kissed him on the lips softly. Raymond then took a seat next to his new girl friend of two months, Tamar.

Dean took Barbette's hand and pulled her towards him. Throughout the ceremony they had eyes only for each other.

Finally the minister said, "You may kiss the bride," and Dean pulled Barbette into his arms and kissed her long and hard.

As their lips separated, the minister said, "Ladies and Gentlemen I would like to introduced Mr. and Mrs. Jenkins," and the people in the church stood up and started to clap.

As the wedding party exited the church, Barbette noticed that a lot of people she had not seen in years had attended her wedding such as, her uncles and aunts, old clients and even her old boyfriend, Lee, who had come with his mother and his new wife. She saw her older brother, Raymond, Jr., and stopped to give him a kiss glad that his international business commitments had not prevented his being there—she was very happy to see him.

Once alone in the limo and on the way to the reception, Dean kissed Barbette again and just as suddenly as he had kissed her, he pulled away.

"Barbette, believe me, I am going to make you happy. I love you girl." Barbette began to cry.

"Hey baby, what's wrong?" Dean asked.

"Nothing, I am just so happy to have you as my husband."

Dean took a hankie out of his pocket and gently wiped away her tears.

"Hey baby, stop crying before you make me cry and you don't want to see a real man cry, do you?" he asked

Barbette started laughing. "No," she managed to say.

The reception was held in the Fox Ballroom on Peachtree Street. When the newly married couple entered the room, people stood up and applauded. Carl approached Dean and they embraced then he escorted them to a table that had been set up on the platform. Once they were seated, Carl joined the rest of the wedding party who were seated at a table next to the couple. The wedding director made a short speech welcoming everyone and introduced the wedding party to the guests. As the music started to play, waiters came from everywhere and began serving the food. The wedding meal started with a salad followed by a choice of chicken-cordon-bleu, salmon or T-bone steak. Two bottles of Crystal was place on each table and the bar was open and free. Most of the guest had come in limos so not many people were worried about over-indulging, which they did all evening long.

After dinner, it was time for the groom and bride to open the dance. Dean took Barbette in his arms and held her tight as everyone watched their every move as they danced to—Musiq's new cut, *LOVE*."

After the dance, Dean escorted Barbette to each of the tables to greet their guests. Barbette happened to look across the room and noticed that her dad was still talking to Donna—she had noticed that they had been talking since she and Dean had first got up to dance. The serious nature of their conversation showed on their faces and it even looked like Donna was crying. As she continued to make her rounds with Dean, Barbette thought that it was probably nothing important, but decided she would address the matter later.

Dean escorted Barbette back to the wedding party's table and as he pulled out her seat for her, she realized that he had not taken his eyes off her all evening. She truly thought that Dean loved her more than any man had or could love her.

EPISODE TEN

The honeymoon

Dean woke up, and upon opening his eyes, remembered that he was in the Bahamas on his honeymoon. He sat up in bed and rested his head on the headboard—Barbette was lying next to him sound asleep. It had been a hell of a weekend for the two of them. First, the flowers had arrived late to the church, then, unbelievably, the caterers forgot to bring the cake to the reception hall, but the worst situation was that they had not been able to find Lance. He had spent the night with a few strippers he'd met at the bachelor's party the night before the wedding and claimed he over-slept. Thankfully, he did arrive at the church just before it was his turn to escort his bridesmaid down the aisle. All in all, everything went off pretty well.

Dean looked down at Barbette whose hair was a mess and spread all over the pillow but her make-up was still in place, lipstick and all. Dean smiled at her and pulled her hair gently from her face. He could still smell her perfume and was turned on immediately. He was surprise by the things that she had done sexually to him and with him, last night. It was like a different woman had come out of her. Thinking back, he was happy that she had cut him off from having sex with her a month before the wedding. Although it had seemed like the longest month in the world, he had managed not to touch another woman since the day he asked her to marry him. Having spent most of his time with Barbette planning the wedding, he didn't have time to be tempted by other woman.

Barbette woke up and turned her head to look up at Dean sitting in bed.

"Hey you," she mumbled in a sleepy voice, "you up already?"

"Yep, I've been up for a while. I'm just sitting here thinking about how happy I am baby." Dean pushed his body down in the bed and adjusted his pillow.

"Dean, I love you," Barbette said as she moved her body on top of his. She began to kiss his neck and worked her lips up to his mouth. Dean placed his arms around her and held her close to him.

"Hey baby?"

"What?" Barbette asked.

"You want to let me do what I did to you last night?"

"What's that?" she asked. "We did a lot of things last night."

"You know. The thing that we were having a little problem with," Dean said.

"No! I told you that I didn't want to try that again." Barbette climbed off Dean and got out of bed. She turned to look at him, and saw the disturbed look on his face.

"So, you're telling me that you're not even going to try? Dean asked. Barbette was getting angry and wanted to end the conversation.

"Dean, please don't tell me that you have to have sex with me that way. Please don't," Barbette said in a pleading voice.

"No baby, I don't have to have it that way all the time, but I do like to think of it as a treat It's something we can do on special occasions and I consider being on our honeymoon, a special occasion," Dean replied.

Dean jumped out of the bed and walking over to the window, pulled back the drapes and looked out at the beach. Barbette went to her luggage and opening it, selected a black swimsuit with a matching wrap then walked into the bathroom to take a shower. Dean was still looking out the window wondered if he had a problem. He had experienced anal sex twice as a teenager and managed to experience it again four years ago with Trina, his girlfriend at that time. Since then he had had many women who were willing to accommodate him. The feeling was so fulfilling to him that he had wanted to have anal sex as often as possible. Now that he was married to Barbette, he felt that she should accommodate his sexual needs in any way that he wanted but apparently—Barbette had a problem with this. She had done it before a few times back in the day, but not liking it, she had decided not to try it again. Dean knew that this would probably be a problem for him and hoped that he could, in time, convince her to please him in that way.

Dean walked into the bathroom where Barbette was just getting out of the shower.

"Hey baby, I'm sorry." Dean said.

"Me too," Barbette said and placed her arms around Dean's neck to kiss him. Dean returned the kiss and patted her ass as she exited the bathroom. Dean took his shower and put on his swimming trunks then they left the room and headed to breakfast.

Dean felt proud as Barbette walked in front of him—other men were checking her out and recognized that he was with a *queen*. For breakfast, Dean ordered eggs, toast, and juice for the both of them and as he sat across from her, he couldn't help but think about just how lucky he was to have her as his wife. After breakfast they walked the beach and discussed future plans that included kids, house and cars.

Even though it stayed on his mind, Dean never mentioned his sexual needs again during their honeymoon. The week was spent with dancing, drinking, swimming, and a whole lot of sex.

By the time they left to return home, they were both too tired to speak and slept all the way back to Atlanta.

Once they arrived back in town they retrieved their luggage with the help of their limo driver, Danny.

Danny Muse had always been Barbette's first choice as a chauffeur whenever she ordered limo service. He was a middle-aged, married man with two daughters who were presently attending college. He often talked about his life, sharing stories about his wife and the girls. Danny had a wonderful sense of humor and Barbette adored him.

"Hey, Mr. and Mrs. Jenkins! How was the honeymoon?" Danny asked as he assisted the bell-cap with their luggage.

"Great!" Dean spoke up and answered.

Once in the Limo, Barbette laid her head in Dean's lap and closed her eye while listening to Danny and Dean talked about the weather and sports. She could not wait to get to the condo and get into bed.

Her cell phone rang and she answered it. "Hello!"

"How's my daughter doing?" the voice said.

"Hey, Dad, how are you?" Barbette replied.

"Just fine, considering some personal things, but everything will work out."

"Did something happen while I was gone? What personal things?" she asked.

"Oh, nothing, I was hoping you and Dean could come to dinner this Friday."

"Sure!" Barbette was sitting up now and was very concerned. "Daddy, what is it?" she insisted.

"Baby, nothing that bad," he said with a chuckle in his voice. "Believe me, if it was that urgent, I would have you over before Friday."

Barbette could hear nervousness in her dad's voice and was getting more concerned.

"Okay, okay, we'll wait till Friday."

"Oh, and by the way, I've invited Carl and Dean's sister, Donna, to join us. Barbette had laid her head back in Dean's lap. "Okay, Dad, I'll talk to you later, OK?"

Raymond was trying hard to hide the shakiness in his voice. He had started to cry.

"Okay baby girl, I love you."

"I love you too." Barbette hung up and looked up at Dean.

"Hey, what's going on?" he asked.

"I don't know. He wants us to come to dinner Friday and he's invited your sister and Carl as well."

"Probably just a family get-together—don't worry." Dean passed his fingers through Barbette's hair and leaned over to kiss her. He realized from her facial expression that she was worried and decided he would call Raymond back later on to see if he could find out what was really going on.

Barbette had fallen asleep but woke up when the limo suddenly stopped. She looked up at Dean, who was smiling at her and said, "Hey baby, we're home."

Barbette sat up and looked out the window. "Hey!" she said with excitement. "Where are we? Who live here? Barbette was pissed off. "I wanted to go home and get into my damn bed. I am tired, Dean. I need a shower and, my hair looks like shit."

"Hey! Hey!" Dean grabbed her hands to stop her from trying to fix her hair. "Calm down," he said softly. "This is *our home*."

Barbette looked at him with amazement. "This is our house? Why didn't you tell me we, I mean you, were purchasing a house? I thought we were going to live in the condo until we had time to look for a house." Barbette pulled away from Dean and looked out the window.

"I wanted to surprise you. Do you like it?" he asked. Barbette was so mad that she could not speak. She couldn't understand how he could make such a big decision, like buying a house, without her.

"Come on in and see it," Dean said as he got out of the car.

Danny extended his hand. Barbette got out and Dean led her to the front door of this very large brick house with black shutters and trimming. He opened the door and flipped on the light switch lighting up the foyer like a Christmas tree. The high ceiling embraced a large chandelier while white walls surrounded pale green pattern marble flooring, a gone-with-the-wind staircase and a balcony that encircled the loft overlooking the foyer. It was beautiful but Barbette still could not deal with the idea that Dean had not asked her input on the purchasing of a house.

Dean turned to her and gave her a hug as Danny came in behind them. "Where would you like me to put these, sir?" Danny asked.

"Oh, just leave them here in the foyer. I'll take them up."

"Will there be anything else?"

Dean reached into his pocket and extended a hand full of bills to Danny.

"No, that will be all. Thanks a lot, man," Dean said as he closed the door behind him. Barbette was still in the same spot—looking up at the ceiling, when Dean turned back.

"Hey baby, let me show you the rest of the house." He led her through their new home one room at a time.

The house had five bedrooms, five and a half bathrooms, a master bedroom with a sitting room, and an office across the hall. Down stairs was a large den off of a huge kitchen, a deck that ran the length of the house, a backyard with in-ground pool. The laundry room was larger than the Laundromats she used to visit every week when she was in college. Barbette was speechless and did not know if she was supposed to be happy or mad—in fact, she was confused.

"So, do you like it?" Dean asked as he led her to their master bedroom.

Barbette sat on the bed and started taking her clothes off.

"Oh so, we're not talking?" Dean said, confused as well. He didn't realize that purchasing a house for them would be a problem. He thought he was doing a manly thing—taking care of his wife.

Barbette finally spoke.

"Dean, the house is wonderful, but I was hoping that we would do this house thing together, or at the very least, the furnishings. To me, this is *your* house, not *ours house*." Barbette walked into the bathroom and began taking a shower as Dean sat down in a chair by the window and looked out into the dusk sky. *"I wonder if I'm going to be able to please this woman. Damn, she's complaining already."* He murmured in a low tone.

The next morning, the ring of the phone woke Barbette from her sleep. She sat up in bed and picked up the phone on the night stand.

"Hello!"

"Hey, Sis, it's me. So, how you like your new house?" It was Lance.

"You knew?" she asked as she wiped the sleep from her eyes.

"Yep, I helped Dean pick out the bedroom furniture."

"I should have guessed that you had something to do with it when I saw that mirrored wall," she said and they both started to laugh.

"Where are you, man?" she asked.

"I'm at home, in bed with my woman."

"Where's Dad?"

"He left on the red eye this morning to meet Raymond, Jr. in Boston on business. He'll be back Thursday evening and if you need him, he did leave a phone number where you can reach him." Lance's new girl friend, Sandra, had just walked out of the bathroom and was climbing back into bed.

"Hum, hey, Sis, do you need that number?"

"No, that's okay."

"Will we see you later?" she asked.

Lance could barely talk now that Sandra had put her head under the cover and he knew where she was heading.

"Hey, I got to go. Yeah, I'll be by later."

"See you then." Barbette had noticed that Dean had gotten up already. She didn't know what she was going to say to him. She wondered if this was the first sign of a controlling man.

Dean entered the room, breaking her thoughts.

"Hey baby, you still mad?" He walked towards her.

"No. Just disappointed that I had no say about where we would live."

Dean sat down on the bed and kissed her on her forehead.

"Baby, I was just trying to surprise you, but I promise that you will pick the next house and any other purchases we make from now on, okay?"

Barbette smiled, "Okay."

The rest of the week was great. Barbette and Dean were like ants, they traveled together everywhere. The only time they were apart was when Dean went to work but two days out of the week he worked home to allow him more time to spend with his wife. Dean felt proud that he was the husband he'd always wanted to be to his wife.

EPISODE ELEVEN

Daddy's House for Dinner

Barbette was excited about seeing her Dad and couldn't wait to find out what was going on with him. Even though she had not been on a scale, she could tell by the way her clothes fit that she had gained a few pounds, and not wanting the extra weight to be noticeable to her Dad, decided to wear black pants and sweater. She knew that black was good camouflaging weight. As she walked out of the bathroom, she noticed Dean hanging up the phone.

"Hey baby, who was that?"

"Carl. He wanted to know what I was wearing." They both started to laugh.

"Well, we better hurry up if we're going to get there on time. I can't wait to find out what's going on."

Dean could tell that Barbette had gained weight also and didn't like it at all. He knew from the comments she had been making about herself that she didn't like it either, but Dean decided not to say anything about it and would give her a chance to lose it. He also didn't like the idea that she hadn't wanted to have sex last night, but planned to make up for it later on when they got home.

There were three cars in the driveway when they arrived at Raymond's house twenty minutes late—Donna's Mercedes, Carl's new BMW, and Lance's Jaguar.

"Well, we're late!" Barbette said in an angry tone. It seemed that Dean could not wait till later on that night to make love. "I know that and since we're already about twenty minutes late, why don't we make it an hour and fuck in the car."

Barbette looked at him in amazement.

"I know you don't mean that."

"Oh yeah I do." He released his seat-belt and leaned over to kiss her.

Barbette turned away. "No, Dean, let's go in now."

"So, does this mean we're not going to have sex later on tonight," he asked.

"No, this means were not having it now."

"Okay, you go ahead. I have to get myself together before I get out of this car." Barbette was surprise to see that Dean had developed a hard on.

As she approached the house, Barbette was greeted at the door by Lance.

"Hey, girl, what's going on?" embracing her.

"Hey, Lance, you look good," she replied.

"Thanks. Come on in, everybody is in the dining room. You guys are late. Hey! Where's Dean?" he asked.

"Oh, he's in the car. He'll be right in."

Lance smiled. "You guys fucking in the car now?" Lance started laughing.

Barbette put on her serious face. "No, we're not!"

As Barbette walked into the dining room, everyone looked towards the door.

"Hey everybody!" she said.

"Well, well, well! We were wondering when you two love birds would get here. Hey where's Dean?" Donna asked.

"He's in the car. He'll be right in."

Dean was in the car on his cell phone. He had decided to call his old girl friend, Trina, whom he ran into on Tuesday. He knew he was wrong but he was in need of something sexual that Barbette was not willing to give him, and he knew Trina would do anything to please him. He was just hanging up when he heard Lance knock on the car window. Dean opened the car door to step out.

"Hey, man, were waiting for you," Lance said.

"Okay, okay, I'm coming."

"What are you doing anyway?" Lance asked

"I was just taking care of some business. So what's up, man? Why are we here for dinner?" Dean asked. Lance opened the door to the house and Dean followed him in.

"I have no idea."

Dean walked into the dining area, greeted everybody with apologies and took his seat at the table. Upon Dean's arrival, Raymond rang a bell and the attendant started serving the food; tossed salad, shrimp cocktail, salmon, with green beans and carrots, and for dessert, chocolate mousse—Barbette helped herself to everything but the mousse. During the meal, the dinner conversation was lively with everyone sharing their opinion on policies, money, and world events. Suddenly, Dean cell phone started to ring.

"Excuse me for a minute, please. I was waiting for an important call." Dean walked into the kitchen and answered his phone.

Barbette wondered who it was, but assumed it was work related. Carl looked at Barbette to see her expression and decided that she showed no concern; it must be someone from work calling him. Dean and Carl's partnership had doubled in revenue and they had expanded their office moving to a high-rise office building located in the downtown Peachtree area—they now had twenty-five employees.

Everyone continued talking until Lance intruded and said, "Hey, Dad, when are you going to tell us what this dinner meeting is all about."

Raymond looked at everybody before excusing himself from the table. As he walked out of the dining room he turned and said, "Please excuse me. I need to take care of some business. I would like to see you, Lance." Lance wore a look of surprise on his face. He looked around the table at everyone and said, "I wonder why he wants to see me."

Everyone tried to guess what was so important that Raymond could only speak to Lance about it in private—everyone that is, except Donna. Barbette remembered her father talking with Donna for a long time at her wedding and wondered if this had anything to do with what was happening.

Lance excused himself from the table and headed towards Raymond's office. As he entered the door, Raymond rose from his seat and greeted him with a hug.

"I love you, my son." Raymond managed to maintain a smile on his face.

"Thanks, Dad. Now what is it?" Lance took a seat on the vintage leather couch as his dad handed him a glass filled with cognac and said, "You'll need this."

Lance reached for the glass and drank the cognac in one swallow.

"Okay, what is it?"

"Dean's sister, Donna, is my daughter." Lance jumped up.

"WHAT? What the hell are you talking about, Dad?" he exclaimed.

"Back in the day, when your mother and I were going through something, I had an affair with Donna's mother. We were both married and even though I still loved your mother, she found out and divorced me."

Lance could not believe what he was hearing. He walked to the fireplace and leaned against the mantelpiece to prevent himself from falling.

"There's more," Raymond said as he walked towards his son with a refilled glass. Lance took it out of Raymond's trembling hand and drank it down fast.

"Okay, I'm ready." Lance said.

"Your mother just divorced me, but when Donna and Dean's father found out that Donna wasn't his daughter, and that his wife had had an affair with me, he shot her in the head and drove their car off a cliff, killing them both . . . . Lance, I'm sorry."

Lance was speechless. The room was veiled in ominous silence. Raymond walked away from Lance and took a seat at his desk. He waited, for what seemed an eternity, for Lance to say something.

"Dad, does anyone else know?"

"Your mother, their aunt Mildred (she just found out), my lawyer and now Donna. Milton told Donna about this on his deathbed and asked her not to tell Dean cause he didn't think Dean would be able to handle it. What do you think?"

Lance did not know what to say. He held his hand up to say 'stop there," keeping his father from saying anything else.

"Dad, I don't think you need to tell anyone else other than Barbette, and I'm not sure if this is the right time. For God sake, she just married her stepbrother! Or is he our brother too?" Lance asked wearing a smirk on his face.

"No!" Raymond exclaimed with tears in his eyes.

Lance walked over to the table and poured himself another drink—he was in shock. He had known that his parents split up had to do with his dad's cheating but had no idea the situation had been this bad.

"Okay, Dad, let's not tell anyone tonight—just let me think." Lance paced the length and width of his dad's office for a few minutes then suddenly stopped in his tracks. "Okay, Dad, when we go out there we'll make an announcement that you've decided to get married to your new girl friend or something like that. okay?"

Raymond looked at his son, who had begun pacing again. He thought about what Lance had said and wasn't sure if he should keep living a lie and was especially hesitant about keeping this information from Barbette. But Lance was right, she shouldn't be unhappy now. She had just married the man of her dreams and was happy in love. How could he take that from her? So he decided not to.

"Okay, Lance, we'll handle it your way, I won't tell anybody else and I'll wait for a better time to tell Barbette so, let's get ready to lie when we go back out there but first I need to know one thing," Raymond said as he leaned over his desk unable to look up at his son.

"Yes, what is it, Dad?" Lance asked.

"I need to know if you still love me. Is this a problem for you?"

Lance walked over to his dad and placing his arm around him, hugged his dad as if he was leaving forever.

"Hey, Dad, I still love you. You're my father and I'll always love you." Lance said, pulled away and smiling at his dad. "It was a long, long time ago and you can't go back and fix it, okay?"

Raymond smiled, "Okay."

Raymond and Lance joined the family and announced Raymond's so called marriage. Everyone had their opinion, but was happy for him. Shortly thereafter, Dean left on business and Carl had offered to take Barbette home. Everyone was leaving when Lance asked Donna to hang around for a while. Lance wanted to welcome Donna to the family and also wanted to explain why Raymond hadn't shared the news about her with anyone else. Not knowing why Lance asked Donna to stay, Barbette was surprised. She wondered if Lance was interested in Dean's sister and hoped Lance's taste in women was changing for the better.

Barbette got in the car with Carl and the first thing Carl did was to light up a joint.

"Hey, want some of this," he asked.

"No, thank you."

"Are you sure? It's some good stuff and It will help you sleep tonight."

"No, I better not." Barbette was concerned about Carl driving under the influence of marijuana, and decided someone had to stay straight and keep an eye on him.

"So, Barbette, how is it being married to Mr. Dean," Carl asked.

"It's great!" she replied as she adjusted her seat belt.

"Hey Carl, I hear you've been dating the same woman for a month now. What's that about? I always knew you to be the player of all players."

Carl laughed. "Hey, I'm getting old. I can't handle a lot of women at one time anymore." He continued laughing.

They drove for about fifteen minutes without saying a word before Carl glancing at Barbette and decided to speak.

"Hey, Barbette, man, I just want you to know, and please don't take this wrong—I just want you to know that the weight you've picked up looks damn good." Carl smiled at her.

"Thanks, Carl, I appreciate you saying that, but I don't think Dean likes it that much, so I plan on starting a workout routine beginning Monday."

Carl wondered if they were really happy, but decided not to ask. "Well, you look good to me anyway," he said as he exited off the highway.

Carl turned into the driveway of Dean's and Barbette's house and cut off the engine. Barbette looked at him and wondered if he planned on coming in.

"Barbette, do you think Dean would mind if I used you guys' bathroom," Carl asked.

"No, I don't think so, just as long as you keep your hands off his wife." She laughed.

Carl followed Barbette into the house and Barbette directed him to the half-bath near the kitchen. She walked into the kitchen and decided to prepare coffee all the while wondering where her husband had gone and hoping he would be home soon. Carl came out of the bathroom and asked for a towel.

"Well, as you know I had nothing to do with this house until my return from the honeymoon so I had no idea there were no towels in that bathroom."

Carl reached for a paper towel and dried off his hands.

"Want a drink?" Barbette had always enjoyed Carl's company and besides, she didn't want to stay in the house by herself anyway.

"I would like some of that coffee, if you don't mind." Carl took a seat at the kitchen table.

"So Carl, tell me about your lady." Barbette placed Carl coffee cup in front of him then took a seat across from him. Carl watched her as she lowered her hips into the chair and thought she was finer now then she was when he first met her.

"She's an auditor for MCV Software Corporation. She is very attractive, built really nice and knows how to please me." Carl smile.

Barbette felt wetness between her legs and could not believe that Carl could still take her there.

"That's really nice Carl. Do you think you might ask her to marry you one day?"

"Hell no, I'm not planning on getting married."

"Why?" Barbette asked.

"Too much work," Carl said as he watched Barbette squirming in her seat.

"Hey, am I making you uncomfortable?"

"Oh, no—why do you ask?"

"Just wanted to make sure you were alright with me being here," Carl said as his cell phone rang interrupting him. Carl reached into his pocket and pulled it out.

"Hello." The voice on the other end was Lance's.

"Hey, man, can you meet me at Joe's Bar in about an hour?"

"Sure! What's going on?" Carl asked.

"Nothing, man, just wanted to have a few drinks." Lance sounded a little stressed.

"Okay, man, I'll be there." Carl hung up and directed his attention back to Barbette.

"What's the problem?" she asked.

"Nothing; Lance wants me to meet him for a couple of drinks."

Carl stayed a little longer visiting with Barbette and shared with her, the business ideas he and Dean had in mind as well as their plans to purchase a new location.

Barbette was surprised that Dean had never shared these ideals with her.

"Well, I better get ready to go," Carl said as he rose from the kitchen chair. "Barbette, will you be alright. I know you're not used to the house yet, but I assume Dean will be home soon." Barbette stood up to walk him to the door.

"Oh yeah, he should be home soon."

"You just be careful out there and don't you and Lance be foolish and drive while drunk."

"We won't," Carl said as he walked out the door.

Barbette walked up the stairs to her bedroom and changed into her pink night grown. She pulled her hair back in a ponytail and took off her earrings. After washing her face and brushing her teeth she decided to watch TV. Dean had told her before he left her dad's house, that he would not be long, so she decided to wait up for him. It was now midnight and the news was on.

Barbette woke up Saturday morning to the sound of the TV and no Dean. She wondered where he could be and if something bad had happened. She got up and walked downstairs to start the coffee, and was surprised to see Dean lying on the couch in the den.

Dean had come in so late that he had decided to sleep on the couch and not risk disturbing her at least that was the story he told her. She continued making her coffee without saying a word.

"Barbette, are you going to cook breakfast?" he asked.

"Sure, Dean, as soon as you tell me why you stayed out all night." She retrieved the cream from the refrigerator and glanced in his direction.

"I got home at 12:30—I didn't stay out all night. What is your problem?" he asked.

Barbette started preparing breakfast, and looking over at Dean, she realized that he still had his clothes on. "Were you drunk when you came in?" she asked.

"Listen, you need to leave me alone with the bullshit. If you don't believe me, that's too damn bad," he replied.

Barbette walked over to the couch, where Dean was sitting. "Dean, you leave my father's house at 9:30 and I don't see you again till the next morning. You tell me what the hell I'm supposed to think?"

Dean stood up and walked out of the room and went upstairs.

"Think what you want, okay?" he hollered.

Barbette could not believe it. She wondered what had happened to the man she loved.

After breakfast, Dean left to meet her father and brother at the golf course.

Barbette was still upset about his coming in late and hoped that he would come home right after his golf game.

She was about to sit down and watch a DVD movie when the door bell rang; it was Donna.

"Hey, girl, what's going on?" she said as she walked into Barbette's house.

"Oh, nothing, I was just about to watch a movie."

Donna followed Barbette towards the kitchen and into the den.

"Man, this house is beautiful," she remarked, looking around in admiration.

"Oh, you've never been here before?" Barbette asked. "I'm surprised since everybody else has been here and knew about the house before I did."

Donna could tell Barbette was upset about something. "Hey, what's wrong? Did I do something wrong?" She asked.

"No, No, you haven't done anything wrong. I'm just upset about Dean staying out last night."

"What? Where was he?" Donna asked.

"Girl, I have no idea."

Donna took a seat on the couch and took her shoes off. "Perhaps he had business to take care of," she said.

"That's what he said." Barbette wanted to change the subject.

"Hey, Donna, what's going on between you and Lance? I noticed he asked you to stay behind when everyone left Dad's house last night. Are you and Lance kicking it, or what?" Barbette was now smiling and waited patiently for Donna to response.

Donna was speechless as she tried to figure out, what to say. She knew she couldn't tell Barbette the real reason behind her strange behavior—which she was her sister—so she had to come up with something quickly. "Not really, we've just been hanging out sometimes."

"Oh, okay."

The two of them watched the movie for two hours making remarks and sharing their opinions about the movie when Dean walked in.

"Hey, what you guys watching?" he asked as he walked over to Barbette and kissed her and then his sister. "The Man Who Loved," Barbette said.

"How was your game?"

"It was great, I won. Dad and Lance went to the Daily Lounge afterwards, but I decided to come home and spend some time with my lovely wife," he said with a smile. The Daily Lounge was a bar down the street from the golf course.

"Dad loves that place," Barbette replied.

"Donna, what brings you over here?" Dean asked.

"Can't I just come see my favorite sister and brother?" She stood up and headed towards the kitchen to put her glass in the sink.

"Hey, I better go, I have a date tonight and you know it'll take me five hours to get ready," she said as she hugged her brother.

"Anybody I know?" Dean asked.

"No, I don't think so," she laughed, giving Barbette a hug before leaving.

Dean knew he had mess up by staying out late the night before and was trying to make it up to Barbette.

"Hey baby, want to go out tonight? he asked, as he put his arms around her waist.

"No, I feel like hanging around the house," she said. She placed her arms around Dean and kissed him as Dean thought, *Damn, I guess I'm out of the doghouse.* He began rubbing her ass in a gentle motion and could tell Barbette wanted him. Dean wondered if he could get her to have sex with him the way he had had sex the night before with Trina. Trina was a freak and liked it hard, rough and from behind. Dean loved it too. He had always been genital with Barbette and wasn't sure if she could handle the rough stuff like Trina and didn't dare ask.

EPISODE TWELVE

One Year and Four months

Time went by so fast. It was Christmas already and Barbette and Dean were still married after a year and four months of ups and downs. Lance could not believe that they were still together. He had bet Dean a dinner that they would not last six months and he was impressed that he had lost his bet. The pay-up was that he would spring for a dinner at The Lark Restaurant. Although Dean and Barbette had managed to remain married, it had not been an easy road for them. After moving into Dean's house, as Barbette liked to call it since he had purchased it without her consent or signature, conflict came from every direction and included sex, old girl friends, and even money.

The issue was that Dean had decided that Barbette should quit her job so that they would only live off his income. Dean knew that Barbette had her own money, but he didn't want her to use it. He gave her an allowance each month which basically took care of the household expenses, but not her needs. Barbette had taken to withdrawing money out of her own account to purchase the things she wanted and needed and made sure that Dean wasn't aware of what she was doing. The money issue along with the phone hang-ups was enough to hit the ground running, but Barbette was trying hard to let Dean be the man of the house. She wanted her marriage to work, especially once she found out that Donna was her sister. Raymond had had a hard time telling the family his story about Donna and her mother. He was grateful that everyone had accepted Donna and had forgiven him. It was Donna who decided not to tell Dean the truth. She was afraid of how he would react and everyone agreed to keep the truth hidden—since Donna knew her brother better than anyone else did. As for Barbette, she just wanted happiness and she was trying very hard to get it and keep it.

Dean was standing in front of the full-length mirror tying his tie. He really didn't feel like going out to dinner, but everyone was expecting him. If he had declined dinner, he would be in trouble with Barbette, and being in trouble with her meant no pussy. He had just gotten out of the doghouse and wasn't about to go back in.

"Mrs. Jenkins," he hollered as he walked away from the mirror, upset about being unable to properly tie his tie.

Barbette stood in the doorway with her hands on her hip.

"Hey, I guess you need my help."

"Yes, I do. Come on over here and help a brother out."

As she stood in front of him and began the process of tying his tie, Dean untied her robe and stated to touch and rub her body with hopes of arousing her.

"Damn baby, let Daddy take care of you before we leave." Barbette smiled as she finished adjusting the tie. She walked away from him and closed her robe.

"No! Maybe later on tonight . . ."

Dean turned towards the mirror to check out his tie.

"Fuck it! You keep your damn pussy," he said as he grabbed his suit jacket off the chair and walked out of the bedroom. Barbette just didn't understand what was going on with him, but she didn't have the time to think about it—it was already 7:30 and she didn't want to be late for the dinner party that Lance had worked so hard to put together for them.

She hurried to slip in to her dress and shoes while Dean waited for her downstairs. When she entered the kitchen, Dean was hanging up his cell phone. "Hey, you call Lance to let him know were running late?" she asked.

"No, just had to handle some business."

Barbette wondered what type of business, but was preoccupied with getting to the restaurant on time when the doorbell rang.

As Dean walked towards the door he checked his watch and realized that it was probably the limo driver.

"Hey, man, we'll be right out," Dean said and closed the door.

"Come on Barbette! We're running late."

Dean helped her into her coat and said.

"Damn baby, you look good as hell."

"Thank you, Dean."

He opened the door and they headed towards the car.

As they walked into the restaurant Dean looked around and checked his surroundings for familiar faces; particularly women's faces. He had dined in this restaurant on a number of dinner dates with several young ladies. Barbette walked in front of him and spotting Lance and everyone else sitting at a table on the left side of the restaurant, passed the bar and began walking towards them.

"Hey everybody!" she said, as she approached the table.

"Hello, my sister," Lance said and walked towards Barbette to give her a big hug. Everyone at the table had already had several drinks while waiting for Dean and Barbette, so most of them where pretty tipsy. The ones that could still talk said their hello's while the other one's just waved.

The table was full. Raymond Jr. and his wife had flown in from New York to attend the gathering as well as Dean's uncles from Chicago. Raymond waved from the other end of the table and Carl's woman of six months, Wanda gave Barbette a warm hug.

"Hey, boy," Dean's uncle said as he rose from his seat to embrace his nephew.

"Hey, I'm glad you guys could make it. When did you get in from Chicago?" Dean asked.

"Last night. We're staying at Raymond's house. I mean Raymond's mansion," his uncle said with a laugh.

The waitress approached the table and managing to get everyone's attention asked, "Well, is everybody ready to order?" As she stood there with a big gin on her face, her eyes were focus on Dean.

Barbette thought she must know Dean, but didn't want to let her thoughts go in that direction since she had promised herself that she was going to enjoy the evening no matter what. The last time her husband had taken her out to dinner, a woman had approached her in the ladies room and told her that she and Dean had been fucking for the last six months. She also informed Barbette that Dean had promised that he was going to leave Barbette so that they could spend their lives together. Barbette had lost it! When the discussion was over, the young woman was crying and let's just say there was hair all over the place and it wasn't Barbette's.

Because the young lady had swung first, no charges were brought against Barbette.

They began to place their orders and Dean ordered for Barbette; he knew what she liked and disliked in the food category. Barbette discussed the décor of the restaurant with Wanda while Dean and Carl discussed business. Carl and Dean's Production Company had grown so that they now had over 100 employees on staff with Lance now one of the members of the board of directors. Raymond was proud that Lance wanted to do his own thing and had taken Lance's leaving of the law firm very well. Even thought he had left the law firm, Lance still owned shares with the company and remained on the board of the law firm as well. In fact, Lance owned a large percent of JJB Law Firm and a fourth of Dean and Carl's Production Company, making him one of Atlanta's richest bachelors.

Everything was going well. The food was wonderful and everyone was having fun—that is until Dean undercover life came uncovered.

The waitress walked up to Dean and giving him a note said, "The young lady over there at the bar would like you to read this and also she wants to buy you a drink. Will you be accepting, sir?"

Dean looked at Barbette, who was now pissed off and it showed on her face.

"No, I'll just go over there to see what she wants," Dean replied.

As Dean excused himself from the table and walked over to the bar towards a very attractive white woman sitting on a barstool, Carl moved into Dean's chair and asked Barbette if she would like another drink.

"Yes, please!" she replied tight lipped.

Carl signaled for the server and ordered a double cognac for Barbette and a martini for himself.

Barbette was watching Dean as he moved towards the woman at the bar and wondered what he was saying to her. She also asked herself why she allowed Dean to offend her in this way and even worse, allow him to do this in front of their family and friends.

Carl took her hand in his and asked in a concerned voice, "Barbette, are you okay?"

"Do I look okay? Tell me Carl, a woman that's has been cheated on ever since she's been married, how is she suppose to look? He's been cheating on me for so long that I've started blaming myself for his actions, and have even begun to believe that it's my fault. I tell myself that maybe if I got a breast job, or a stomach tuck or lost ten more pounds, he would want only me."

Carl couldn't say anything to her. He knew that Dean had been cheating on Barbette for a while and when he had confronted Dean about it, they had a big argument. Dean was clear in telling Carl to mind his own business and that Barbette was his wife. He informed him that he could do what he wanted to do to her and with her. Dean returned to the table and started to explain that the lady at the bar was wanting to audition for a group that he intended to promote but Barbette interrupted him by saying in a nasty tone,

"So, why didn't you invite her over to meet your other partners?"

"Baby, I hope you're not getting upset about my handling business. You knew before we got married that women would be approaching me and calling me. That's the type of business I'm in but—Baby, believe me it's just business." Dean replied.

Suddenly, Barbette remembered that Carl had said the same thing to her on their first date at the jazz club, when he stopped at the bar to talk to another woman.

"Okay baby, I understand—it was just business," Barbette replied with an attitude.

Everyone at the table pretended that there was nothing going on, but they saw what was happening and they *knew* what was happening.

The rest of the evening was spent with everyone having a good time. Barbette didn't let the incident with Dean's mess up her evening; she just wanted to enjoy her friends and family.

They were saying their goodbyes as they stood at the exit of the restaurant, waiting for their limos to pull up when Carl hugged Barbette and whispered in her ear. "If you need to talk, don't hesitate to call me, okay?"

Barbette nodded.

Over the past year Barbette and Carl had been able to build a good friendship, partly because of his relationship with Lance—they were like brothers. Carl had come to her rescue after she had confronted Dean about some girl calling the house and he had lost control. Carl called to check on her every day when Dean went out of town on business. Although he was still a dog when it came to women, Carl treated her with nothing but respect—just like a sister.

Barbette hugged Wanda, before she and Carl got into their limo to go home. On the way home in their own limo, Dean and Barbette talked about children. They had been trying to have a baby for the past six months but had had no luck and in his disappointment, Dean had tried to blame Barbette for their lack of a child. Barbette had recently made a doctor's appointment to have herself checked out just in case.

When they arrived home, Barbette went up stairs to the bedroom while Dean went downstairs to the recording studio which he had built a month after they had moved into the house. Barbette wondered what he had on his mind as she continued up the stairs. She knew if she didn't do something, her marriage would be over. She wasn't sure what was bothering Dean but at that moment Barbette made up her mind that she was going to try and save her marriage. Whatever Dean wanted her to do for him; she was going to do it, starting tonight.

Once inside the bedroom, Barbette removed her clothes, hopped on the bed, and struck a sexy pose as she waited for Dean. Her heart began beating faster when she heard Dean's coming up the stairs.

Dean walked into the bedroom and looked in her direction.

"Hey, what are you doing?" he said, as he walked pass the bed giving her a quick glance over.

"I hope you're not waiting for me because I've got some business to take care of," he said as he walked into the closet and pulled out a wine and cream Vascase shirt and a pair of wine colored snake skin Laval shoes. Dean changed his clothes without looking her way and Barbette knew he was trying to avoid eye contact with her, because he didn't want to give away the fact that he was going to see another woman probably the women he had interacted with at the restaurant. Barbette positioned herself on the side of the bed and watched him as he stood in front of the mirror buttoning his shirt.

"Why, Dean?" she asked. "Why don't you love me anymore? What did I do to deserve the way you treat me?"

Dean never turned around to look at her as he continued dressing.

"I don't know what you're talking about. I treat you good and I still love you," he replied. "Dam baby, I'm just going out. You've never felt good about my being in the entertainment business. Every time I have a late business appointment you get upset."

Barbette looked at Dean in disbelief as he walked across the room to the dresser to pick up his watch. She wondered if he thought she was crazy or just plain stupid.

"Dean, I know you've been cheating on me for the past three months or more. And I was hoping that there was some way we could save this marriage, but it seems that you're not interested in saving it."

Dean turned to look at Barbette as she walked towards the bathroom without looking in his direction. She had nothing else to say.

"Hey!" he shouted. She turned around to focus her eyes in his direction.

"Are you accusing me of cheating on you? You think this motherfuckin marriage is in trouble? You're fucking crazy! And don't think you're leaving me either." Dean had lost it.

Barbette decided not to say another word, she knew she was going to have to leave Dean and there was nothing else to say to him, especially since he was acting crazy. Barbette round her eyes and walked into the bathroom.

Dean walked out of the bedroom, down the stairs, and out the door without so much as a "good bye," or "I'll be back later," or even a "fuck you." She heard his car pull off and knew he wouldn't be back till morning. Barbette refused to cry; she had no more tears left. This situation had to be corrected and she promised herself that from this day forward, she would not rely on Dean to make her happy; she would make herself happy.

Barbette laid back in her zebra print lounge chair thinking about the changes she would make in her life. *First,* she thought, *I'll call Daddy tomorrow to let him know I'll be coming back to work.* She had missed her co-workers and the pressure of the job was what she needed to keep her mind occupied. *Secondly,* she thought, *I'll move into the spare bedroom until I decide when to move out.*

Suddenly, the phone rang, interrupting her thoughts. Barbette thought it might be Dean calling to apologize.

"Hello?"

"Hey girl. What you guys doing?" It was Carl.

"I'm just sitting here doing nothing. What's up?" she asked glancing at her clock and noticing that it was almost 12:00.

"Carl we just left each other. Did you forget something or is something wrong?"

"No, I got home and found unexpected guests in my home so I've decided to invite some people over to party with us. My cousins just came in from Chicago with a few friends and I was hoping you and Dean could come join us."

"We plan to be partying till the morning," Carl added.

Barbette could hear the people and music in the background.

"Well, Carl, Dean's gone out and probably won't be back till morning, but I would love to come by." She wondered if Carl was uncomfortable with her coming by herself, but she knew she had to start doing things solo and this was a great opportunity for her to start doing just that.

"Okay then, come on but be careful. It's late and there are a lot of crazies on the road. Oh, and I'll try to reach Dean on his cell," Carl said.

They ended their phone call and Barbette got up to get dressed. She put on a long black knit skirt that had a split to the thigh on the side and paired it with a black fitted ruffle-trimmed top. She went into the spare bedroom closet, where she stored her expensive designer shoes and pulled out a pair of 4 inch black leather Lanely Jones boots. She sat on the bed and slid them on her feet. Barbette was not sure what the dress code was, but she was dressing the way she felt—sexy and horny. She wanted her life to start over; with or without Dean. As she walked out of the bedroom, she wondered what had happened to them. Dean had loved her so much and now he didn't love or respected her. He had changed so much in the past three months and she couldn't help wondering who the other woman was.

Barbette entered the house and was greeted by Carl, who had a woman hanging on his arm. "Hey, girl, glad you made it safely. I was worried about you." As he unlatched himself from the young lady, Carl hugged her and helped her out of her coat. "What can I get you to drink? Wine?" Carl started to laugh uncontrollably, remembering the first time Barbette came over the house and got drunk and sick from drinking wine.

"Funny Carl . . . No, thank you. Do you have anything else?" she asked.

"Sure, I got your drink. Cognac right?" he asked.

"Right!" she answered.

Carl led her into the kitchen. Unfamiliar faces looked at her and smiled as she passed them. Carl introduced her to his cousins, Jerry, Victor and Perry. They were all good looking men and appeared to be between the ages of 25 to 35. Barbette realized that she hadn't seen Wanda, Carl's lady friend. "Hey, Carl, where's Wanda?"

"She has to work in the morning, so she went home."

"So, who are these women?" There were five, very attractive women walking through the house. They were women that Barbette had never met before. All five were wearing very sexy clothing and very high heels.

Carl started to laugh as he watched Barbette watching them. "Those ladies are friends of mine. Two of them work at Magic City and the others are just friends." Carl handed Barbette her drink and a napkin. He noticed that Barbette looked pretty sexy herself and couldn't help saying.

"Damn, Barbette, you look good as hell. If you weren't married, I would, I would . . ."

"What? Fuck me?" she responded.

Carl quickly grabbed Barbette by the hand and pulled her pass the crowd and down the hall to his bedroom. Barbette wondered if he had taken her seriously. Carl still lived in the house that he shared with Dean when Dean was single.

Carl closed the bedroom door behind him.

"Sit down Barbette;" he said. We need to talk. What's going on with you?" Barbette sat on the bed and crossed her legs. She didn't know if she felt disappointed or relieved that he was not trying to pull her clothes off and get her into bed. "Nothing's going on with me," she replied.

Carl pulled out a joint and had lit it without her even noticing. He took two puffs and held the joint out towards her.

"You need this. Go ahead and take a puff."

Barbette took the joint from Carl's hand, and took a puff. She started to cough and heard Carl laughing at her.

"Been a long time hum?" Unable to speak, she nodded and handed it back to him.

"So, what's going on?" he said as he pulled a chair up to the bed and took a seat across from her.

"Dean is cheating on me," Barbette said as tears welled to the rim of her eyes and he has been for the past three months or more. He stays out all night and comes home smelling like perfume. We don't have sex that often because I'm afraid I'll catch something from the girls he's been sleeping around with. I've found hotel receipts. I know he's been cheating on me, and I . . . I . . ."

Carl got up from his seat, sat on the bed next to her and placed his arms around her to comfort her as she broke down in tears.

"It's alright, it's alright. Now you stop that crying. You want me to try to talk to him?" Carl asked.

Barbette pulled away from Carl.

"No, No, don't do that. He'll raise the roof if he knows I've said anything to you about our situation." Barbette adjusted her posture and dried her eyes. "Let's just have a good time tonight. I know you're expecting a crowd because I saw three cars looking for parking space when I got out of my car. And by the way, I parked in your driveway." She managed to laugh. "I'm going to try to enjoy myself tonight and worry about my problems tomorrow."

Carl smiled. "Okay. So lets start with a couple more puffs of this stuff and another drink," he laughed as he lit up the joint and placed it in his mouth.

"Oh, and, Barbette" he said, "I'm not going to let anything happen to you. I won't let anyone take advantage of you no matter how drunk or crazy you get tonight. I take full responsibility for you so you can let your hair down, baby, and enjoy yourself." Barbette trusted Carl. He had become like a big brother to her.

The party was jumping when they returned to the living room. Someone had moved the dining room table against the wall and placed Kentucky Fried Chicken and slaw, bowls of chips, dip, bake beans and biscuits on it. People were dancing everywhere and the kitchen cabinet was completely covered with liquor and bottles of wine and the sink was filled with ice and beer. The glassed-in garden room, located off the kitchen, was filled with women and men in conversation.

Barbette poured herself another drink and leaned against the doorway leading into the garden room. Feeling good about coming to the party, she looked up from her drink and came face to face with a very tall, attractive, brown skinned man. She quickly turned away but heard him ask the gentleman he was talking to about her. She looked up again and realized that the tall, attractive, brown skinned man she had noticed was Maurice Moore, the number one player for the Atlanta Jays Basketball team, and a client of her dad's law firm. Barbette decided to sit out in the garden room and finish her drink. After about five minutes she headed back towards the kitchen. Janet Jackson was playing and everyone was dancing. The

Magic City ladies had taken over the floor and were rotating and grinning their hips all over the place. Maurice was now standing next to Carl along with another man that she had seen before, but had no idea who he was.

Carl spotted her standing over by the cabinet and started towards her.

"Hey, he hollered as he approached her. "You're doing okay?"

Barbette smiled.

"Sure, man," she yelled back over the music. "I had no idea that you knew Maurice Moore."

"I don't, I just met him. He came with a buddy of mine—a sports agent, Mike Parks. Do you know Maurice?" Carl asked, raising his eyebrows.

"No, I've never met him, but he is a client of our law firm."

"What? Did you guys represent him in his divorces?" Carl shouted.

"Yep," Barbette replied flatly.

Another song came on. "Oh, man, that's my song. You want to dance?" Carl asked.

"Sure." Barbette took his hand and Carl led her into the living room. They started to move in rhythm to the music. Barbette could not remember the last time she had danced other than at the 'Rec Center', where she had been spending her evenings teaching each Tuesday and Wednesday, but she was enjoying her dance. She spun her body around and locked eyes again with Maurice who smiling, said "Nice, I like the way you move baby."

Barbette continued moving to the music and turned around to face Carl who was so into the song he was singing the words. When the song ended, Carl grabbed her hand and led her back into the kitchen and Barbette noticed that Maurice and his friend were following them.

"Hey, man," Maurice said as he tapped Carl on the shoulder. "Man, introduce me to this nice-looking woman."

Carl looked at him in amazement but was excited that Barbette was getting action. He felt that since Dean was acting like a fool, and besides, she could use some attention—she needed to know that she still had it going on. "Barbette, this is Maurice Moore." Barbette looked at Maurice and smiling extended her hand.

"Nice to meet you Baby," Maurice said as he leaned over and asked, "Are you here with anyone?"

"No," Barbette said.

Then Maurice whispered something in Carl's ear. Carl took Barbette's hand and led her out of the kitchen as Maurice followed. All three of them walked down the hall and into Carl's bedroom where Carl closed the door to allowing them to talk to each other without the interference of the music.

Carl disappeared into the closet and returned holding a joint in his hand. He lit it and taking a couple of puffs passed it to Maurice.

"So, are you having a good time?" Maurice asked.

"Oh yes, it's been a ball," Barbette replied.

Maurice took a seat in the chair across from where Barbette was sitting. "Hey you two, I'm going to check on everybody. I'll be right back," Carl said, as he looked Barbette in the eye for any sign that she was uncomfortable being left alone with Maurice.

After the door closed, Maurice asked her if she knew anything about him.

She informed him that she was aware that he played basketball for the Atlanta Jays, but that was all she knew about him. He passed the joint to her.

"Hey baby, tell me what you do for a living?" he asked as Barbette took a puff.

"I'm a lawyer," she replied.

"A lawyer," he said with excitement. "What firm are you with?"

"L.R.B—my father's law firm."

"Oh no, man, that's the firm that handles my legal stuff."

"I know."

"So, you must be Lance's sister, right?"

"Yes, I am," Barbette said proudly.

"Oh hell, you are finer than they said you were."

"And just who is '*they*?" Barbette asked with a smile.

"*They* are the people who recommended your law firm to me." Maurice started to laugh. He was feeling really relaxed with her. "Your father saved me a lot of money on my divorces," he added.

"Yes, he told me about it," Barbette said.

"Oh, so you do know more about me than I know about you?"

Barbette nodded. Maurice leaned over and spoke softly. "Have you ever seen me play?"

Barbette decided that Maurice was a little conceded.

"No."

Maurice reached into his pocket and gave her a business card while at the same time inviting her to come see him play on Tuesday. He promised that the team would win if she was there. Barbette looked him straight in the eye and said, "Thank you so much, I would love to come see you play, but I think you should know, I'm a married woman."

"Oh yeah? Anybody I know?" he asked

"Probably; his name is Dean Jenkins?"

"OH, HELL, NO. You're Dean's wife?" Maurice was stunned. "I know of Dean, I met him one night when I was out with my man, Paul. Okay, okay." Maurice was shaking his head. She could tell he was a little disappointed she was married.

"Well, bring your husband with you, if you like," he said.

Right then, Barbette decided she liked Maurice. She thought that he was a very nice person and definitely attractive. Maurice was about 6'5" tall, very sexy and seemed to have a great sense of humor.

"Oh, I'll bring him if he's around," she responded.

"Hey, I'm not going to ask you what you meant by that, but I hope to see you there," Maurice said.

Carl walked back into the room carrying two drinks. "How you guys doing?" he asked as he handed the drinks to Maurice and Barbette. Carl could tell by the look on Barbette's face that she liked Maurice.

"I'm doing fine, but I don't think I should drink this. I have to drive home in a few minutes," Barbette said, depositing the drink on the nightstand.

"You know, you can stay here for tonight if you want," Carl offered as Maurice looked at Carl and Barbette in turn.

"No, I'd better go home," Barbette countered.

Standing up to leave she said, "Maurice, it was very nice meeting you and I think I will be able to attend the game on Tuesday, so don't you file out. Better yet, I hope you can pass the drug test. "she said and started to laugh.

"Oh, don't worry, I always pass drug testing baby. You need to know that I'll be showing out for you Tuesday, girl." Maurice stood up and downed his drink while Carl retrieved Barbette's coat and helped her into it.

"Now, are you alright to drive?" Carl asked.

"I believe so."

Maurice took her hand and held it in his. "Barbette, I can't wait to see you Tuesday. I'll leave your tickets at the gate. Just give them your name."

"Thanks, Maurice," she said and pulled her hand from his.

Carl walked her to her car and gave her a hug. She was feeling pretty independent and liked the feeling.

When Barbette reached her house, there were no lights on so she knew that Dean had not made it home yet. Barbette checked the time; it was 4:00 in the morning. She went straight to the bedroom, changed into her nightgown and went to bed.

Barbette woke with Dean lying beside her. She wondered what time he had gotten home and decided to wake him. Shaking him, she asked, "Dean, Dean, what time did you get in?"

Dean opened one eye and looked at her as if she was crazy. "Barbette, I don't know, I wasn't looking at the clock," he replied.

"Where were you?" she asked. Dean turned his back to her without answering. Barbette got up and moved to the other side of the bed to face him, hollered "DEAN! ANSWER ME!"

Dean opened his eyes and said, "You better leave me alone, girl. I'll talk to you when I get up."

Pissed off, Barbette hurried into the closet and pulled out a white sweater and a pair of jeans and began dressing loudly, kicking things here and throwing things there. Dean heard the commotion and turned his body around to see what was going on.

"Hey, where do you think you're going?" he asked as Barbette looked at him with fire in her eyes.

"Fuck you, Dean, I'm going out. I'm getting the fuck away from you."

Dean closed his eyes and responded, "I don't care what the hell you do."

Barbette left the house and drove over to her dad's. Pulling in the garage she saw that Lance and her father's cars were missing and assumed that they weren't at home. She found that she was glad they weren't so that she could have time to herself to think about what to do about Dean. The past month had been hell for her and she had decided to make plans to leave him. Barbette knew she still loved him, but she also knew that she could not live like this anymore.

Once in the house she went upstairs to her old bedroom and fell across the bed and went to sleep.

She was awoken by the call of her name. "Barbette, Barbette, wake up."

"What's wrong? Why are you here?" Raymond asked.

"Oh hi, Dad," she said as she looked up at him.

"Hello, my little B."

That's what he used to call her when she was little. "You're in trouble or something?" he asked.

"No, Dad."

"Then what's wrong?"

"Dean and I are having problems," she managed to say. Barbette then went on to tell her dad what had been going on between her and Dean as her father listened quietly.

"Wild baby, I'm sorry to hear that. What can I do for you?" he asked.

Barbette sat up on the bed while her father took a seat next to her.

"Dad, can you take a look at my prenuptial agreement and see if there is anything in it that will help me? I want the house, the car and alimony." Dean had suggested they both sign prenuptial agreements before getting married and Barbette was not about to disagree.

Barbette's father looked at her in shock.

"Baby, why would you want all of that? You still have your condo. You still have your Jaguar, and you have your own money."

Barbette stood up and walked away from the bed. She turned around slowly and said, "I want payback, for the hell I've been through. He's taken almost two years of my life. He's verbally abused me, cheated on me and . . . ."

Raymond stopped her in mid-sentence. "Okay, okay, that's enough."

Barbette sat back down on the bed next to her father and began to cry.

"Okay, I'll see what I can do." Raymond got up and started for the door.

"Dad, what about the condo; will he be able to fight me for it?"

Raymond turned back around. "No baby. The day I had you sign the prenuptial; I had you sign the condo back over to me, just in case something like this happened. I also had you sign over your shares of the company to me as well. Don't worry. Everything is going to be alright." Raymond said as he walked out of the room.

Barbette laid back on the bed and managed to smile through her tears. Her father had always been a step ahead of her. She thought, *I should have known he would protect me, especially if it involved money.*

Raymond went to his home office and looked over the prenuptial agreements, and decided that from what he read, Barbette could get half of the purchase price of Dean's house, but she would probably have to go to court for it. He didn't want Barbette to go through anything else. He had not seen his daughter in such bad shape since the day her mother had missed her 16th birthday party.

Lance came home and noticed Barbette's car in the garages next to his dad's and hoped everything was cool. "Barbette! Where you at?" he yelled.

"I'm upstairs, Lance," she answered. Lance walked up the stairs singing "Sake that Stuff," a popular rap song and entering Barbette's room, spotted her lying on the bed.

"You sick, girl?" he asked as he lay on the bed next to her. "If I was, I guess you would be too, since you're lying up in my face." Lance laughed.

"So, sister girl, what brings you to this neck of the woods?" Barbette looked up to the ceiling.

"Dean and I are having problems and that's all I want to say."

"Okay then. I understand; you don't want me in your business and all, but tell me this, do I need to kill him?" he asked wearing a crazy look on his face.

Barbette started to laugh.

"You are so crazy, man. No, man, please don't kill him, just keep your phone turned on at all times, just in case I need you." She was still laughing as she jumped up and adjusted her clothes. "I got to go home."

Lance raised his head off the bed and supported it with his hand. "You sure I don't need to bust a cap into that motherfucker's ass?"

"I told you no Lance. No, no, no."

Barbette headed down the stairs to say her goodbyes to her dad. Raymond was on the phone when Barbette entered his office and he motioned his hand for her to enter. "Hold on one minute. I'll let you talk to her." He handed the phone to Barbette.

"Who is it?" she asked.

"It's your mother."

Barbette had not talked to her mother since her call of two months ago when it was her birthday. "Hey, Mom," she said.

"Hello baby. I'm not going to keep you long. Raymond has been telling me about you and Dean and I just have one question," she said.

"What's that?" Barbette asked.

"Has he been physical with you? Has he hit you baby?" she asked.

"No, Mom. He's been cheating on me and very disrespectful to me but he hasn't hit me"

"Okay baby, I just wanted to make sure. Listen, I'll be praying for you guys and I'm going to send you some bible verses that will help you through this, okay? GOD will work things out for you, Baby. You just pray. Matter of fact, have you been going to church?" she asked.

"No, Mom. It seems like I've been lost since I've been married. Sometimes I don't know who I am anymore." Barbette sat down in her dad's desk-chair and spun round and round like she had so many times in her childhood.

"Oh baby, you are God's child, and he wants you to be happy. You just have to stay in pray and be faithful and true to God, that's all."

"Okay, Mom, I'll pray. Where are you anyway?" Barbette asked.

"I'm in Boston attending a bible conference. Do you need me to come there? You know I will," she replied.

"No, Mom, I think I can handle it with Dad's help."

"Okay baby. I have to go." I'll talk to you the end of next week.

"Okay. Good bye, Mom."

"Good bye, my darling daughter."

Barbette left for home and arrived home to find Dean lying on the couch in the den; dishes were still in the sink, clothes were all over the chairs and floor needed to be swept. The place was a mess from the kitchen to the den and Barbette was afraid to go up stairs to see what it looked like.

"Hey baby, where you been?" Dean asked.

"Over my dad's," she replied.

"Oh, so you've been over there, talking about me, hum?"

"What would make you think that we would waste our time talking about you, Dean?" she said as she went through the mail that was lying on the counter. She noticed that most of it was junk mail except for one envelope. Barbette couldn't tell who had sent it since there was no return address on the peach-colored envelope that smelled of perfume. Barbette decided to open it even though it was addressed to Dean and not her. The front of the card read, "I LOVE YOU" in large silver letter with a white background. She opened the card and reading the hand written note that said,

"The test was negative. Please call me when you get a chance. Love You, Trina."

Barbette placed the card back in the envelope and stuck it in between her mail to hide it from Dean who was now walking into the kitchen. He headed to the refrigerator to retrieve a bottle of water. As he closed the refrigerator door he turned in Barbette's direction. She had picked up a magazine and was pretending to be reading it.

"Hey baby, you want to talk?"

Barbette looked up at him and smiled. "Sure."

Dean returned the smile.

"Well, first of all I wanted to explain to you why I was late coming home last night." Dean walked towards the den.

"Come on in here and have a seat," he said.

After folding the letter and placing it in her jeans pocket Barbette headed towards the den. She sat in a chair next the couch and directed her attention towards Dean. She considered asking him about this Trina person, but knew he would lie and was not sure this was the right time to confront him anyway.

"Barbette, you know that bringing in new groups keeps my company growing and the money coming in, Right?"

"Right," Barbette answered.

"Well, the reason I was late coming in last night is because I had to drive to Carterville, in North Georgia, to see this new group and it took longer than I thought it would." Dean could tell that Barbette wasn't buying it. Barbette could not take it any longer.

"Dean, who is Trina?"

Dean's facial expression changed to stone.

"I used to date her a long time before we got married, why?" he asked.

"She sent you a card." Barbette pulled the card out of her pocket, balled it up and threw it at him. "Now you listen to me Dean. From now on, you'll be sleeping in the guest bedroom. I will not cook for you and I suggest that you start cleaning up behind your nasty ass self too."

She stood over Dean and while looking down at him, said in a low tone.

"Dean, I'm not sure what went on between you and her but it must not be over. Evidently, you don't understand that marriage means that you get to fuck only one person, and that's me, your wife. If you want this marriage to work you'd better start acting like a husband or we will be getting a divorce." She headed for the stairs.

"You know something, Barbette? You are fucking crazy!" Dean hollered. He was sitting up now and had lit a cigarette. Dean knew he was wrong and he also knew that he didn't want his marriage to end.

Barbette reached the bedroom and saw that it was a mess. She walked through the mess and into the bathroom to take, a much-needed bath, and thought to herself, I *am not dumb*. She knew that Dean was lying. Barbette ran bath water in the garden tub and poured bath oil under the running faucet. As the tub filled, she undressed and stood in front of the mirror to admire her body. Barbette noticing that she had gained more weight in addition to the ten pounds she had gained within the past two months and knew that if she did not get it together, she wouldn't have a bit of clothing to wear. She wasn't sure how Dean felt about the weight since he hadn't mentioned it at all. Barbette slowly stepped into the tub, sat her body down into the water, and lay back. She released a sigh and closing her eyes, gave in to the relaxation of the water instead of Dean's bullshit.

EPISODE THIRTEEN

The Other Man

It was Tuesday and Barbette was excited about going to the basketball game. She had invited Carl and Wanda to come along. She had also asked Dean to come with her but he had declined; something about a recording session. Barbette was glad he wasn't going. Wanda and Carl met her at the gate and they retrieved their tickets. The seats were up front—A1, 2, and 3. Maurice was already on the floor warming up with his team. He waved at them and smiled in her direction. Barbette realized that she was more attracted to him than she should be or wanted to admit. The game started and Maurice was awesome. He was up and down the court like Superman. During half time a security officer approached them and gave Barbette a note that read, *"Please wait for me after the game. I would like to take you out for drinks."*

Barbette smiled and showed the note to Carl and Wanda who teased her. Barbette didn't know if she was ready to spend time with another man—she didn't trust herself. After all, she had not had sex in about a week. After the game ended, they remained in their seat to wait for the crowd to leave.

"So, Barbette, are you going for drinks with Maurice?" Carl asked. Carl was not feeling too good about being in the middle of the Dean-Barbette situation but felt that Dean was wrong. Dean had told him that he had been cheating on Barbette, but he was going to get his act together.

"No, I don't feel right about going out with another man. After all, I am still married to Dean and just because he doesn't act like it, I don't think I should."

Carl was glad to hear that. He did not want to keep any unnecessary secrets from his boy, even though he never would have told him. They left and went to Joe's Bar for a couple of drinks. When Barbette got home at about midnight Dean was there.

"How was the game?" Dean asked.

"It was great. We won."

"Carl called me and told me you were on your way home, so I waited up for you. Dean was lying across the bed wearing an undershirt and pajama pants. "Barbette, why don't you let me sleep in here tonight? I won't try anything; I just want you near me." Dean had been sleeping in the guest bedroom all week at Barbette's insistence.

Barbette had walked into the bathroom and was standing in front of the sink. She walked back out to the bedroom where Dean was now sitting on the bed.

"Okay," she smiled and thought to herself, *Maybe things will work out and if not, I don't want it ever said that I didn't try.*

Dean was elated. "Oh, by the way, your father called and said to tell you not to forget that you have to be at the Taboo 2 Nite Club next Friday to support the Rec Center—something about a dance contest."

"Oh yeah, that's right! My dance team from the Rec Center is going to participating in a dance contest. If they win, they have an opportunity to be in one of Puff's music videos. Would you like to go with me?"

"I have to check my calendar. I have a recording session to attend sometime next week, but I'll see what I can do."

Barbette and Dean got into bed and said their good nights.

* * *

Dean had been down stairs in his recording studio, working, almost every day, on a demo for a female singing group. He let Barbette know on Thursday that he had to go out of town on business and was leaving Friday morning and returning Sunday evening. That meant that he would not be able to attend the dance contest with her. Barbette knew Dean was up to no good, but decided that she was not going to let Dean mess up her plans.

Barbette and Dean had started sleeping together again but weren't having sex—Barbette wasn't ready to trust him yet. Her father had prepared the paper-work and had told her to give him the word if and when she wanted to file for divorce. Raymond was upset with Dean and not only because of his treatment towards Barbette, Raymond had found out that Dean purchased a substantial amount of LRB company shares from one of his shareholders, without his knowledge or approval. Without Barbette's knowledge, Raymond had scheduled a meeting with Dean for the following Wednesday to discuss his stock purchases. He had also discussed, with Donna, the possibility of her disclosing the news to Dean that she was his daughter. Donna didn't think it would be a good time. She was aware of Dean and Barbette marriage problems and wanted to wait until everything was resolved, one way or the other. Donna had always been very protective of Dean and knew that Dean had suffered with mental and stress-related problems throughout his life and didn't want to put anything to heavy on him right now.

Carl had tried talking to Dean about his marriage, but Dean had accused him of wanting Barbette for himself, so Carl had backed up off him and decided not to confront Dean again.

* * *

Barbette arrived at the club in a limo and as the limo pulled in front of the club, she was amazed to see all the people lined up outside. She stepped out of the car and walked past the people standing in line. Barbette couldn't help but hear the adoring comments being made by unknown men who were waiting anxiously to enter the club. She walked up to the doorman, handing him her pass, and walked into the club. The music was loud and people were everywhere. She spotted Lance right away—he was standing and waving his hand to get her attention. She started towards him and noticed Maurice Moore coming towards her.

"Hey baby," he said once he reached her. She was surprised to see Maurice there.

"Hey, what are you doing here?"

"I'm a judge and you look damn good," he said as he took her hand and cup it in his. Barbette had worn a black two-piece suit. The skirt flared at the bottom and fit tightly around the hips, mostly because of the weight she had gained.

"Thank you, Maurice." Barbette was excited about seeing him again.

"You want to sit at my table? That is, if you're alone."

"Sure, and I am alone," she said with a smile. At that moment, Lance walked up and joined them.

"Hey, Sis," he said and leaned over to kiss her on her cheek, "You guys know each other?"

"Yes, I met Mr. Moore at Carl's party last week," she informed him.

Maurice turned towards Lance. "Would you mind if your sister sat with me, man?"

"No man, not at all. You two better get to your seats cause the contest is about to start," Lance said as he walked away. Maurice's table was in the front near the stage. He pulled out the chair for her before he took his own, leaned over and asked her what she wanted to drink.

"I would like a Hypnotic, please," Barbette responded. Maurice disappeared and came back with her drink just before the first contestant started their performance. In no time at all the first three groups of dancers had finished their performances and the emcee announced that there would be a twenty-minute intermission. A waitress approached the table and placed a drink in front of Barbette and Maurice.

"Baby, are you enjoying yourself?" Maurice asked.

"Yes, I just hope my dance group wins."

"Which one is yours?" Maurice asked.

"I'm affiliated with the Deane Carter Recreation Center. My father is on the Board of Directors and Lance and I are volunteers; I work with the dance team." Barbette said.

Maurice was surprised. He had seen Lance earlier in the club and wondered why he was there and if he had anything to do with the event.

"I should have known you were a dancer from the moves you displayed at Carl's party. I would love for you to give me a private dance lesson sometime soon." Maurice took a sip of his drink. He continued.

"Barbette, I guess your answer was 'no' to going out with me since you didn't wait for me after the game Tuesday?"

Barbette really liked Maurice but she didn't want to try and explain her marriage to Dean.

"I'd already made other plans that night. I'm sorry."

Maurice decided this would be a good time to ask her out again.

"So, do you have other plans after this—because, if not, I would love to take you to this little jazz club down the street and spend some quiet time with you? I just want to get to know you better sweetheart." Maurice could tell he caught her off guard. He knew she was married to Dean, but he had heard that the marriage was in trouble and he didn't mind being part of the trouble.

"Okay, but I can't stay out late."

The contest ended about 12:30 and Barbette's dance-team won the contest. She was elated, and like a proud mama, couldn't stop talking about her dancers as she and Maurice walked out of the club.

"Barbette, is that your limo?" Maurice asked.

"Oh yes. Are we going in your car or shall we take the limo?"

"I'll drive, if it's alright with you," Maurice replied.

"Cool. I'll just let the driver know I won't need him for the rest of the night."

Maurice stepped in front of Barbette as she headed towards the limo.

"Hold up baby, let me take care of it" he said. Maurice walked up to the limo and the driver stepped out of the car. Barbette noticed Maurice slip the driver some money after exchanging some conversation that ended with a handshake and laughter. She waited patiently as Maurice retrieved his car from the valet parking station and headed back to where she was standing at the bottom of the stairs.

"Okay baby, everything is taken care of. Is there anything else I can do for you?" he asked as he took her by the hand to lead her to his car.

"No, I'm just fine, Mr. Moore." Barbette smiled.

Maurice drove a white two-seater Mercedes that had been custom made to comfortably fit his tall body. On the way to the jazz club, Maurice told Barbette that he was making it his business to learn more about her and the more he learned, the more he liked her. He continued his conversation as they walked into the club and took a seat at a table in the back. The club was very small and was packed with people with some standing against the wall and others sitting at the bar that was raised above the floor where the tables were laid out to the far corner of the room. People constantly came to their table to greet Maurice and he was nice to everyone whether he knew them or not. He introduced Barbette to a few people, including the waitress who waited on them.

"You comfortable?" he asked as he adjusted his chair to sit closer to her.

"Yes, I'm alright."

They talked about their high school years and Barbette shared the fun times with Maurice but left out the bad times, like when three girls beat the hell out of her for messing around with their boyfriends or the time

196

when she was suspended for smoking in the bathroom. Maurice talked mostly about his high school basketball years. Suddenly he changed the subject by asking her how much she knew about his divorce.

"Barbette, did you work on my case at all?" he asked, wearing a serious look.

"No, but my brother did."

"Did you know that I had to give my ex the house and a large amount of money." Barbette was starting to feel uncomfortable but tried not to let Maurice know.

"No, Lance didn't share anything about your case with me."

"She's living in the house right now but she's trying to sell it because she wants to move back to Detroit where her family lives. The girl was cheating on me and I found out, but I was willing to try to make it work . . . Believe me when I say that I tried hard, but it was just a waste of time." At that moment, Maurice was interrupted by a man who wanted his autograph. The jazz band had started. Barbette focused her attention on the band while Maurice focused his attention on her. The crowd was really into the music and the female signer on stage, who was the attraction for the evening, sang "*All Of Me*," bringing down the house. Maurice excused himself from the table and came back carrying one red rose.

"This is for you," he said as he handed the rose to Barbette.

"Thank you, Maurice." Barbette wanted to kiss him, but knew it would move their relationship to another level and she wasn't quite ready for that just yet.

The band ended their set and left the stage with everyone clapping and having a good time. Maurice touched her hand to get her attention and leaning in close to allow her to hear him.

"Barbette, I know you're not happy in your marriage."

"How do you know that?" She was wondering where he had gotten his information.

"Because, if you were happy you wouldn't be sitting here with me, am I right?" he asked as he took a sip from his glass. Barbette turned her head away from him.

"Oh, come on, Barbette, I didn't mean to make you angry. I was just trying to find out what was going on with you baby," Maurice placed his hand on her cheek, pulled her head around, slowly leaned over and kissed her softly on her lips.

"Come on, Baby, talk to me. I've been there."

Barbette looked into Maurice's eyes and knew that she wanted him, but she wasn't sure if she wanted him in revenge for the things that Dean had done to her or for some other reasons that she couldn't figure out.

"Dean is cheating on me, and I've been trying to give him a chance to come to his senses, but I don't know how much more time I can give him."

Barbette took a sip from her drink and waited for Maurice to respond.

"Well, baby, I'm here for you if you ever need to talk. I'm an expert on the subject of being cheated on; as a matter of fact; I wrote the book." They both started to laugh and Maurice ordered another round of drinks.

After they left the club, Barbette asked Maurice to drop her off at her downtown condominium since they were already on that side of town and she didn't want him to have to drive her all the way across town to her house. Besides, Dean might have come home and she didn't want to have a run in with him. Barbette called Lance on her cell and asked him to meet her at the condo; she didn't feel like being along and he could keep her company. Lance knew she probably wanted to talk about Dean and agreed to meet her. Barbette had caught him at a party with Damika, an old girl friend of his.

"Just pull up in front of the building," Barbette said as they approached the high-rise.

"Hey, I live about four blocks down from here!" Maurice exclaimed.

"Really!"

"Yep. I purchased a condo after my divorce and. I stay there during the season. I also own a house up in the Georgia Mountains, in Jasper. That's where I live off-season when I'm not traveling. You would love it." Maurice had put his car in park and had started to get out.

"Wait! You don't have to get out—the doorman will see me in."

Maurice chuckled. "Okay, okay, but I just wanted to tell you, I really enjoyed your company and would like to take you out again, soon. Very soon."

"I would like that too," Barbette replied as she opened the car door and got out. She waved as she walked into the building. The doorman greeted Barbette with a smile and informed her that the cleaning staff had done a great job at keeping the condo clean. Barbette was pleased to hear that since she had not stayed there since the day before her honeymoon.

When she entered her place, she smelled the delightful scent of lemon lime as evidence that the cleaning staff had been there. She immediately decided to take the guest bedroom since Lance would probably bring a guest with him to spend the night. Barbette took off her clothes and finding a gown in the dresser drawer, put it on and got into bed. She lay there thinking about Maurice and how wonderful he seemed to be and wished Dean would come back to his senses and be the man that she had fallen in love with. She wondered where he was since he had not told her where he was going other than to say he would be out of town.

Suddenly, Barbette was awakened by sounds coming from the other bedroom. At first she thought it was Lance and looked at the clock noting it was 4:45 in the morning. She lay still in the bed listening to the sound of two voices, a man's and a woman's, that didn't sound at all like Lance. Barbette was afraid that someone had broken in and picked up the phone to call the security guard.

"Yes, Mrs. Jenkins."

"Yes, I believe that someone has broken into my place." She was speaking in a low tone while getting out the bed to put on her robe.

"Oh no, Ms. Jenkins, your husband, just came through the parking garage gate. It's probably him but if you still need me to check it out . . ."

Barbette stopped in her tracks and tried to gather herself.

"No, no, that's okay. Thanks"

Barbette hung up the phone and sat down quietly on the bed and listened to the voices in the next room once again. She heard the man say, "You know I like it like that don't you girl?" The only sound she could hear from the girl was; "Ohh, Ohh baby, yes, baby . . ."

Barbette knew it was time to confront them. She quickly walked out of the bedroom and across the living room towards the door of the master bedroom. The door was opened wide enough for her to look in. She had no idea that what she was about to see would change her life. As she peeked into the room, she saw a girl bended over on a chair and Dean's body lying over her entering her from the back; he was, moving in and out of her. They were naked and so into what they were doing they hadn't notice that Barbette had entered the bedroom and was watching them in shock. By now, Dean had grabbed the girl's hair and was riding her like a horse.

"DEAN, YOU MOTHERFUCKER. HOW COULD YOU DO THIS TO ME? Barbette screamed. Dean turned around and pulling himself away from the girl, stared at Barbette in total astonishment.

"Baby, let me explain," he stammered as Barbette ran out of the room.

"Barbette, listen, listen, please, listen to me." Dean was trying to grab Barbette and make her stop while the girl had started gathering her clothes and was trying to get dressed.

"DEAN, YOU'RE FUCKED! GET OFF OF ME!" Barbette hollered. Dean had grabbed her and was holding her tightly around her waist while at the same time trying to dodge her swinging arms. "GET OFF ME, YOU BASTARD," she was screaming at the top of her lungs.

"Trina, you need to leave. Get some money out of my pocket and go downstairs; the doorman will call you a cab," Dean said while still holding onto Barbette.

Barbette broke loose from Dean and like a mad woman, went for Trina but Dean managed to catch her just before she could reach her. Trina had finished dressing and was standing calmly by the door.

"Dean listen to me; when you can decide which one of us you want, let me know," she said as she went out the door.

Barbette pulled away from Dean and kicked him in the leg, then ran into her bedroom and locked the door behind her. Barbette paced the floor, and with tears pouring down her cheeks in anger—Barbette wanted to kill him. She could not believe he would do this to her.

Dean knocked on the door. "Come on, baby please, let's talk"—but soon Dean realized that Barbette was not about to open the door. He went back to the master bedroom, got dressed and sat on the side of the bed and tried to understand why Barbette was there anyway. He had been bringing Trina to the condo for over two months without Barbette's knowing about it; why was she there tonight? The sound of the door opening interrupted his thoughts and he walked out of the bedroom to come face to face with Lance.

"Hey man, I didn't know you were here with Barbette," Lance said. He introduced Damika, and they all walked into the kitchen.

"Lance, what are you doing here?" Dean asked, as Lance was about to answer, Barbette appeared in the doorway.

"DEAN, GET THE FUCK OUT OF MY HOUSE!" she screamed at him. Dean turned around, wearing a stunned look on his face. "Baby, let me explain . . ."

"There is nothing to explain. I knew you were cheating on me, but I had no idea you had the balls to use my condo and now that I've seen you in action, fucking that bitch, man, you are so out of here and out of my life. So, GET THE FUCK OUT BEFORE I KILL YOUR ASS!"

Lance looked at Barbette and saw that her eyes were red and swollen and her hair was all in a tussle. "Excuse me, but what the hell is going on here?" Lance asked Barbette with an edge in his voice.

Dean strode out of the kitchen deciding that he should leave before Lance found out what had just happened. He didn't want to have to deal with Lance physically or verbally and common sense told him that leaving was the best thing that he could do.

Barbette had not moved and stood in the kitchen doorway waiting to hear the door close, indicating that Dean had left the building. Dean walked out the door without saying a word.

"Barbette, what's going on?" Lance asked in confusion. Suddenly Barbette legs gave way and she fell to the floor crying. Lance picked her up to carry her into the master bedroom but Barbette screamed, "NO, NO, I don't want to go in there. Please take me to the other bedroom. Please! Oh God, help me!" she cried out.

Damika had followed them, carrying a glass of cognac she had poured for Barbette. She placed it on the nightstand while Lance placed Barbette on the bed and covered her with a blanket.

"Barbette, please tell me what happened? From what I gather, Dean had another woman in here."

Barbette nodded, "yes." She was unable to speak and could not stop crying. Lance sat on the bed next to her and held her hand.

"It will be alright. I'll handle it."

Barbette managed to speak. "No Lance. Leave it alone." She knew that Lance knew people and he could have Dean killed, if she gave him the word.

"No, Lance," she said again softly. "Dean and I are over. I can go on with my life now. Please, just don't leave me here by myself, okay?" she said in a little girl voice.

"Sure, Barbette, we had planned to spend the night anyway."

"Barbette, is there anything you want me to do?" Damika asked concern showing in her eyes.

"No, I'll be alright. You two go to bed and I'll call you if I need you."

Lance took Damika's hand and left the room.

"Come on. Let's leave her alone for awhile. Barbette, we'll check on you in a few hours, but if you need us, just holler, okay?" Lance said.

Barbette nodded.

Damika and Lance went to bed but. Lance did not sleep all night. He was worried about Barbette's state of mind and kept checking on her. He was furious with Dean and couldn't believe that Dean would bring a bitch here. He had no idea that he was that dumb.

Lance wakened by the sound of music coming from somewhere in the condo. He quickly jumped up and went into the living room but didn't see anyone and Damika was still asleep. He heard noises in the kitchen and went to check it out. Standing in the doorway, he spotted Barbette sitting at the island drinking coffee—she looked like hell.

"Hey, Sis," he said as he walked towards her and placed his arm around her shoulder. Barbette looked up at him.

"Hey, Lance, you want some coffee," she asked, forcing a smile.

"Yes, I wouldn't mind if I do."

Lance walked over to the counter and poured himself a cup of coffee and took a seat next to Barbette.

"So, you want to talk?" he asked.

Barbette looked Lance in the eyes. "Tell me Lance, how other men who don't even know me, can find me attractive, intelligent, and classy, and treat me like a queen, while my own husband, think I'm worth shit."

"I knew he was cheating on you," Lance said unable to look her in her eyes.

"You knew and you never told me?" Barbette gave Lance a look of disgust.

"Hey, wait one damn minute. You knew it too and anyway, I never saw him with anyone, but I could tell by the things he said to you and the way he treated you that he was cheating on you," Lance went on to explain. "See, Dean is the worst kind of man."

"Why do you say that?" Barbette asked as she got up from her seat and adjusted her robe.

"He acts like a perfect gentleman around women, but he is really a snake. He's always been very private about his dating, even when he was bachelor, which makes me believe that he was a stone freak, in the worst way. He always acted as if he was better than Carl and I because, as you say, we *dog women*, but really, we don't do anything but let a woman know where we're coming from, so there won't be no surprises. See, me and Carl know what a woman wants and how to treat them good; take them out, wine and dine them and when we're not interested anymore, we tell them instead of keeping them hanging on. We don't play games. At first the woman might feel rejected but after a while, our honesty is appreciated. You see, there are no surprises when you are upfront about who you are; everyone in the relationship knows where he or she stands. On the other hand, Dean, he's full of surprises."

Barbette looked at Lance with understanding.

"You got that right."

"Tell me Lance, how do you know so much about women?" Barbette asked.

"I listen. I listen to what they say, I watch how they walk, talk, and their reactions to situations and the way they laugh. A man can learn a lot from a woman by just listening to her. Sometimes I have to read between the lines, but overall, I know what they're saying. I have learned to read well. For example, Damika and I used to date about three years ago, but we still get together once in a while between breakups. We have an understanding and, you know something else? I still remain friends with 90% of the women I've dated. WHY?" Lance extended his arms. "Because I fucking listen." He started to laugh as Damika walked into the kitchen.

"You know, he's right. He does listen. Damika said as she walked over to Lance and kissed him on the cheek. "But if he knew how to listen to my heart he wouldn't spend his time out in the streets messing around with other women. He would know that I am the one for him," she explained, and they laughed.

Damika directed her attention to Barbette. "You alright this morning?" She gave Barbette a hug.

"Yes, I'm fine," Barbette answered when suddenly her cell phone started to ring.

"Oh God, I hope it's not Dean," she said as she looked at her caller ID that show an unfamiliar number. She wasn't sure about answering, but she did.

"Hello." The voice on the other end was familiar, but she couldn't figure out who it was.

"Hey baby, I just wanted you to know that I was thinking about you and how much I enjoyed your company last night." Barbette realized it was Maurice.

"Oh, thank you. I enjoyed your company also." Lance motioned her to tell him whom she was talking to. "Hold on please," she covered the receiver.

"Lance, its Maurice. Now will you let me talk?" Lance laughed. She put the receiver back up to her ear. "Yes, I'm sorry Maurice, now what where you saying?"

"Hey, am I interrupting something?" Maurice asked.

"Oh no, that's just my brother, trying to be nosey." They both laughed and Maurice continued . . .

"Well anyway, I was just watching the weather report on TV and there's supposed to be a snow storm coming this way. I was hoping you'd like to go with me up to my house in the mountain and keep me company during the storm."

"So, let me get this straight," said Barbette. "You want me to go with you to your house so that I can be stranded in the mountains with you," she asked.

"Yes, that's right. "Now don't think you'll have to do anything that you don't want to while you're with me. I just want your company," he explained.

"When are you leaving?"

"In a couple of hours."

Barbette didn't know what to say. She wanted to go, but was not sure if she should. "Hold on, Maurice." she covered the receiver again and relayed Maurice's request to Lance.

"What shall I do?" she asked

"You should go—say, yes," Lance said.

Barbette agreed to go and hung up. She wasn't sure if it was the right thing to do since she was still married, but she knew she had to start a new life without Dean. She hurried to gather her toiletries and dressed in a pair of Levi jeans, a red turtleneck, and a polo sweater that she found amongst some clothing that she had left in the condo when she lived there.

Damika came into the bedroom to keep her company and helped her choices the clothing she would need for her trip, while Lance went to the grocery store to stock up on foods since he and Damika planned to stay in the condo and have their own snow party.

EPISODE FOURTEEN

MAURICE

The drive to Maurice house was beautiful and very comfortable. He chose to drive the Hummer he had just purchased and even though it was a three-hour drive, Barbette didn't mind at all. Maurice was good company and he had her laughing all the way. He talked about his childhood and people he had met on his way to fame. She felt comfortable with him and warm inside. As they took their exit off the highway and on to a long road, it began to snow. Maurice could barely contain his excitement and said, "I love snow! It reminds me of the Christmases I used to spend with my family when I was a little boy!"

Barbette smiled. "Maurice, can I ask you something?"

"Hey baby you can ask me anything," he replied.

"Have you ever thought about having children of your own?"

Earlier in the conversation, on the drive up to his house, Maurice had shared with Barbette that he was volunteer for several children benefits. He had also talked a lot about his nephews and nieces.

"Oh yes, my ex and I tried having kids till we found out that she couldn't have any. We considered adopting, but it never happened. What about you?" Barbette looked out the side window and thought about how she and Dean had talked about having three children.

"Yes, I was hoping Dean and I would have children, but it will never happen, at least not with him," she replied.

Maurice decided not to ask her about what was happening with Dean, he would wait and let her tell him on her own.

They reached the house, and as they got out of the Hummer, the snow began coming down harder. Maurice grabbed their luggage and hurried her into the house. The house was built in the style of a wooden cabin, but much larger and contemporary, there were three levels. The lower area was used as a recreation, billiards area. On the second floor, there was a kitchen with a great room located off it that housed a large fire place, two bedrooms, two large bathrooms that could be entered from the bedrooms, a living room, dining room and a small library that displayed many book shelves of old books that he had collected from his international travels. Maurice's bedroom was on the top floor and contained a master bathroom, two fire places, one located in the bedroom and the other in the bathroom, and a large office with a sitting area that he called his private TV/video room. Barbette really loved the house, especially the bedroom fireplace area where Maurice had placed pillows that covered the floor like a bed. He told Barbette that the house was built last year but that he has not spent as much time in it as he would have liked. Maurice's bedroom windows went from the ceiling to the floor and Barbette noticed that they framed a breathtaking view of treetops and sky. After touring the upstairs, Maurice led Barbette back to the second level of the house, while pointing out his very expense collection of art that lined the walls along the stair case. She walked with him to the back door and watched him as he gathered wood for the fireplace. He made three trips back and forth before taking on the task of making a fire in the living room fireplace as Barbette looked on.

"You're pretty good at that," she said.

Maurice turned away from the fireplace and looked at her.

"Baby, I'm pretty good at a lot of things, and if you give me a chance, I'll show you," he smiled.

Barbette returned his smile and thought; *this man has got it going on.*

"Hey baby, let's cook now, just in case the power goes out." Barbette got up from the couch to look out the window and couldn't believe how fast the snow was coming down.

"Okay, I guess we better," she said. It looks like the storm has already arrived.

Barbette and Maurice worked together as a team in preparing their meal of turkey burgers and pasta salad. After they ate, Maurice asked her if she would help him start a fire in the bedroom; Barbette helped him carry up a pile of wood. Once the fire was lit and on its way, Maurice invited her to sit on the pillows that were placed in front of the fireplace.

"Barbette, why don't you relax, lay back and get comfortable. Now that we've finished our chores, I'll make us a hot drink, that is, if that's okay with you."

"Sure, Maurice," Barbette said as she lay back on the pillows and pulled a blanket over her. The house was still warming up and despite the fireplace, Barbette felt a little chilly. After about ten minutes, Maurice came into the room carrying a tray with two hot coffees, which he had laced with rum, and a plate of cookies. He sat it on the floor beside them and handed her a cup.

"Tell me something baby," Maurice said. "How do you feel about me?"

Barbette didn't know what to say. "What do you mean?"

"I mean do you like me enough to spend more time with me or am I just a fling or something like that?"

"I don't think you're a fling and yes, I think I would like to spend more time with you."

"I'm glad you said that because I am what you see. There are no games with me other than basketball and you don't play that, do you?" He leaned over and kissed her softly at first and followed it up with a long sensual kiss. Maurice lay next to Barbette and pulled her on top of him.

"Listen baby, if you let me, I can do some things to you that will take you to a level of pleasure you've never reached before but I'll only do that when you're ready, okay?"

Barbette had no idea what he meant by a 'level of pleasure,' but answered "okay" anyway. She laid her head on Maurice's chest and felt safe and secure. She was trying not a fall asleep, but her body gave in to the sleep monster and she felt into a deep, much needed sleep. Barbette continued to lie on top of Maurice as he stroked her hair and body. He had not dated anyone seriously since his divorce and he knew that his relationship with Barbette could be a very serious one if she let it. He just wasn't sure if that was what she wanted.

The phone rang and Maurice woke her up.

"Baby, I got to get the phone. Lay here for a minute." he said, as he shifted her body on to the pillows on the floor and ran for the phone.

"Hello."

"Hey, man." It was his friend, Paul Dodson, a professional basketball player for the New York Tigers, a married man with two children. Paul and Maurice had been friends since high school and had attended the same college. Paul was checking in on Maurice since he hadn't spoken to him in two days. Sometime ago they had made an agreement amongst themselves that if two days went by and they had not heard from each other, they would contact one another to confirm their safety. It was a security thing.

Paul and Maurice updated each other about what was going on in their lives and Maurice told Paul about the relationship he was having with Barbette, letting him know that she was at the house with him. Paul and his family were in Florida visiting relatives and he and Maurice agreed to meet during the Christmas holiday, if the weather permitted. They said their goodbyes promising to touch bases over the next couple of days.

Maurice hung up the phone and walking over to the bed to pulled back the cover. He walked over to Barbette to pull her up from the floor saying,

"Come on baby, let's get ready for bed. Would you like to take a hot bath with me? I promise I won't harm you." He could see the uncertain look on her face and did not want to alarm her. "Okay, I just think that a hot bath will help you sleep better."

Barbette wasn't sure if she should, but she *sure* did want to. "Okay, just keep your promise," she said with a smile.

Maurice ran the bath water into the very large custom tub made for his tall body and lit the candles that circled the edge of the tub. He turned on his CD player, and music came out of built-in speakers in the ceiling and the walls throughout the upstairs area. "Baby, look in the linen closet and grab us some towels and wash cloths," he requested, as he disappeared downstairs to put out the fire in the living room fireplace and lock the door. By the time he came back up, Barbette was in the tub and was lying back with her eyes closed.

"Mumm, now that's what I'm talking about," Maurice said as he looked at her and placed their drinks on the side of the tub. "Does it feel good baby?" he asked as he started to take off his clothes.

Barbette watched him disrobe and was speechless at what she saw. Maurice had well defined muscles in his arms and legs and his small waste accented his perfectly round butt, however, it was his private parts that took Barbette by surprise; He was larger than she had expected. She kept her eyes on him as he slid his body into the water at the other end of the tub while facing her.

"OOhh, this feels good as hell," he said as he laid back and closed his eyes. They laid there silent for a while, listening to the music.

"Hey baby? You know what? This isn't fair."

Barbette opened her eye.

"What do you mean? What's not fair?" she asked.

"Well, you saw my body but I didn't get a chance to see yours. So, why don't you stand up so I can check you out, Baby?"

Barbette wondered if he knew he sounded like a child. *I showed you, now it's your turn to show me.* She knew he was fucking with her and she knew that he wanted to fuck her and she was willing to participate in playing the game he started. Barbette stood up and the water ran off her body like a running faucets. She stood in front of Maurice who now was sitting straight up. He slid his body up to her, leaned over to place his hands on Barbette legs while positioning his self so that his head was facing her private area allowing him to finger and lick her. Barbette's legs went weak. Maurice noticed that she had started to shake and wasn't sure if it was because of the air hitting her body or his tongue teasing her.

"I'm sorry, Baby, go ahead, and sit back down in the water." He assisted in helping her to lower her body back into the water but before she could sit back down, he pulled her on top of him.

"Come on Baby, lay in my arms—I'm not going to hurt you," Maurice knew she was wet, inside and out, but did not want to rush things. He was a man who could get pussy at the drop of a hat but had made up his mind to take his time with Barbette; he was enjoying being able to subdue her. Barbette laid in his arms, listening to jazz and feeling relaxed and at ease. It was easy to surrender to Maurice.

"Maurice, I haven't asked you this, but are you dating anyone at this moment? I mean is there any one special in your life?"

Maurice started to laugh. "Baby you would not be in this tub, laying on top of me if I had someone special in my life. I guess I can say, you are *that someone* special baby."

Barbette looked up at him and gave him a puzzled look.

"What, you didn't know that? Hey, you better recognize it baby." Maurice chuckled and gave her a kiss on the forehead. They continued listening to the music, while their bodies lay wrapped together.

"Barbette, I got to tell you," Maurice said seductively, "I want to make love to you so bad baby." I've had a hard on since I've met you." He laughed softly. "And I believe you've been moist between them legs of yours too. So, tell me this baby, should we wait to know each other better, or should we just do what we've both wanted to do since we met?"

Barbette realized that Maurice sure knew how to talk shit to a woman. He was damn good and he knew it. She had not expected him to get this far with her, but she accepted that he was the type of man that could get whatever he wanted from a woman.

"Maurice, I haven't been with another man since I met Dean over two years ago, and I'm not sure if I want to, or if I even can please another man. I thought I was pleasing Dean but evidently, it was not good enough for him because he cheated on me to accommodate his sexual needs."

Maurice didn't say a word. He just pulled her tighter and thought, *this is a woman who has been hurt* and he wasn't about to add to the wound; he cared about her too much. He knew that Dean had fucked up and messed up a good thing and now he had the opportunity to have Barbette. He smiled and continued holding her.

Once they got out of the tub, Maurice dried himself off then approached Barbette took her towel out of her hand and began drying her off.

"Now, don't get nervous," he said as he placed the towel on her enter thigh—I just want to touch you right here," Maurice was now on his knees looking up at her as he placed his finger on her private area. "And now I am going to do this," he whispered moving his finger in a circular motion till he reached the entrance to her private area which was now very wet and not from the bath water either. "Relax." he said.

"Hummmm yes, it's wet, good and moist," Maurice continued playing with her wetness until Barbette let go and surrendered her body to pleasure.

"Oh yes, that's it," he said. She was beginning to feel her pleasure reach its peak when Maurice suddenly removed his hand from her pleasure zone and got up from his knees. He didn't say a word to her as he went back to drying himself off with his towel.

Barbette couldn't understand what had just happened and when she asked him what was going on, Maurice just smiled and said, "You're not ready yet baby. Come on let's get in bed." They lay in bed naked, facing each other and talked till they fell asleep.

The next morning, Maurice checked outside to find just what he expected—they were snowed in. He was happy that the electricity was still on and went about making coffee before going into his office to send messages to his family and friends to let them know he was all right. He was glad he had gotten the DSL line put in two months ago even though he didn't spend much time in the house.

Barbette woke up to find Maurice had already left the bed. She grabbed his robe that was lying across the foot of the bed and started down the stairs until she heard Maurice in his office.

"Good morning, Maurice. What you doing?" she asked as she entered the office.

"Oh, just letting everybody know we're safe. Why don't you take a look outside?" he replied. Barbette walked over to the window.

"WOW, we must be snowed in!"

"Yes, we are baby." Maurice said as he raised his cup to her before placing it back on his desk. Barbette walked over to his desk and, picking up the cup and began drinking from it. Maurice stopped typing and leaned back in his chair, focusing his attention on Barbette who was now sitting on the desk. He was smiling.

"Do me a favor Sweetheart."

"What's that?" Barbette asked wondering what he could possibly ask of her.

"Open up your robe."

Barbette was taken aback, but was about to obey his command. She was horny as hell and needed it.

"Why?" she asked.

"I just want to see what I can't have." Maurice moved his laptop aside and slid Barbette's body over to him and untying the belt of the terry cloth robe she wore, exposing her nude body.

"Now," he said with a grin on his face, "let me type on you." He placed a hand on each of her breasts and slowly caressed them. Barbette's head fell back with pleasure and she knew she didn't want to hold back any longer. Maurice knew exactly how to seduce her and she loved how it made her feel and wanted him bad. Maurice pushed her legs apart and placed his hand in her jade garden and begins playing with her wetness.

"Ohhh hell yeah baby, you're cat is so dam wet," he said as he slid two fingers inside of her, moving them in and out of her juice box while paying much attention to her 'g' spot. Barbette closed her eyes. She could hardly breathe as she allowed her body to rise up to meet the pleasure she was receiving.

"Yeah, that's right baby," Maurice murmured. Barbette couldn't hold it back any longer and was on the brink of climaxing when Maurice suddenly pulled his fingers out of her. He placed his fingers into his mouth and sucked them like a Popsicle. Barbette looked at him in amazement.

"Maurice, what's wrong?" Barbette questioned him.

He started laughing, as he closed her robe. "Nothing wrong, Baby—everything is right."

"So, why did you stop?"

"Well, because, like I said last night, you're not ready for me yet baby."

Maurice placed his hand on Barbette's chin and pulled her lips towards his and bestowed a kiss on them. He pulled back to assist her in removing her body from the top of his desk and Barbette walked into the bedroom to get dressed.

She was pissed. This was the second time Maurice had left her unfulfilled and she didn't really like the feeling of unfinished business. She hoped this wouldn't happen again.

Barbette started to get a turtleneck shirt and a pair of jeans from her suitcase when Maurice entered the room wearing a pair of pajama pants and a tee shirt.

"Hey baby, there's no need for you to put on clothes. We're not going anywhere and besides, I want your body available for me when I feel you're ready."

Barbette wondered what the hell he was doing but obeyed his wishes—she was curious.

They spent the day talking and laughing, and telling each other stories about their lives. At no time during the day did Maurice touch her as he had last night in the tub or that morning on his desk—that is, until later that night, when she was in the bathroom, combing her hair that had been in a ponytail all day.

"Hey, Baby, why don't you leave your hair down? I like it like that."

Barbette laid the comb on the counter. "Okay, if that's what you want."

Maurice approached her from the back and started kissing her neck.

"Damn baby, you smell so good," he said as he turned her around, picked her up and placed her on the counter. Maurice kissed her hard and long. Barbette wanted him and wanted to show him that she was ready for him. She pulled her lips away from his, opened her robe and started playing with herself, rubbing her finger across her clitoris.

"Oh damn, Baby, that shit turns me on like a motherfucker," he said. She had closed her eyes and was moving her body in a sensual motion while Maurice watched. She had started rubbing faster and harder as her body kept up with her. She was about to reach the mountain top when Maurice grabbed her wrist and gently moved her hand from her wetness stopping her from releasing herself. Barbette opened her eyes and looked at him in confusion.

"Baby, don't move your body at all. Now, take deep breaths and calm down. I'm not ready for you to cum yet. Trust me, okay?"

Barbette did what she was told and Maurice continued to watch her, never taking his eyes from hers, until her heart rate had gone back to normal. Barbette had never experienced this kind of thing with a man before, and didn't understand what Maurice was doing to her.

"Come on. Let's go laid down in front of the fire place, okay?" Maurice said as he helped her off the counter and led her into the bedroom. They lay on the pillows in front of the fireplace and after sharing over three hours of conversation decided to sleep there. Maurice pulled a blanket on top of them.

"Baby, I need to know one thing."

"What's that?" asked Barbette

"Do you still love Dean?" Barbette did not want to answer him nor have conversation about her marriage, but she knew she would have to talk about it one day and this was as a good time as any.

"I still love Dean—I'm just not in love with him anymore. He has hurt me really bad and I could never forgive him. What about you, Maurice? Do you still love your ex-wife?" she asked.

"No, not anymore. I love her in general like a friend. I mean I still care about her, but there are no emotional feelings anymore. I can tell you this though; it took time to get over her. We were college sweethearts and she was all I knew for a long time."

"Why do you think she cheated on you?" Barbette asked. Maurice looked in her direction.

"I wasn't home enough."

"She was bored."

"At least that's what she said."

Barbette leaned over and kissed Maurice on his lips.

"Well, I'm not bored with you. Matter of fact, I've been enjoying your company."

Maurice started to get a hard on, but he still wasn't ready to have her. He knew Barbette didn't understand what he was doing and he wasn't about to let her know that he was using a sexual technique that was taught to him by a older women while traveling overseas.

"Baby, my body wants you," Maurice confessed. Barbette smiled.

"So, why don't you let your body have me?"

Maurice laughed. "In time Baby, in time."

"Maurice, why won't you make love to me? Why are you doing this to me? I know you're not gay, or are you?" she asked.

"HELL NO, baby, I'm not gay!. I'm doing this to you because, there are a lot of things that people do not experience in their sexual life time; they never realize how intense their climax could be. Now, you might consider this as a control thing, but in the end it is going to be rewarding for the both of us. Baby, I want to show you what I can do for you sexually and mentally, if you ever became my lady."

Barbette lay back down and thought about what Maurice had said. They cuddle up under the blanket and shortly afterwards, fell asleep.

The snow had been plowed and the roads had opened, allowing Barbette and Maurice to leave the next day. They packed their stuff and headed back towards Atlanta. Barbette had gotten a lot of rest and she was feeling better than she had in a long time. She had decided to stay at her dad's house and made arrangements to move her stuff out of Dean's house, as soon as possible. She was able to reach Lance on his cell once they had gotten closer to town.

"Hey, Barbette, did you have a good time?" asked Lance.

"Oh yes, Lance, I did."

"Are you going to be staying with me and Dad?" he asked.

"Yes, I'm on my way there as a matter of fact. Are you still at the condo?" she asked.

Lance started to laugh, "Hell yeah! My girl Damika is the shit man. We had a good ass time, so we've decided to stay here another day,"

Barbette had always liked Damika. Damika had just completed her Master's in health management and was now looking for a job. Of course, Lance had helped to finance her schooling, but Damika had always been supportive of Lance in everything he had done.

"Barbette, just so you know, Dean called you here at the condo and I told him I didn't know where you were. I talked to Carl and he said Dean had called him crying and asked for his help in getting you back. Dean also told Carl that he was going to get some help, because he's hoping that if he does, you'll come back to him." Barbette listened quietly as Lance finished.

"Lance, I don't give a fuck. Now, is there anything else you need to tell me?" she asked.

Maurice glanced over at her, wondering what was going on.

"Hey, I'm just giving you an update, but no, there's nothing else."

"Oh, Lance, have you talked to Dad?"

"Yep, Daddy and Chi Chi are on their way back from the Bahamas. He called this morning and said something about a meeting with Dean on Wednesday. I have no idea what it's about." Lance waited for a response.

"Okay, I'll call you later."

Barbette said her goodbyes and turned towards Maurice who was now in bumper-to-bumper, stop-and-go traffic.

"You alright?" she asked, seeing how upset he was with the traffic.

Maurice smiled, "Yes. I should be asking you that." She started to laugh.

"Yes, I'm fine," she replied.

EPISODE FIFTEEN

Dean is crazy!

On Monday morning, Barbette rode to the office with her father. On the way, he explained that he had additional business to discuss with Dean that didn't concern her. Barbette knew that Raymond would be discussing their divorce with Dean, but couldn't help wondering what other business they would have to talk about. Raymond also let her know that he would call her into the meeting when they started the procedures for the divorce. Barbette was about to ask her father a question, when her cell phone rang. It was Donna. Donna told Barbette how sorry she was about the situation with Dean and how she had wanted to come by to see her to try to help her through this situation; Donna couldn't go on any further and she broke down crying. Barbette informed Donna that she would be fine. She didn't have to worry about her and that Dean would soon have the freedom to do whatever he wanted.

Once she reached her office Barbette set up her laptop and signed on; she wanted to send Maurice a message. He was in Boston preparing for a game. The phone rang as she began to type.

"Barbette Jenkins, I mean Jackson," she said.

"Hey baby, you don't know your name anymore, hum?" It was Maurice.

"Maurice, I was getting ready to send you a message. How is everything going for you?" she asked.

"I'm ready. Just have to win this one, and we're in the play off. SWEET!" Maurice was excited.

"That's great!"

"Hey, what time is your meeting with your dad?" Barbette had told Maurice about the upcoming meeting with Dean to discuss divorce when he had called Sunday night.

"9:00."

"Well, good luck; I know everything will work out just fine. By the way, I'll be back in town tonight about 12:30 and I was hoping you could meet me and tell me all about it."

Barbette smiled just thinking about the opportunity to spend time with him again. "Sure, where should I meet you?" she asked.

"How bout you pick me up from the airport. My flight comes in at 12:45 so you can meet me in front of Delta baggage terminal around 1:00 am."

"Okay Maurice, I'll meet you there." They ended their conversation and Barbette sat back in her chair, resting her head against the headrest. She closed her eyes and thought about how Maurice was just what she needed to make it through this divorce thing.

Dean exited the elevator and approached the receptionist desk at the entrance to the law firm.

"Yes, how can I help you?" the receptionist, Lillian asked.

Dean adjusted his tie. "Yes, I have an appointment with Mr. Jackson," he informed her. "A nine o'clock meeting," he added.

She looked down at her appointment book and then back up at him.

"Oh, yes, Mr. Jenkins. I'm sorry, I didn't recognize you. Mr. Jackson will be right with you." Lillian noticed that Dean's face looked a little puffy around the eye and he walked as if one of his legs was bothering him.

Dean took a seat and waited. After five to ten minutes, Raymond's secretary, Jasmine, approached him. Dean stood up to greet her and she escorted him into a very large conference room. Dean took a seat at a huge table and pulled two folders out of his brief case, laying them on the table in front of him. Jasmine returned carrying a cup of coffee in one hand and a small tray that held a small pitcher of cream and several packets sugar in the other.

"Mr. Jenkins, I thought you might like a cup of coffee while you wait." she said. Dean nodded his head and picked up the cup from the table, drank the coffee, without any cream or sugar, which was unusual for him since he always liked cream and sugar in his coffee.

Dean was just sitting back in his chair when Raymond entered the room.

"Mr. Jenkins," Raymond said as he approached Dean to shake his hand and then he walked around the table to take a seat across from him. "How are you doing this morning?"

"I'm just fine. Now, can we just get down to business, Raymond?"

Raymond raised his eyebrows as he looked in Dean's direction. "Sure. We can start with the business of my company stock and how you purchased them without my knowledge. This purchase gives you ten percent ownership of my company—I must say, very smart move."

Raymond gave Dean a smile and locking eyes with him. "Dean, I want my stock back," he said in a cold demanding voice.

"I know purchasing your stock was a smart move," Dean replied in a smart-ass tone. "I also know that my sister, Donna is your daughter, Raymond." Dean leaned back in his chair and wondered if he had crossed a line with Raymond that most people never had the opportunity to cross. The very thought of it being true excited Dean. He felt that he had real power over Raymond.

Raymond glanced down at a pile of papers, trying to hide his surprise at Dean's knowledge.

"How did you find out?" Raymond asked

"When Uncle Milton died, I went through the papers in his office and found the shares of stock that he had purchased when you first started your company. Along with the stocks, I found letters from you discussing me and Donna."

Raymond remained silent, listening and watching Dean's performance and wondered what he had up his sleeve.

Dean continued. "So, Raymond, I purchased additional shares to give to Donna so that she would have as much in your company as your other children. You see, because of you, we lost our mother." Dean lowered his head and continued. "If it wasn't for you our mother would still be alive." He ran his hands over his face and continued looking down at the table. Raymond stood up and walked over to the window, standing with his back to Dean.

"Dean, I'm sorry about your mother. I want you to know, that I really loved her and she was a very special woman to me."

Dean was about to interrupt but Raymond stopped him by raising his hand.

"Hey, I let you talk; now you listen to me. I have always taken care of Donna as well as you; the trips to Europe, college tuition, the new cars you both got for graduation, and the deal you and Carl made with Motown." Dean looked up at Raymond in shock.

"Yes, that was me," Raymond continued. "I had done so many fucked up things in my life, and have hurt so many people. Believe me; I live with what I've done every day of my life. Barbette's mother left me for cheating on her, something I had done many times while married to her, but with your mother it was different. I was in love with her and my wife knew it. She couldn't deal with it and left me.

"I hurt my wife terribly and my children never spend much time with me because I was working all the time or just didn't want to be bothered. But, I'll tell you one thing, Dean—I have always taken care of Donna. Every year at Christmas time, I give my children shares of stock. Each one has the same amount of shares and that includes Donna. I was unable to give them to her in the past, for fear of her finding out about me, so I saved her shares for the day I would be able to give them to her in person."

Raymond slid a folder across the table to Dean. "Here, take a look." Dean opened the folder and looked over the contents.

"As you see, Donna has the same amount of shares as Raymond, Jr., Lance and Barbette. I've even saved some for you."

Dean didn't know what to say; he had been wrong about Raymond and felt like a fool. Raymond walked over to Dean and took a seat next to him. "Man, can I purchase my shares back from you internally, or even off the record? I will talk to Barbette about not taking you to court for your house, car and alimony."

Raymond saw that Dean was astounded. He placed his hand on Dean's shoulder and said, "Hey, Dean, you and I, we're just alike." Dean looked up at Raymond.

"What do you mean by that?" he asked.

"Two things, we're both shrewd businessmen and we've both cheated on our wife's and have lived to regret it."

Dean pushed away from the table, stood up and turning his back to Raymond.

"Raymond, I don't want a divorce."

"Dean, I'm not sure if you can fix the relationship between you and Barbette, but you do have time to try." Dean turned around to face Raymond with a questioning look on his face.

"What can I do?"

"I'll file separation paper instead of divorce papers. This will give you time to try to make your marriage work." Raymond walked over to Dean and placed his arm around his shoulder.

"Dean, my son, get your shit together. Everyone makes mistakes but you really need to figure out what you want—is it your freedom or my daughter?"

Dean nodded his understanding of what Raymond was saying to him and walked over to the table to place his folders back into his brief case. In the meantime, Raymond walked around the table and retrieved the separation papers. He laid them on the table and slid them in Dean's direction.

"Dean, I'll need you to sign these papers." Dean sat down in his chair when he realized what the papers were. After about five minutes of reading, he decided to sign and slid the papers back across the table to Raymond.

"I'm going to get her back somehow," Dean said in a low tone. As he walked towards the door, he turned around and meeting Raymond eye to eye informed him that he would sell the stocks back to him at cost. Raymond thanked him and Dean walked out of the conference room.

Barbette remained in her office waiting for her dad to call her into the meeting. It was now 10:00 and she began to wonder if something had gone wrong. Just as she was about to make her way to the conference room to find out what was going on, Raymond walked into her office.

"Hey, Barbette, everything has been taken care of. I just need you to sign these papers." Raymond placed the separation papers on her desk in front of Barbette and took a seat in her seating area. She looked at Raymond in annoyance and demanded,

"Why wasn't I called into the meeting, Dad?"

"Dean and I had business to take care of and it took a little longer than I expected, but he signed the papers and now all you have to do is to sign them," Raymond said, as he rose from the couch and walked over to the window to look out. Barbette sensed that there was something else going on, but had no idea what it might be.

"Hey, Dad, what's really going on?" she asked. Raymond continued looking out the window.

"Nothing baby, but I told Dean that I would talk to you and ask you not to take him to court for his house, or car or alimony."

Barbette walked to where her father was standing and stood beside him.

"Dad, why did you tell him that when we discussed what I wanted to do? I thought you were on my side."

"Baby, I am on your side. Believe me, I have my reasons, but right now I don't care to share them with you. Please, just trust me everything will work out."

Barbette could tell that her dad was hiding something and didn't understand what had happened between her dad and Dean but she knew that whatever her father's reasons were they had to be very important ones and thought it was best to just let it go.

Barbette signed the papers and began to cry.

"Oh, Dad, I tried so hard to make this marriage work." Raymond started towards his daughter but before he could reach her, Barbette rose from her seat, grabbed her coat and walked out of the office and headed to the elevator.

When she arrived at the parking garage level, Barbette walked towards Raymond's car and got in.

The day before, Raymond had given Barbette a set of keys to his brand new Mercedes and she was about to, what people say, *break it in*. With everything that was on her mind, Barbette was driving so fast that she couldn't believe how quickly she had arrived at the condo. She managed to get past security without a lot of conversation and once she entered the condominium, she laid on the sofa and fell asleep.

The sound of the door opening awakened Barbette. It was Lance. He had come to check on her.

"Hey, big sister, Daddy sent me to check on you. Well, not really. He sent me to check on his car and to make sure that it was in one piece since you took off in it faster than hell." Lance was laughing. "Oh, and he also asked me to bring these papers to you to sign; you forgot to sign this one," Lance said as he placed the paper on the end table.

Barbette was in a daze, but reached for the paper and the pen and signed her name. She just wanted to get on with her life.

Lance walked into the kitchen then back into the living room carrying a coke and a bag of chips. He took a seat across from the couch where

Barbette was still laying. "Hey girl, you're going to lie there all day or what?" he asked.

Barbette sat up. "Hey Lance, does Dad need me to pick him up, since I have his car?"

"No, he's going over Chi Chi and she's going to pick him up from work."

Just then, Barbette's cell phone rang; it was Diane, her friend from New York.

"Hey girl, I finally have some time off and want to come see you next week and maybe spend Christmas with you. This is, if you're available."

Barbette had kept in touch with Diane, calling her at least once a month to say hello and to get an update on her boy friend and work.

"Sure, I'll be here. I'll make some plans for us to do something special, like shopping." They both laughed.

Diane told Barbette that her son was spending Christmas with her mother in California and that her boyfriend was going to Buffalo to spend Christmas with his children which left her pretty much open to do anything she wanted. They continued their conversation, with Lance butting in every other word and agreeing that Barbette would pick Diane up from the airport next Tuesday, the day before Christmas. After Diane had hung up, Barbette decided to take a shower and go to bed. She asked Lance to stick around till she got out of the shower and asked him to stay a while longer to keep her company. He agreed, mainly because he had started watching a movie and wanted to see the ending.

The water felt good on Barbette body. After washing her hair, she lathered her body, caressing it all over, which brought back memories of Maurice which in turn, remind her that she needed to pick him up from the airport at 1:00 in the morning. Barbette hurried to finish her shower since she was concerned about her hair being wet and knew she would have to blow dry it before she stepped a foot out of her house. She walked passed Lance, who had now taken her place on the couch, on her way to the kitchen.

"Lance, I almost forgot that I have to pick up Maurice from the airport at 1:00am tonight," she said in passing.

"Oh, that's right; the game is about to come on. They play Boston. Let me see if it's already on," Lance said as he flipped the channels. He was happy that Barbette had someone in her life to take her mind off Dean.

"Hey, is there anything I can do?" Lance asked as Barbette came back, wearing a terry-cloth robe, head wrapped in a turban and a glass of coke in her hand.

"No, I just have to make sure my hair is dry before I leave."

It was only 7:00 o'clock pm and Lance couldn't understand why she was so rushed about drying her hair and getting ready. He realized that she was probably excited about seeing Maurice again. He got up and walked into her bedroom, turned on the TV, found the game and lay across the bed.

"Hey, Barbette," he hollered.

"Yes, Lance?" she replied as she poked her head out of the bathroom door.

"What you wearing?" Lance loved to see women dressed up, especially in black; black dresses, black shoes, black stockings, you name it. He thought black was a sexy color on a woman.

"Black, I guess," she responded and continued drying her hair.

Barbette was parked outside the airport at 1:00am on the dot. She had chosen, with Lance's help, to wear a black low cut—moderate length—fit in the waste—flared out at the hips, Ann Donaldson, designer dress. Her under garments consisted of a black and red stripped ribbon garter with matching bra, black shear hoses and a pair of plain black ankle tie-up high heel boots. Due to the cold temperature, she had wrapped herself in her black diamond mink coat that her father had purchased for her on her twenty-first birthday.

She waited patiently for Maurice's arrival, after discovering his plane was going to be late. It was 1:40 before she finally saw him walking out of the terminal. She quickly rolled down her window and waved him in her direction. Maurice walked toward the car carrying a tote bag and wearing a black cashmere over-coat; black pin striped suit, white shirt and a yellow and black print tie. He placed his luggage in the trunk of the car, which she had already opened as he approached her.

"Hey baby," he said as he got in the car. He looked around with admiration on his face.

"You got a new car?" he asked.

"Oh no, this is my father's car," she said as Maurice leaned over and gently kissed her on her lips Barbette pulled out from the curb and headed into the airport traffic all the while paying close attention to other cars, as she congratulated him on his teams win. She shared her work day explaining that she had signed the separation papers and she also shared her suspicion that her dad was hiding something from her. Maurice assured her that everything would work out. Maurice asked Barbette to take the exit for the downtown area so that he could stop by the jazz club they'd gone to last week He wanted to distributed gifts to the waitresses and bartender. Barbette was excited about being with Maurice and really didn't mind where they went, just as long as they could be together. She was trying hard not to think about Dean, and frankly, was doing a damn good job of it. The nightclub was not as crowed as the other night when they'd been there, but there was a fairly good sized crowd. Maurice escorted her to the bar and ordered drinks. He gave the bartender several envelopes and conversed with him for awhile, but never took his eyes off of her. After ending his conversation with the bartender, he gave her his undivided attention.

"Hey baby, what are your plans for the Christmas Holidays?" he asked as he ordered another round of drinks.

"Well, tomorrow we're having an office party at my dad's house. We also give a Christmas brunch for our red carpet clients on Sunday after church, which will also be held at the house, and my friend Diane will be here on Tuesday. I'm supposed to make some special plans for us but I haven't come up with anything yet other than shopping, that is." They both laughed.

Maurice rubbed his hands together as if they were cold and took her hands into his, while glancing down at her breasts that were exposed in her low cut dress.

"Baby, I'll be in Detroit spending the holidays with my family, so I'm afraid, that with your busy schedule and my being out of town, we probably won't get to see each other until New Year's Eve. That is, if you would like to be my date," he asked.

Barbette was thrilled. "Oh yes, I would love to be your date for New Year's Eve."

Maurice leaned over and kissed her tenderly on the mouth as the band started to play. After they had listened to a few selections, Maurice used hand motions, to indicate he was ready to leave. He helped her into her coat, said their good bye, and left.

As Maurice sat in the car waiting for Barbette to turn on the ignition, he said, "Hey baby, let's go to my place, unless you have a better idea. It's about four blocks away."

Barbette agreed to this idea and Maurice directed her to his condo. Once they were in the house, Maurice took her coat and hung it up in the foyer coat closet. He watched her as she walked around the room checking out the paintings and pictures of him and people in his life.

"Maurice, who is this?" she asked as she turned in his direction. Maurice walked over to look at the picture and saw that she was pointing to his brother.

"Oh that's my brother. He plays college basketball for Georgia and is hoping to go pro."

"Wild! How many children in your family?" she asked.

"Four boys, one girl," he answered proudly. Barbette smiled and continued looking around. Maurice's condo was fashioned in loft style. He had used gray and black in his décor with cranberry red as an accent. The sofa and two loveseats were covered in a gray mock-suede material and the floor was a cherry hardwood with huge West Indian rugs thrown over it. There was a long, black marble top bar with six black leather bar stools and the bar divide between the kitchen and the very spacious living room. An imposing black marble fireplace stood at the center of the wall off the living room, in front of the sofa that was in the middle of the room.

Maurice picked up a remote from the table and pushed the buttons to release the smooth sound of Jill Scott that flowed out of the wall speakers before going into the kitchen to prepare drinks for the two of them. By now, Barbette was already feeling a little tipsy from the drinks they had had earlier at the jazz club, but she felt that one more wouldn't hurt. She took a seat at the bar to watch him.

"Barbette, do you want something to eat?" Maurice asked as he focused his eyes on her enticing breasts which he'd been waiting for an opportunity to touch all night.

"No, thank you, I'm on a diet," she replied as she picked up her drink that he had placed in front of her.

"Why?" he asked and walked around the bar towards her.

"I've gained too much weight and I'm trying to lose about 10 pounds."

"Baby you don't need to lose a pound." Maurice said, and smiling, he took her hand to help her down from the bar stool. He invited her to join him on the couch, started up the fireplace, and lit a large candle that sat in a holder on the table in front of them. Maurice leaned over to kiss Barbette on the lips and as he pulled his lips away from hers whispered, "Come on over here Baby and let me hold you in my arms." Barbette leaned her head in the pit of Maurice arms as he adjusted his position to suit her. They talked for a while about their Christmas plans and Maurice shared some highlights of his game. Suddenly Maurice asked Barbette in a low deep voice, "Barbette, will you spend the night with me Baby?"

Barbette liked Maurice and she liked him a lot, but she didn't think she should take their relationship any further. Of course, she had considered that weekend in the mountain with him as unfinished business, but wondered if she really wanted to finish the business tonight. She didn't answer.

"Hey, girl, you can't answer my question or what?" Maurice asked softly while hoping she would say "yes."

"Maurice, I don't know if I should," she answered. Maurice pulled his arm from around her and turned his body to face her.

"Listen baby, I'm not going to do anything to you that you don't want me to do. All I'm asking is that you spend some time with me. I'll be leaving Friday and won't return till after Christmas. I just want to be near you for a while before I leave."

Maurice smiled and placed Barbette's hands into his. He silently waited for Barbette to respond to his request. He knew he wanted her and believed that if he could just get her in the bedroom, the shit would be on. Still, Barbette still did not answer. Maurice laid back on the couch with a disgusted look on his face.

"Okay, why don't you just think about it for now? In the meantime, let's just enjoy each other and the time we do have together." Maurice could not believe that she would even have to think about spending the night with him; after all, they had already been intimate with each other. They just hadn't gone all the way.

Maurice stood up and walked into the kitchen for a drink—he felt like he needed another one to soothe his disappointment. He was not pleased, nor was he happy that he had to beg for pussy, usually he could get it from any woman he wanted but the problem was that he wanted it from her. "Would you like another drink?" he called from the kitchen.

"No, thank you," Barbette replied as she walk into the kitchen and toward him. "And the answer to your question is, "yes." She paused for a few seconds and then continued. "I don't think it will be wise for me to drive home after having so many drinks anyway." Barbette walked over to the fireplace, and seemed to be looking into the fire for a sign that she had made the right decision. She thought when she married Dean that these dating days would be over forever. Barbette was feeling as if she was going in circles and couldn't help herself. She wanted and needed Maurice to please her and she needed to know if she could still please a man.

"Hey, what are you thinking about?" Maurice asked as he took her by the hand and led her to a staircase leading to the bedrooms in the loft.

"I was just admiring the fire." After a couple of steps up the stairs, Barbette pulled her hand away from Maurice.

"Hey, where are we going?" she asked.

"Hey, I just wanted to show you the upstairs, if you don't mind." He smiled and continued leading her up the stairs.

The upstairs' loft consisted of a very large master bedroom and bathroom, a large sitting room with a corner that was set up as an office area. When Maurice and Barbette entered the bedroom, the first thing that caught Barbette's eye was the poster-bed—it was huge. It was covered with a black and green pattern comforter and lots of pillows. Maurice walked her over to the ceiling to floor windows so that she could see the view of high rises and city lights. As she looked out the window, she felt the touch of Maurice's hands around her waist as he turned her around to face him. He began to kiss her more passionately than he had before and moved his lips to nibble her neck as he moved one of his hands up to caress her breasts.

"Maurice, please stop," Barbette said breathlessly. Maurice took a step back and without warning, slowly pulled up her dress exposing her black lace garter belt and hose. As usual, Barbette wasn't wearing any under wear.

"Damn baby, I know you wore this shit for me, so stop playing." He placed his hand between her legs to test her wetness while watching her reaction.

"You passed the test baby" he said softly as he began to rotate his fingers to give her pleasure.

"Maurice, oh Maurice, please, oh, please stop," Barbette mumbled, as she attempted to pull his hand away from her. Maurice moved his hand and stepped back from her.

"Listen, Baby, all you gotta do is relax. If you're afraid that we're going to have to fuck, don't be. I'm not going to take a damn thing from you, that you don't want to give me. I just want to make you feel good."

Maurice pulled her close to him and looked into her eyes. "Hey, when you can tell me to stop and mean it, I will. But we both know you can't, so let me do this shit. You want it as bad as I do."

Barbette acknowledged that he was right. She wanted him badly and decided to let him do whatever he wanted to do to her.

Maurice walked over to a large armless black leather chair on the other side of the room and took a seat while she remained standing where she was, watching his every move.

He looked in her direction and wearing a grin on his face said with authority, "Now if you think you're ready, bring your fine ass over here."

Barbette didn't hesitate; she was ready. Barbette walked across the room towards Maurice. Once she reached him, he pulled her down onto his lap and started running his fingers through her hair.

"I want you to do something for me," he said,

Maurice was breathing hard and she could see from the imprint in his pants that he had a hard on. She knew that she would probably do anything he wanted her to do. She was getting into his control game and loving it. Barbette had always been attracted to men who could over-power her sexually. She just wasn't into the hard-core stuff anymore and was hoping Maurice didn't request anything too 'out there'.

"What can I do for you?" she said in a sexy tone.

"I want you to stand up and take your dress off, but leave on the pretty under garments."

Barbette was about to stand up but he pulled her back into his lap.

"Let me unzip you first." Maurice unzipped her dress than allowed her to stand up in front of him. He then laid back in the chair and whispered, "Go ahead, Baby, show me that shit."

Barbette stepped away then turned to face him. She let her dress drop to the floor and stood waiting for his next command. Maurice adjusted himself in his chair to allow him to unzip his pants and release his hard on. Barbette tried to act cool and unaffected as she checked him out. She was fucked up to see Maurice was much bigger than she remembered.

I hope this motherfucker can hang all night and that's not just show, she thought,

"Come on over here, Baby," he said

As Barbette approached him, he gently took her hand in his and instructed her to sit down on his lap facing him. He positioned his hard on to enter her wetness as she slowly moved herself down on him.

"Oh fuck, you're bigger than I . . . than I thought," Barbette said quietly.

Before he began to move inside her, Maurice kissed her and said, "If this become too much for you just let me know and I'll stop." Even though he had made the statement, Maurice was not about to stop; he had gotten this far and he was planning to take it home.

When Barbette made no response, he placed his hands on Barbette hips and directing them to follow his lead; he began to move in a rotating motion.

"Shit, Baby, I knew your shit was good," he said as he tried to concentrate on not releasing too soon. Barbette had unbuttoned his shirt and started kissing his chest, nipping on his nipples and fondling his ear. She stuck her tongue into his ear, Maurice started to move faster.

"Oh, man, you're fucking me up, GIRL," he said as he rolled his head back and side to side. Barbette love canal had adjusted to his rod. She was now riding him like a horse. She was on her way to the gate that was now open to receive all that Maurice was giving. She started to move faster as he lifted his hips, jamming his cock all the way up into her wetness. She was about to win the race and Maurice was holding on tight while managing to reach her anal entry where he position his finger at the opening to enter.

"Come on, Baby, let Daddy pop that pussy," he said softly as he gradually pushed his finger up into her. Barbette's legs started to shake as she felt the built up of pleasure taking over her body. "OH FUCK, MAURICE, YOU'RE, YOU'RE SO FUCKIN GOOD, she screamed as she released like a volcano exploding in her body.

Maurice's body started to jerk as he followed Barbette's explosion with his own.

"Yes, yes, oh yes. You are going to kill me, GIRL, GIRL, GIRL," he hollered.

They were both exhausted and couldn't move. Barbette laid her head on his shoulder as tears flowed down her cheek, not knowing if they were tears of joy or sorrow. She hoped Maurice would not notice.

"Baby, you got some good shit there," he said and started to laugh. "I can't believe you were trying not to give it up to me. Damn, Baby, has anyone ever told you that your pussy is like a drug? I think I'm hooked like a motherfucker," he said as he noticed that she wasn't responding and pulled her head back from his shoulder to look at her and asked,

"Hey, what's wrong? Did I hurt you?"

"No, no, it's just that the answer to your question is yes."

Maurice was confused. "What are you talking about?"

"Dean told me once that my pussy was like a drug," she responded and began to cry harder. Maurice held her tight and wondered what type of fool Dean had to be to give her up. She was fine, had money, and could make a motherfucker dick hard just from eye contact alone.

Barbette gently pulled away from his hug and stood up.

"I got to go to the bathroom."

"Okay, just get your ass back here as soon as possible," Maurice said, with a smile.

Barbette went into the bathroom and when she came out, Maurice was already under the covers in the bed.

"Come on Barbette get in," he said as he pulled the covers back on her side of the over-sized king-sized, post bed. Maurice laid on his back looking at Barbette as she undressed. He instantly became aroused and wanted to fuck her again. Barbette climbed up into the bed and laid her naked body next to him.

"Barbette, I'm going to miss you over the Christmas holidays baby. Oh, and by the way, you'll be receiving a gift from me when I get back."

"I'm going to miss you too, and you don't have to get me anything," she replied while they lay snuggled up against each other naked bodies.

"I know, but I want to," Maurice said as he closed his eyes and let his mind rest on the day and its happenings. He thought about how well it had been—three women in one day—two of them in Boston and Barbette. He wondered why he hadn't put on a condom before entering her, as he usually did. He didn't forget, he just didn't want to and he couldn't figure out why he had made that decision.

"Baby?"

"Yes, Maurice." Barbette was half asleep now.

"Are you on any type of birth control?"

Barbette opened her eyes. "I was just laying here thinking about how stupid we were for not using a condom. But, just to put your mind at rest, I'm not HIV positive. As far as birth control is concerned, no, I'm not on anything."

"Well, I'm not HIV positive either and I'm not on birth control either."

Barbette chuckled softly. "Let's just hope nothing happens and let's not let this happen again."

Barbette left the next morning, after Maurice had fucked her doggy style before going to sleep. He then started the morning with requesting that she stand up, lean over, and support herself on the bedpost while he entered her for breakfast—she was happy to oblige. This time, they used a condom.

ABOUT THE AUTHOR

While growing up, L.M. Sharp had always been a daydreamer. Whenever things in her life became too stressful she would go to another world that she had created in her mind; a world that allowed her to have some control over her trials and tribulations. In this world she could let herself live the life of someone else and do whatever she wanted to do.

This story has been on her mind for several years. She finally got the push from her husband, who has always believed in her, to put it on paper. "I believe God blesses us with talents and we should use them to survive," Lady Sharp concludes. "I'm hoping that you would consider this book worthy of being read."